The Missing Years

Also by Terri O'Mahony

The Windbreaker Season
The Seamstress of Fortune

The Missing Years

Terri O'Mahony

POOLBEG

This novel is entirely a work of fiction. The names, characters and incidents portrayed in it are the work of the author's imagination. Any resemblance to actual persons, living or dead, events or localities is entirely coincidental.

Published 2006
by Poolbeg Press Ltd
123 Grange Hill, Baldoyle
Dublin 13, Ireland
E-mail: poolbeg@poolbeg.com

1 3 5 7 9 10 8 6 4 2

A catalogue record for this book is available from the British Library.

ISBN 1-84223-235-5
ISBN 978 1 84223 235 4 (From January 2007)

Typeset by Type Design in Sabon 11.4/14.2
Printed by Litografia Rosés S.A., Spain

www.poolbeg.com

About the Author

Terri O'Mahony is a native of Limerick and is a natural storyteller. She has been writing from an early age, and has contributed short stories and articles published in *Woman's Way*, *The Messenger* and *Ireland's Own*. She has also had articles and short stories published in Limerick's *Gazette* newspaper. She was runner-up in the Ian St James Awards in the early 1980s and has had short stories broadcast on radio.

She works full-time as a clerical officer with Limerick City Council. Her first novel, *The Windbreaker Season*, was published by Poolbeg in 2004 and her second novel, *The Seamstress of Fortune*, was published in 2005.

Acknowledgements

Thank you all at Poolbeg for your encouragement and friendship. It is very much appreciated especially in the early hours just before dawn when inspiration seems to be hiding from me! All of you have given me the professional guidance and reassurance a fledgeling author appreciates when deadlines have to be met.

A grateful thank you to my editor, Gaye Shortland, who has been so kind and professional in her editing. Thank you, Gaye, for your assistance and encouragement.

Thank you to my family, to Mam, my confidante and staunch supporter always, to Joy, Laura, Roseanne, Valerie and John for their love and appreciation, and to Fred, my dog, for his consideration in keeping his barking to a minimum when I'm trying to concentrate on a storyline!

To my sisters, Eleanor and Audrey, and my brother, Roger, thank you for being proud of me.

To Dad, for watching over me always and guiding me in making the right choices.

To Geraldine, my friend, I hope she enjoys reading *The Missing Years* as much as she enjoyed reading my other books.

With love always to dear Mam, Joy, Laura,
Roseanne, Valerie and John.
I love you all very much – thank you
for your love and support.

To my dad – a posthumous dedication –
I hope he is proud of me as I was
always of him.

Chapter 1

The walls were closing in on her again. She could see the grey, damp streaks on the wallpaper merge and form various shapes and patterns, sometimes coming so close to her that she could feel ghostly fingers touch her cheeks, almost mocking her anxiety. Sheila clasped her hands firmly against her chest, feeling her heart beating wildly. If I relax, she told herself desperately, it will go away, this terrible, overpowering sensation of being out of control, this unbearable longing to have Sam close again . . .

She closed her eyes tightly, afraid that if she opened them again she might see *his* face – the familiar features, the tilt of his stubborn chin –

etched unmistakably on the shadowed wall. It was just the way the light through the tiny crack in the curtains spotlighted a certain notch in the mottled wallpaper, a certain incongruous line drawn smoothly across the pale shadows. For the past week, Sam's face had appeared there, to the left of the old wardrobe, even the dark hollows of his eyes with that unbearable, taunting reproach in their depths. She missed him so much. The word went round and round in her brain until she thought her head would explode. 'Miss' him, 'miss' him – such a small word, that 'miss', but with a wealth of poignancy behind it. Her mind was a fog of memories and certain moments in both their lives when they had been close, so close that she thought nothing could ever separate them. She looked up blankly at the ceiling, counting the cracks in its shadowed surface. She knew now what it meant to miss somebody. Her life had a large portion taken out of it since Sam had left, a time of missing him, a time of being out of the mainstream of life, time that would never be given back to her again.

Why, Sam, why? she asked herself over and over again, but there was no answer in the silent room, only an echo of self-accusation. Had she been at fault? Had he grown tired of her because she hadn't given him enough attention, hadn't asked him more frequently how he was getting on in the job? She tossed and turned on the pillow and tried to reason logically. Who was it who had walked out on them, herself and the girls and the little fellow? What father could do the likes of that to his own? Surely it couldn't be all her fault? She had been a good wife, she couldn't have done more . . .

She would go mad thinking like this. The sweat stood in small beads on her forehead, and she reached for the bedside lamp, switching it on to see the time on her watch. Two o'clock. Another six hours to be got through before it was time to get the children up for school. She picked up her book, a romantic thriller, from the locker, but her thoughts flitted wildly across the pages until she tossed it angrily from her hands, her head pounding from lack of sleep.

She sat up in the bed, throwing back the duvet. Going across to the window and opening the curtains just a little, she looked out into the deserted avenue. Nobody knew. Not yet, anyway. It was as though they were waiting for normality to return to the house. Sam might walk in the door any minute, tell them he'd had to go away urgently on a business trip for the firm, he was sorry for worrying her, for making her think that she had started a journey down the 'missing' years of living without him . . .

She had tried to make things right between

them, but he had laughed in her face. Her whole body stiffened as she watched the mirage appear once more on the wall.

She could see his sneering mouth form the words: "I need to be on my own for a while, make some time for myself – Jesus, Sheila, twenty years wasted of my life and I don't know what it's like to spend a few days on my own without you lot hanging out of me! I'm sick of it – my life is passing me by, and I have nothing to show for it!"

"Nothing to show for it!" Sheila repeated to herself in the dark. He had a good job, selling computer software, always on the road, from Monday to Saturday. His salary had trebled in the last three years because he was a popular, outgoing type, especially with the ladies. The telephone was constantly hopping with firms wanting to contact him about expanding their business abroad, computerising their overseas offices.

And then he had left. Just a few lukewarm arguments about how short life was, they should never have married in the first place, they were so unsuited – and Sheila had looked after his tall figure striding towards the front gate, suitcase in his hand – "I'll collect the rest of my things later" – and then she felt her whole world crumble about her. The girls had stood by her side, not saying anything, because at fifteen and sixteen there wasn't very much they could say to console her – not when they were hurting inside themselves.

Their father was leaving them. Tom, six years old, had sat inside watching cartoons on television. He had never seen much of his father, anyway. Dad was just off on another business trip – maybe he'd bring him back something nice . . .

It was no use. Sheila swung her legs out at the side of the bed, pulling her dressing-gown around her thin shoulders. She had lost a lot of weight since Sam left. Food just didn't seem to interest her any more. A boiled egg and a slice of brown bread was all her dinner consisted of most days. She padded silently out on to the landing and went downstairs, pausing before the telephone in the hallway. She supposed she could have used her mobile, but it was cheaper on the landline. Shakily, she let her hand touch the receiver, fingers tentatively poised as she picked it up, then put it down again. They'd think she was mad, telephoning at this hour. She looked at the clock on the wall. Ten to three. Five more lonely hours before she could justify her getting up, five more endless hours until the blackness outside made way for the morning. She grabbed the receiver, tears of frustration running down her cheeks. She dialled the number without hesitating, listening to the 'beep-beep' sound before a soft, friendly male voice finally answered.

"Samaritans here – can I help you?"

She took a deep breath, her thoughts frozen for a second. "I know this is an unearthly hour to be calling, but I . . ."

"What's the matter? Do you want to talk about it?"

The man's voice sounded so patient, so kind. She imagined him sitting at the other end of the telephone, his chin cupped in his hand, a concerned look on his face. Or maybe they were trained to sound like that, and he could detach himself from his work. He could be thinking of his wife, lying in bed at home, waiting for him to get in beside her, to put his arms about her . . .

"I'm sorry – I shouldn't have bothered you," Sheila faltered, her hand trembling as she tried to separate the receiver from the side of her head, but her hand just wouldn't obey. She felt a wave of terror inside her, her heart pounding, hearing the man's voice talking calmly to her, urging her to talk about whatever was troubling her. Maybe she was having a stroke – the ambulance men would have to prise the telephone from her grasp, her ice-cold fingers locked in a death-grip.

The voice sounded again, coming to her from a blur of words, indistinct and unfamiliar, so that her feeling of panic intensified.

"Please – I want to talk to you – won't you tell me what's the matter?"

"I want to put the receiver down – but I can't – I think I'm having a stroke, or something – maybe a nervous breakdown – it's my husband, you see – he's left me – us – and I don't know what to do."

"I'm going to give you the number of somebody who will be able to help you with some things – social welfare, your entitlements as a deserted wife. Take a deep breath and slide your hand along the receiver – go on – let your fingers relax . . ."

Sheila did as she was told. He sounded so sympathetic. Tears flowed unchecked down her cheeks. Her grip loosened and she was once more in control, her mouth close to the mouthpiece, wanting to be closer to this wonderful sympathetic man with the voice of an angel.

"I don't know where to start – maybe I shouldn't have been going on at him about things that had to be done in the house – the tap in the kitchen needs a new washer for the past six months – but every time I asked him about it, he asked me was that all I had to worry me, a leaky tap? Do you think it was my fault – whoever you are – I wish I knew your name – p1ease tell me it wasn't my fault!"

"Please – you mustn't blame yourself – these things happen – nobody's fault, just human nature asserting itself."

She liked the sound of his voice. It seemed to caress all the hurt she felt inside, relieving the torment for a little while. She didn't want to end the conversation – not just yet. It was still dark outside, only the light from the streetlamp near the front gate casting a lukewarm shadow on the patterned carpet in the hall.

"Please, can you tell me your name – or is that not allowed? If I knew your name, it would be just like talking to a friend . . ." Her voice was barely a whisper, afraid that if she spoke even louder the girls might wake up – or, worse still, Tom might come running down the stairs and see her crying into the receiver. That wouldn't do. His life was messed up too much already.

"That's all right – I can give you my name – Peter. Any time you feel like talking to someone, just ring the number and ask for Peter. I'll be here, or if I'm not here, I'll ring you back – if that's what you'd like – there's no commitment – just you do what you think might help you at this time."

Sheila sat on the bottom step of the stairs, hunched over the receiver. She didn't want to give anybody her number. Everybody would know who the loony was who rang the Samaritans at three in the morning – maybe one of them was a neighbour. And yet, if she didn't trust somebody, she would surely go mad. Peter seemed to read her thoughts as his concerned voice crackled comfortingly in her ear. "It's all strictly confidential – anything you say to me will not be divulged outside – not even to my own family. Please, don't be afraid – I just want to help."

Sheila's lips moved mechanically as she volunteered her telephone number. There was a short pause and she knew he was taking it down.

"And can you give me a name? It doesn't matter, it needn't be your own – just a name you feel comfortable with – it's nicer talking to a name rather than a number."

"Gerardine."

She wasn't brave enough yet to reveal more than she had to. This man wanted to be a friend. She would take advantage of his kindness, because it was all she had right now. Her Confirmation name would have to do him. "Ships that pass in the night," she whispered to herself, forgetting for a moment the presence at the other end of the telephone.

"The darkest hour is just before dawn," came his voice.

Startled, she almost dropped the receiver.

"We can talk in clichés, Gerardine, or we can be real friends."

A flush spread across her face. She thought he might be scolding her, maybe even reproaching her – for what? He thought she was to blame, for all the mess, all the upset she had caused – by letting her husband go, walk out of her life, and the children's . . . "I'm sorry – I just thought – that's what we're like – two ships, passing each other in the night – we'll probably never speak to each other again."

"Floating ships reach safe harbour, Gerardine. You sound like a good woman. Get rid of those skeletons in your mind, don't shoulder all the burden of blame. The seas look a bit choppy for you right now, but things will improve – you wait and see. Please ring me again – that's what I'm here for – to listen."

Maybe that was his winding-up statement. Maybe he was tired with her. Probably had other calls waiting for him, other loonies waiting to talk to Peter.

"Thanks for listening – maybe I will call – the nights are the worst."

She replaced the receiver without saying goodbye. If she had said goodbye, she knew she would never have rung again. She had left the lines of communication open. Maybe she was getting over it, just a little. She no longer wanted to be on her own, stuffing her mouth with Valium. It was a first step.

She sat for a moment on the stairs, listening to the ticking of the clock, the sound confusing in the thick silence. She put her hands to her ears, trying to block out the mechanical tick-tock, trying to remember the man's name. Peter – that was it – his name was Peter and he had asked her to ring him whenever she felt she needed a friend. She looked at the scribbled number on the telephone pad. *Social Welfare* people. She put the two words in italics in her brain. *Social Welfare* were dirty words to Sheila. *Social Welfare* spelt failure. Sam had walked out on her, she didn't know where he was, what he intended to do with the rest of his life – and she was left with a telephone number and the humiliating words *Social Welfare* etched painfully in her mind.

"Mam, are you all right?"

She looked over her shoulder, at the girl standing uncertainly behind her in the Mickey Mouse nightdress, the pale face, dark eyes smudged with tiredness.

"I'm sorry, Deirdre – I didn't mean to wake you, love – but I couldn't sleep." Deirdre went and put an arm about her. It was a clumsy gesture but one Sheila welcomed, leaning against her, feeling her daughter's long blonde hair sweep gently against her face. There was an irony in the cameo picture of mother and daughter, sitting so close together, the young girl taking on the mother role. Flashes of the past came into Sheila's mind – the little girl, just six years old, big dark eyes full of tears and a teddy clutched in her hands. "I'm frightened, Mammy – there's a black dog running after me. Every time I try to sleep he keeps running after me – and I can't get away from him. Can I sleep in your bed?"

She looked at Deirdre and cursed Sam for making the girl grow up before her time.

"Do you want me to sleep with you, Mam – would you feel better with somebody near you? Just like when I was little, you remember – I used to scramble over Dad and tuck myself in between the two of you – it helped." Deirdre spoke calmly. In her young eyes, there was a solution to the problem, if only temporary.

"I'd like that, love – but don't worry – I won't disturb you like this any more – maybe some more sleeping tablets would do the trick."

"Jean at school – her mother takes two kinds of sleeping tablets every night – and she's awake all night. They don't do a thing for her."

The adult mentality already, Sheila thought wryly.

"Lay off the pills, Mam – please!" Deirdre pleaded, helping her mother up the stairs, leading her gently into the bedroom.

"I'll try, love – but just now I need them."

She lay, eyes open, staring up at the ceiling until Deirdre got in beside her, shoving her cold feet up against hers.

"You should wear bedsocks, love – your feet

are like ice-blocks!"

She heard the comforting sound of Deirdre's shallow breathing as she drifted into sleep, and wondered if she would ever get used to sleeping on her own again, after twenty years of Sam's bulky shape lying next to hers on the lumpy mattress. That was the next thing she had to do. Get rid of the bed.

She laughed, her whole body shaking, causing Deirdre to mutter "Take it easy, Mam …"

She was thinking of the faces of the neighbours when they saw the old double bed go out the gate and the new single bed come in to take its place. Not that they didn't have enough to talk about already. Sam was gone almost three weeks now.

Esther Looney next door had casually mentioned to her over the back fence only last week how lonely it must be for her without Sam all week.

"Sam is taking his time coming back this time round, isn't he, Sheila?" she had asked with just a hint of 'tell me more' in her inquisitive tone.

"Yes, he's making the money all right," Sheila had answered her flippantly. "Not a bad thing to be doing in these times, eh, Esther?" and she had pointedly closed the back door in Esther's face.

They would all know soon enough. Yes, the bed would definitely go – by the end of the week at the latest.

The shadows in the room were lifting. Pale streaks of early-morning light were coming through the flowered curtains. She turned over, nestling close to Deirdre's warm body and closed her eyes thankfully. Just a couple of hours' sleep, that was all she needed …

She woke with a start to see the alarm clock staring her in the face. 9.30! "Deirdre, we're late – come on, love – get Sharon – I'll dress Tom – there'll only be time for cornflakes this morning – maybe you can get a drink at school for elevenses …"

Sharon came into the bedroom, rubbing the sleep from her eyes. Her hair was as dark as Deirdre's was fair, her cornflower-blue eyes looking reproachfully at her mother and sister lying in bed. "Oh, Mam! You never set the alarm – and I have a test this morning at ten! I don't care, I'm not taking Tom in to school – I'm late enough as it is!"

"Give over, Shar – *I'll* take Tom in to school. Mam, stay in bed – I'll get him dressed." Deirdre threw back the quilt and hurried Sharon from the room.

Sheila could hear her angry whispers on the landing outside the bedroom door. "Can't you see she can't help it? Give her time – Dad is only gone three weeks, and he won't be coming back, or so he says. How do you think she feels, for God's sake, Shar? Cop on!"

Sheila felt the tears burn her eyes. She lay back on the pillow, pulling the quilt up about her, closing her eyes against the splash of sunlight coming through the window. What was she doing to them? Wasn't it bad enough that their father had left them, without their mother turning into a zombie, not even capable of making a simple decision like would she get up or stay in bed this morning?

She slid out of bed and almost tripped as she hurried into Tom's bedroom. She shook him gently awake. He protested and kept a tight grip on the quilt she tried to wrench from his grasp.

"Come on, up out of that, my boyo! Time for school – and I'll have a surprise ready for you when you come home today – I promise!"

He looked up at her suspiciously. "What kind of a surprise?" But he threw back the quilt and got out. He struggled to get dressed, pushing her hand away as he tried to knot his school tie.

"Here – let me, Tommy – you'll be late if we don't hurry – you can do it yourself every other morning!"

"*No!* I want to do it myself – I'm six now – Sister Regina says we should all be able to dress ourselves and tie our laces now – and I'm the biggest in the class, so I *can* do it!"

Sheila tried to hold back her frustration. It was

at times like this that she missed Sam the most. Just one word of reprimand from his father and Tommy was like a lamb. "Think of that surprise, love," she tried to coax him.

He reluctantly allowed her to finish his dressing, and by the time they got downstairs Deirdre had the breakfast cereal poured into the bowls on the table, giant-sized slices of bread spread with butter and marmalade at the side of each bowl.

"I've made the tea, Mam – it's not so late – I'll have plenty of time to take Tommy in to school."

Sheila looked at her gratefully. It was a pity Sharon wasn't more like her sister. She could be so obstinate at times, like this morning, as she sat at the breakfast table, a dark scowl on her face, her hair falling into her eyes as she played about with the bowl of cornflakes, some of the milk splashing onto the table.

"Look, Mam – Sharon is just like a baby messing all her breakfast!" Tommy looked delightedly at his sister and Sharon stuck out her tongue at him.

"Please, Sharon, stop the messing and get on with your breakfast! You're not too late – still time enough for your exam –" She could feel the tight band of tension about her head as Sharon got up angrily from the table, overturning the chair as she grabbed her schoolbag.

"What does anyone in this house care whether I fail or not? I'm sick of you going around the house like a freak, I'm sick of dirty dishes left in the sink, and sheets almost three weeks old left on the beds – I'm sick of having to mind *Tom* all the time!" She pointed an angry finger at Tommy, now happily munching through his cornflakes. Sharon was always cross about something.

He heard his name mentioned and looked up for a minute, then resumed his eating. He preferred Deirdre. Deirdre was great. She always played games with him when he came in from school while Mam was getting the dinner ready.

Sheila stood in front of her younger daughter, barring her way as she went to shove past her. "Listen to me, madam – I have something to say to you." Her eyes blazed angrily in her thin pale face, shadowed with tiredness.

Sharon reluctantly cast her eyes downwards, her annoyance increasing as she saw the dirty yellow tiles. She couldn't bring any of her friends home to this place any more. It was a dump.

"Sharon – I can't put it more bluntly. Your father has left us. He couldn't care less what happens to us from now on, and it's going to take some adjustments until we're on our feet again." She took Sharon by the shoulders, forcing her to look up into her face. "There's nothing I can do to fix things, make it like it used to be. We have to forget the past – look to the future from now on."

"*You* must have done something to make him leave like that!" Sharon said loudly, her anger like a slap in Sheila's face.

"Maybe I did – I don't know – I don't know what went through your father's head . . ." She looked at her daughter pleadingly. "Please, Shar – give me a break – meet me halfway in this."

"It was great when he was home – we were always laughing and joking. Nobody laughs any more." She turned away from Sheila, wiping angry tears from her eyes with the back of her sleeve.

Sheila put her arm about her, pulling her close until she felt the girl's body yield to her embrace, her tears muffled against the pink towelling dressing-gown. "We'll laugh again – I think we can if we put our minds to it. I can promise you one thing though – all of you." She looked at Deirdre sitting at the breakfast-table, her head bent over her untouched cereal, and knew she was crying. Tommy was looking at her, a frightened look in his eyes. "Things will get better – I'll get a little job and we have enough money in the bank to tide us over until I've got things fixed up with your father. He can't just leave us like this – there are people who'll help us – he has to see we don't go short, even if he doesn't want to live here any more . . ." Her voice broke and she thought of the big, lonely bed upstairs, the years stretching endlessly ahead, long lonely nights and nightmares breaking through her troubled sleep …

"I'm taking Tommy to school this morning," she said firmly.

Today was the first day of the rest of their lives. She had read that line in a book about a group of people who had just been through separations. She couldn't have imagined then that the motto would one day apply to herself.

She took a five-euro note from her purse and gave it to Deirdre. "Here – buy yourselves a snack for elevenses."

Sharon was about to protest again, but Deirdre was looking at her with a "don't you dare" look in her eyes, so she remained silent. Five euros wouldn't go far for something decent to eat, Sharon thought, irritated. Mam must really be going round the twist.

Chapter 2

They left the house together ten minutes later, Sheila having hastily thrown on her lime-green tracksuit over her pyjamas, her bare feet encased in Deirdre's runners because she couldn't find her own. She had combed her dyed blonde hair carelessly, looking in the mirror in the hallway before she went, noticing that the roots badly needed redoing. If she met your one next door right now, she'd have enough to talk about. Esther never went outside the door of her house without a pound of expensive make-up on her face and a designer outfit encasing her anorexic figure. Sam had always been ridiculing her, saying how could her husband bear to make love to a bag of bones – a bit of flesh on a woman, there was nothing like it. Sam could have all the bit of flesh he wanted, now, Sheila thought as she hurried Tommy out the door, pausing for an instant as she looked at the empty driveway, Sam's car missing, the rain from the previous weeks having washed away all trace of tyre tracks until there was no longer any evidence of a car having been parked there.

He hadn't even left her that much, she thought angrily, feeling the reluctant Tommy pull at her hand as she hurried him towards the bus stop, the bus driver beckoning to her impatiently as the last of the passengers disappeared into the already crowded bus. She managed to get a seat at the back, squeezing herself between a woman with a laptop already open as she tapped her way expertly through her emails, and a schoolboy who made faces at Tommy, encouraging him to return the same. After a while reprimanding Tommy, she gave up, closing her eyes and relaxing against the seat. Life was just too complicated at the moment to worry about teaching Tommy the rudiments of good manners.

When they reached the school steps the yard was already deserted, the pupils gone into classes and Sheila hurried towards the main entrance, feeling the welcome heat warm her as she stepped into the corridor.

She could see Tommy's teacher standing in the doorway of his classroom, looking at her watch pointedly.

"I'm sorry, Miss Casey – I'm afraid we overslept this morning," Sheila explained breathlessly.

There was no answering smile from the other woman. Bitch! Sheila thought. How would *she* feel if her husband left her to cater for three children? But she wasn't even married, of course. Then Sheila felt cold at the thought that the teacher might guess what the situation was like at home. If Tommy should say anything, however innocently. 'Separated' was a dirty word still in some people's vocabulary. 'Separated' meant you keep your distance, especially if the 'separated' one was a woman. Separated meant game for anything, a disruptive influence on the status quo . . . maybe a husband might develop a roving eye for the 'separated' one. Miss Casey looked like a vigilante, protecting the sanctity of the marriage vows.

Sheila smiled suddenly at her wild imaginings. She could imagine Miss Casey hanging a bell around the neck of the 'separated one', shouting out at the top of her voice, 'Unclean!' Miss Casey should wait until she had a man of her own, and was married twenty years with a few children before she judged the lot of the 'separated ones'.

"Sister Regina was just on the intercom, Mrs Shaughnessy, speaking about latecomers, and in future they will be marked absent if they are more than ten minutes late." Her face was expressionless, her voice grating on Sheila's nerves as she reluctantly handed over her son to the tall, thin woman.

"I'll collect you at lunch-time, love – and I'll have that surprise for you." She winked conspiratorially at him.

He smiled, sighing happily – it was nice to have the old mam back again.

Sheila fixed the teacher with a cold look. "It won't happen again, Miss Casey."

The teacher nodded. "Well, come along, Tommy."

For an instant, Tommy looked back at his mother, and she wanted to pick him up and run home with him. They could sit in front of the television all day and watch cartoons and whatever other sort of nonsense Tommy liked, and eat popcorn until it came out of their ears. She couldn't, though. She had things to do today.

She squared her shoulders determinedly, and with her head of black-rooted greasy hair held high, marched out the door and down the front steps of the school.

Once outside, her decisiveness began to waver. Where could she begin? Would she go to the

Social Welfare office first, or to the bank? Should she go to Sam's firm and look for information as to his whereabouts? She didn't want to, it would be so degrading, and then the gossip would spread and everybody would know and she might as well bury herself and be done with it. No. She'd go to the hairdresser's first. She needed to do that before she approached the bank manager. She had some emergency money left in her purse from the last Children's Allowance. She'd have her hair fixed nicely – a wash, cut and blow-dry. She hadn't enough to have the roots touched up, but at least it would make her feel a bit more human. Then she'd go to the bank and she'd see what the money situation was like. Sam had opened a joint account just three years ago – "for our old age" he had joked with her. She had never taken much interest in it since, because she wasn't working outside the home, and she had never contributed to the account. How naive can a woman be, she thought bitterly as she made her way up the steps of Tasha's Hair Salon. She had relied too much on Sam, had never for a moment thought that he would ever do the dirty on her. She looked at two men fixing a lock on the door of Tasha's place, laughing about some television programme they had seen the previous night on telly.

Telly, booze, fags, sex and football, she said to herself as she passed them. You could sum up the opposite sex in those five words. Kids, the lot of them. She knew she was being unfair to most men, but nobody could blame her for being prejudiced just now, she thought darkly. In Sam's case sex would come first. She had never really been up to par in his opinion – always telling her it was her fault when she didn't climax at just the right moment. So she had faked it, marvelling sometimes at how well she played the part, rolling about in ecstasy beneath Sam's heaving body, and feeling so relieved when eventually she could turn over and sleep, knowing that in spite of his contrived macho-like antics, Sam's performance was only adequate for one 'fix' in the night.

Soon Sheila was sitting at the washbasin, leaning her head back as Tasha gently caressed her scalp, the light, herb smell of the shampoo like a breath of fresh air as she closed her eyes, listening to Tasha's incessant chatter.

"You weren't here for a while, Sheila – it must be almost a month now – God, your roots are very black – are you sure you wouldn't let me do them for you now? It's no good getting a new hairstyle when the roots are all black."

"I'm a bit short this morning, Tasha – maybe at the end of the month – I can wait until then."

Tasha looked down at her client, observing lines of strain about the eyes. Tasha was the type who thought all women were underdogs in a man's world. If she could do a woman a favour, she felt she had struck a blow for Women's Lib. Her auld fella had left her almost ten years ago. She had set up the hair salon since then. She had taken a Fás course in hairdressing and worked as a trainee for a pittance until she got the grant which allowed her to rent the salon space and transform it, giving it the ambience of a successful hairdressing salon with a relaxing peaches-and-cream decor. She had never looked back. Her auld fella had come back several times when he had heard that she was making money, whining about the good times and the mistake he had made in leaving her. She had given him the two-finger salute and shoved him out the door, warning him never to come near her again.

She finished shampooing Sheila's hair and, as she placed a fresh towel about her shoulders, was shocked at the way her shoulder bones protruded through the top of her tracksuit. The woman was in trouble – just a hunch she had – and could do with a friend right now. But Sheila Shaughnessy was proud. In the five years she had been coming to have her hair done, Tasha had never heard her gossip about anybody – she had never a bad word to say, most times just sitting quietly while Tasha manoeuvred her hair into the bob she usually asked for. She would never confide to Tasha, no matter how bad things were with her.

"Look – I'm not busy this morning – I'll have the roots done in no time, and you can pay me for the lot at the end of the month – honestly, I'm only looking for something to do this morning. It's a bit slack."

Sheila hesitated. She looked about the salon. There was one woman in the corner with perm curlers in her hair, waiting patiently until it was rinsed out, her forehead swathed with cotton wool. It would be nice to have her hair fixed properly, especially if she had to go to see Michael Bates at the bank. She didn't want to let herself down, not in front of him.

"Well, if you're sure ..." she started hesitantly, but Tasha had sat her firmly in front of the mirror, taken down the bottle of dye and fixed the nozzle to the top of it before she had a chance to change her mind.

"I'll have you going out of here looking like a million dollars – your man won't know you when he sees you. And you're having a new hairstyle – that bob of yours has seen its day. I have this great new hairstyle that I'm just dying to try out and you're perfect for it!"

"I don't know, Tasha – I'm too old for anything new." Sheila looked doubtfully at the sketch Tasha presented to her. It was a beautiful cut, short at the sides and short and wispy at the back, the top full and curling seductively on to the model's forehead. "It looks lovely on her, but would it suit me?"

Tasha looked at Sheila's face, studying it carefully. "Your face is too thin for all that hair. This is just the style for you – it'll take years off you. Just wait and see!"

Sheila shrugged her shoulders resignedly. She had nothing to lose. There was no Sam at home now to criticise – she could dye her hair purple if she wanted to.

Two hours later, Sheila was walking down the steps from Tasha's salon, one hand self-consciously feeling the wispy curls of hair on her forehead. The girls would get a shock when they saw her. She had never had her hair cut so short in her whole life. "Time to make a change, love," Tasha had said intuitively, and Sheila had nodded. There was no need to say anything more. Sheila's silence had told Tasha that here was another woman with man trouble.

She had reached the end step when she heard the whistle. A piercing wolf-whistle that made her look round in surprise. She saw the two workmen at the top of the stairs grinning down at her, the admiration obvious on their faces.

"Keep it like that, love! You look just like that film star – you know the one – Michelle Pfeiffer – your auld fella won't know himself tonight!"

Sheila blushed and turned away. The wolf-whistle was a blast from the past, calling up bittersweet memories of Sam's admiring glances at her whenever she had a particularly sexy outfit on, or when she had got her hair styled differently. Now she had no Sam to dress for, no Sam to tell her she was looking good, a message in his eyes conveying how much he wanted her ... When she was in her twenties, she had been annoyed whenever a man showed his appreciation by whistling after her. Now it was different. She was forty, and two men had whistled after her, and she could have kissed them both, they had made her feel so good about herself. She turned back to them and smiled. "Have a nice day!"

She crossed the road to the bank. She walked through the swing doors and up to the receptionist who sat behind a desk overflowing with potted plants and evergreen creepers.

"I'd like to speak to Mr Bates, please," she said in a low voice.

The girl looked up at her and smiled. "Mr Bates will be free in just a few moments. If you can just take a seat ... what name shall I say?"

"Shaughnessy – Sheila Shaughnessy – I have an account here."

She felt a little uncertain now that she was actually in the bank, waiting to see the manager. She had never been in the bank before, always leaving the paying of bills and any other money matters to Sam. He had just given her the housekeeping money, and told her that he would take care of the rest. She cursed herself now for being so complacent about everything. Would anybody believe that she had never had cause to go to the bank in all the years they had been married? What if the manager didn't believe that she really *was* Sheila Shaughnessy? The humiliation of it, if he had her checked up on ... she had the Children's Allowance book in her bag – that might be enough identification ...

Sweat began to form on her forehead as the anxiety attack took hold. She stood up suddenly, about to turn and walk out through the swing floors again, when the office door opened behind the receptionist.

The girl smiled at Sheila. "You can go in, Mrs Shaughnessy – Mr Bates will see you now."

Her legs felt like jelly as she went into the office and crossed the red-carpeted office to sit in front of the tall, distinguished-looking man.

Chapter 3

Michael Bates had the compassionate look of a man used to dealing with people who had reached the end of their tether. He could spot a client with more money than they could handle just as readily as he could see the despair in the eyes of a woman, just like this one before him now, who probably hadn't even the price of a good dinner in her purse. He could tell by the way she gripped her handbag, the muscles on her hands tense, that Sheila was a woman with a lot of problems and not only financial ones.

"Mrs Shaughnessy? Take a seat there, won't you? I'll get you a cup of coffee – there's a bit of a nip in the air this morning, not quite spring yet by the looks of it!" Sheila started to protest that coffee wouldn't be necessary, but he was already buzzing his secretary, querying Sheila if she liked it black or white, sugar or –?

"White, please – no sugar," she answered him faintly.

The mini-skirted girl with the crisp white silk blouse came floating into the office, balancing two cups of coffee delicately in her hands, the beautifully manicured nails painted deep red, fascinating Sheila as she looked at the cup of coffee with a confused detachment. The girl smiled as she placed the coffee on a table next to her, a whiff of expensive perfume – Passion, Sheila thought – filling the room as she went as swiftly as she had come.

"Now – what can I do for you, Mrs Shaughnessy?"

Sheila had lifted the cup to her lips, her hand shaking, and now she replaced it quickly in the saucer, almost overbalancing it in the process.

Michael Bates nodded reassuringly at her. "I believe your husband has an account with us, isn't that right?" His fingers were busily checking the computer in front of him as he spoke and Sheila felt as if her whole personal life was wide open to this stranger, imagining him tapping suddenly into the terrible revelation emblazoned like some incriminating sentence on the screen: *Her husband has left her!*

She took a deep breath. She had to calm herself, stop her mind playing these terrible tricks on her.

"Yes – it's a joint account and I was wondering if perhaps I could withdraw some money – or get a loan – would that be all right?"

Michael Bates fingered his chin thoughtfully. He'd have to look into this account more thoroughly. Sam Shaughnessy had been putting large sums of money into his account for some time. A salesman's salary would never amount to the substantial deposits he had lodged on the first of every month. If his wife wished to withdraw some of that money, he would have to clear it with her husband first.

He looked at her appraisingly, noticing the worried lines on her forehead, the lips almost frozen in a thin, anxious line. It was funny the pictures one conjured up of a person's spouse. He had always pictured Shaughnessy's wife as a tall, elegant, probably blonde woman, with one of those false St Tropez tans, sophisticated in appearance. This small, fair-haired woman sitting in front of him dressed in a green track-suit, her pale face dominated by the big frightened eyes, was not at all how he had imagined her.

"I'll just check on that account for you ..." He buzzed the secretary once more, asked her for ledger details of Sam Shaughnessy's account, and minutes later she came slinking back into the room, her slim hips beneath the mini-skirt moving seductively as she floated behind his desk, handing him the necessary information.

Sheila watched her enviously. She hoped that Michael Bates' wife wasn't the sort who went about the house in a dirty dressing-gown until midday with spots of baby food spattered across the front. If so, then she'd better watch out for seductive *femmes fatales* like his secretary.

"Now – let me see . . ." He opened the ledger and looked down the columns of figures, one eyebrow raised incredulously as he surveyed the final total.

"I'm sorry, Mrs Shaughnessy, but I'm afraid I'll have to investigate your husband's account further – you see, he has withdrawn everything, all except one hundred euro – and he has changed the account name. The joint account is now obsolete – the account is now in the sole name of Sam Shaughnessy."

Sheila was beginning to lose her hold on reality. The money she thought was safely put away for them in the bank – even the hundred euro he had left in the account – was no good to her, because it was in Sam's name only – she had no claim to it. She didn't understand – surely he needed her permission to change the account's name? She looked at Michael Bates, her eyes pleading with him. "I didn't sign any papers to transfer the account into his name – surely there's some record of it in your files – *I signed nothing,* do you hear me – my husband had no right!"

She felt the room getting warmer. Michael Bates was saying something to her but she couldn't focus properly. His face was a kaleidoscope of colour, the sun's rays coming through the window behind him blinding her, making his features swim before her eyes. Then she slumped forward onto the desk, sending the coffee cup and saucer flying to the ground, overturning its dark brown liquid onto the pale-coloured carpet.

From far away she heard somebody, a female voice, saying "Shall I fetch a doctor, Mr Bates?" Then the scent of Passion perfume was in her nostrils,

"Mrs Shaughnessy, are you all right?" said Michael Bates. "I think she's coming round – a glass of iced water, I think, Muriel." He gripped Sheila firmly about the shoulders. "Here you are – take some of this, Mrs Shaughnessy. It will make you feel better." He held the glass to her dry lips.

She sipped gratefully, the feeling of disorientation gradually dispersing as she finally lay back against the leather-covered chair. "I'm sorry – it was just a shock, you see – I hadn't realised Sam had closed the account – it was all we had."

Her voice trembled and Michael Bates

wondered what kind of man could leave a woman in such a state, not caring where her future lay, or even if she was capable of making a future for herself now. In fact, observing the state the woman was in right now, he wondered if she could ever get over her husband's actions.

"I'll have to check on this further, Mrs Shaughnessy – I think it could be a police matter."

Sheila looked up at him in horror. "Oh no! Please – I'm sure he wouldn't be capable of doing anything illegal – please, wait a little longer. Perhaps he'll contact you – give you some explanation."

He thought of his own wife at home. Shirley had just turned forty and was expecting their third child after a break of almost fifteen years. They had been devastated at first, Shirley ranting and raving about how tied she was going to be, having to give up her job in interior design, her life brought to a standstill. Gradually they had both come to terms with it, Shirley begging him to forgive her for her outburst, he in turn apologising for his lack of understanding – things were never so bad when you had the support of a good partner. It was when that support was lacking that everything fell apart. Sheila Shaughnessy had lost the crutch she had obviously over-relied on over the years. She had nobody to turn to now. Michael looked at the hollowed cheekbones, the too-thin frame of her small body, and made a quick decision.

"I'll do a bit of investigating on my own, just for now. I'll have to try to trace your husband. There's nothing I can do about the money situation, I'm afraid – he had lodged approximately 10,000 euro in his account over the last year, and now he has withdrawn the lot." He looked at her stricken expression and couldn't help the feeling of guilt he felt at that moment, knowing that in some way he had contributed to this woman's predicament. "Did you know he was lodging that money, Mrs Shaughnessy?"

"No," she whispered. "I have no idea where he would get money like that. It couldn't be from his salary."

"Well, whatever about his sources of income, the fact that the money was withdrawn while the account was in both your names warrants a full investigation by the bank." He would have gladly given her money out of his own pocket at that very moment, because she obviously needed a Good Samaritan to give her a helping hand, yet instinctively he knew that any such offer on his part would be met with a firm refusal. This woman wouldn't take charity.

"Have you any other means of support, Mrs Shaughnessy?" he asked urgently. "Are you working – have you a family that maybe could offer you support at this time?"

Sheila shook her head, her thoughts whirling about in her head until she felt it might burst. "I haven't got a job – I was a secretary before I married Sam – he wanted me to give up working then, stay at home to look after the house and the children." She gave a stifled sob, lifting her tear-stained face to Michael Bates. "I made a big mistake by not holding on to my independence, Mr Bates – you can never rely on anybody to look after you for the rest of your life – not even your husband!" She bit her lip as she tried to hold back the tears. With an effort she controlled herself, and looked at him, her gaze steady, a determined light in her eyes. "Don't worry. We'll manage – now that I know where I stand. If you could just help me to trace my husband – if he has all that money then I think his family deserve some of it – I think twenty years of loyal service to a partner deserves something in return, don't you, Mr Bates?" She got up unsteadily, holding out her hand to him.

He grasped it in his for a second, feeling the chill of her ice-cold skin against his warm palm, flinching for a second at the cold touch.

"I must go now," she said. "I have to collect my son from school."

He didn't know what to say to her. He stood there in the centre of the room, watching her as she left, closing the door silently behind her. He waited for a second, staring blankly at the wall of his office before pressing the intercom button on his desk.

"Muriel – get me everything you can about Sam Shaughnessy's account – and hold all my calls for an hour or so – I'm going to check everything connected with this guy." He sat back in his seat, his mouth set in a grim line. The bank had a lot to answer for, if Sam Shaughnessy had been allowed to breach every security measure drawn up to safeguard customers' money. Sheila Shaughnessy had been an unwitting victim and he was going to see to it that she was well compensated for this negligence.

Chapter 4

Mechanically Sheila walked in the direction of St Finbarr's church. She had half an hour yet until she collected Tommy. She sat in the dark corner on the left-hand aisle, in front of the statue of the Sacred Heart, his hands opened wide to reveal his bleeding heart.

"Sweet Jesus, please help me to stay sane, for my children's sake," she whispered, her shoulders now heaving as she gave up the battle to keep the tears in check, her sobbing echoing in a hollow sound around the silent church.

She didn't hear somebody approach her, didn't feel the light touch on her arm until a voice spoke softly in her ear.

"There now – things can't be that bad – do you want to talk about it?"

She looked up, startled. The man was tall and well-built, a mop of dark curly hair falling untidily on to his forehead, his brown eyes gentle and sympathetic as he looked down at her. Almost without thinking she blurted out, her voice catching in a sob "I wish I was dead!"

He gave no response, showed no surprise at the words. Instead he helped her to her feet. "Stephen O'Hara is my name. I'm the parish priest in these parts. You're not from this parish yourself?" He sat down next to her on the seat.

Sheila shook her head miserably. "No – I'm from St Gabriel's."

He put up his hands in resignation. "Ah well, you can't blame a guy for trying to recruit some new members to the congregation!"

She gave a polite, lukewarm smile.

He tapped her on the shoulder. "Come on – we'll go inside and have a chat."

He guided her through to the sacristy, across the cobbled yard and into the little bungalow next to the church.

He ushered her into the living room, then looked at her apologetically as he saw her noticing his lunch on the coffee table – a big wedge of cheese and some roughly cut tomatoes sandwiched between two uneven pieces of bread on a paper napkin. "Mags – the woman who does a bit of cleaning and cooking for me – she has a day off today. I have to get my own lunch ready. Don't worry – I won't ask you to join me," he said with a grin and Sheila had to smile in spite of her misery.

He led her to the chair by the warm, open fire, throwing another sod of turf on to the dying flames, kindling it once more into life.

"Now – I'll go and make some tea – tea and sympathy go well together, so they say – and you can tell me about whatever it is that's troubling you."

"I can't stay long, Father – I have to collect my son from school." Sheila looked at her watch agitatedly. Now that she was more in control of herself, the dark depression that had come over her in the bank now dissipated somewhat, she felt acutely embarrassed in front of this stranger.

He handed her a cup of tea, indicating the sugar and milk on the coffee table, and reluctantly she accepted. She seemed to be doing nothing this morning only accepting cups of tea from people who had really no idea what she was going through. She fought back angry tears and he looked at her, waiting, then picked up the sugar bowl and, without asking her, popped a spoonful into her tea.

"Plenty of sugar, that's what you need – just

the job, so the experts say, for an attack of the miseries!"

She took a sip from the cup of strong, sweet tea, then sat back in the chair, her gaze on the orange flames as the fire once again took hold, sending sparks flying up the chimney.

"I don't know what to do, Father – nobody can help me," she said, her face a pale mask of misery. "What does a woman do when her husband leaves her?"

The anguish in her voice made him sit up and listen.

"We have no money – maybe even the house might be taken away from us." She put down the cup on the coffee table, a thought suddenly coming to her. She looked at him, her eyes anxious. "We have a mortgage on the house until next year – where will I get the money to keep up with the repayments? Does God rain money on people like me, Father? Is it fair?" She talked on, her words tumbling out, angry words, frightened words, a torrent of bitter accusations against her husband.

When she had finished Stephen O'Hara looked across at her, seeing the lines of strain beneath her eyes. "I have no answers for you – but I might have some temporary solution to your predicament, such as it is, at the moment." He stood up and paced the room, silent for a while, then turned to her as if he had suddenly come to a decision. "The first thing you have to do is to go to the Garda Station, tell them your husband has left you, you don't know where he is – and you must find him as you need money to keep yourself and your family." His tone was matter-of-fact – no questions as to why her husband might have felt so desperate that he had made a decision to opt out of his responsibilities.

She felt suddenly at peace. She was tired of thinking, of trying to put the pieces of a jigsaw together that would never be completed until she found out where Sam had gone.

"I didn't want to get the gardai involved, Father. I thought it might be something of a betrayal – telling people about him, having him followed, when maybe there's a perfectly good explanation for it ... something he didn't want to tell me at the time ..."

She looked like a small child hoping that her dreams might come true, Stephen thought sympathetically.

She looked at her watch and rose to leave, explaining again that she had to go to pick up her son. He rose to accompany her.

With one hand on the door-handle, she turned to him and said, "Maybe it was all my fault, maybe I was to blame ... I used to nag him about doing the garden at weekends when maybe he needed a rest – or sometimes I'd ask him to look after the children while I went for a swim to the leisure centre on a Saturday evening – maybe it was me, Father ..." Her face was ashen, the misery in her face making the bones stick out, skeletal, dark circles outlining her eyes.

"We'll have none of that – no blaming yourself – explanations are what we need now, and we're going to have to start somewhere." He followed her to the door, picking up his car keys on the way. "Come on – I'll run you down to the school – then we'll go to the Garda Station and you can tell them everything." He led the way, through the hallway and out onto the pebbled driveway where his car, a Starlet, was parked.

In a daze, Sheila fastened her seat belt and they set off through the lunch-time traffic. When they reached the school, Father O'Hara manoeuvred the car into a narrow parking space, while she closed her eyes, afraid to look at the car in front, the gleaming silver paintwork in danger of becoming streaked with the dark blue of the Starlet.

"There you go – perfect parking, eh?" He looked at her, a satisfied grin on his face. Sheila nodded, taking a deep breath. He had parked in a double-yellow-line area and she felt a sudden urge to burst out laughing that she could only suppose was a prelude to hysteria.

"Go on in and get him, like a good woman – or we'll have our own personal escort to the Garda Station if they come along and find me parked here – right in front of a lorry exit!"

Sheila laughed aloud. She was surprised at the sound, couldn't remember when she had laughed last, certainly not since Sam had left them.

Stephen O'Hara looked pleased. "That's more like it – chin up and bugger the begrudgers, that's what I say – and I'm never wrong when it comes to advice!"

She was still smiling as she went in to collect Tom, and she sighed in relief as she noticed the smile on the teacher's face, her humour obviously improved from this morning.

"There you go, Mrs Shaughnessy – he's a great boy – he got a book this morning as a prize for his reading and spelling."

"Will you read it to me tonight, please – when I go to bed?" said Tom eagerly.

"Just try to stop me!" said Sheila smiling.

Sheila took Tom's hand firmly in hers. She looked at the teacher gratefully. The woman wasn't so bad, after all. Everybody had their bad days, teachers included.

"Thank you, Miss Casey – and I'll have him on time tomorrow morning, don't worry."

Elinor Casey looked at Sheila Shaughnessy's pale face, the tired lines around her eyes, and knew instinctively that this woman had problems. She felt a pang of remorse as she remembered how impatient she had been that morning. She resolved to be more considerate in future. If teaching young children had taught her anything, it was that not every child's tardiness was caused by a lazy parent. "I'm sorry about this morning – I know it's a hassle for every mother trying to get the children to school on time – let's just forget about it, okay?"

"Thank you, Miss Casey." Sheila smiled gratefully. The day was beginning to look a little more promising. She had met kindness in Father Stephen when he had given her a sympathetic ear, and now in Miss Casey, who didn't seem to be the ogre she had thought her to be that morning.

Tom spoke up as they left the school. "Miss Casey was very nice to me today, Mam – and I got all my sums right, too – Daddy will be proud of me when he comes home, won't he?" He looked up at her anxiously and it was as though a dark cloud had descended, her optimism vanishing in an instant, leaving her with the dull weight of depression that came upon her whenever Sam's name was mentioned.

"He will be very proud of you, son." She turned her face away from him so that he couldn't see the sudden tears in her eyes.

The nightmare was never-ending, the 'missing'

time heavy on her heart as she tried to get through the days and nights without him. It wasn't fair, she thought tearfully. Life wasn't fair to her or her children right now!

Chapter 5

"How long has your husband been gone, Mrs Shaughnessy?" The garda was polite, the yellow form in front of him, his pen poised for action as he waited for Sheila's reply.

Father O'Hara nodded encouragingly at her. Tom stood near the desk, playing with a miniature toy car the friendly garda had taken from a drawer in his desk and handed to him.

"He's gone three weeks, almost four."

The garda raised his head and looked at her doubtfully. "Are you sure you want to fill out a missing person's form, Mrs Shaughnessy? He isn't really gone long enough to warrant a full investigation."

"He's gone long enough for me to know he's not coming back – long enough for him to close our joint account in the bank and leave me and the children without a penny to keep us!"

Her voice rose as her anger filled the room, and he looked down, embarrassed, at the paper in front of him.

"I'm sorry – I realise this is a bad time for you – I was only trying to point out to you the way things are done here."

Father O'Hara gave him a pointed look, his eyes indicating Sheila's worried face in a silent request not to push too hard, afraid that Sheila might break down altogether. "That's okay," he said to the garda. "We understand you have to go through the procedures – but we're talking desperate circumstances here if the man isn't found soon." He looked around at Tom, but the boy seemed oblivious to what was being said, the book he had won at school open in front of him, his face screwed up in concentration as he tried to read the more difficult words.

"The thing is – this woman and her children have been deserted by a husband and father, and it might take a while before she gets some financial assistance from the State – maybe you could hurry things up a bit for her, eh?"

Stephen O'Hara fixed the young garda with a determined gaze. He was used to getting his own way, following things through, for the most part, to a satisfactory conclusion.

Tom was sitting on the wooden bench behind the door now, swinging his legs backwards and forwards. He was getting tired, and hungry. Every now and then his heels would bang against the wall, sending some of the cream-coloured plaster in a powdery shower to the floor. Sheila looked across at him and he expected a sharp rebuke – 'Stop kicking the walls, Tom! Sit quietly!" – but there was no reaction, just a glazed, troubled look in his mother's eyes.

The young garda finished completing the missing persons form, then handed the pen to Sheila. "Just sign your name there, Mrs Shaughnessy." He indicated with his finger and Sheila took the pen, signing her name mechanically. "You know, this might take weeks, months even. If a person doesn't want to be found, then he can make it very hard for us." He got up and shook hands with Sheila, his eyes behind the regulatory impartiality of his office warm and sympathetic.

"Thank you. If you hear anything, please contact me," said Sheila, beckoning to Tom. "Come along, love. There's no more we can do now except wait."

"Will they find Daddy, Mam? When will he be coming back? I don't like it when you're sad."

His bottom lip started to tremble and, seeing

all the signs of a tearful outburst, Father Stephen grasped him firmly by the arm, steering him through the swing doors of the garda station and into the bright spring sunlight. "Come along now – I think an ice cream might be in order, eh, Mammy? And maybe you could manage a double cheeseburger beforehand at McDonald's, or maybe that appetite of yours isn't up to it?"

Sheila looked at him, embarrassed. "Oh no, Father – you've done too much already – really – we'll go home now, try to get things sorted out –"

Father Stephen, much to Tom's delight, shook his head vigorously. "I'll not take no for an answer – I'll bet you could do with a bite to eat yourself, and as for me – well, that stale cheese and tomato sandwich didn't go down too well, so I think I'll indulge myself."

Fifteen minutes later they were sitting in McDonald's, Tom's mouth embroidered with a ribbon of tomato sauce, his face ecstatic, as he bit into a Big Mac. Sheila was surprised to find that she felt quite hungry, and when the plate of french fries and a crispy chicken salad was placed in front of her, she made short work of it, finally settling back in her seat, the tension in her head dissolving slowly as she sipped a cappuccino.

Stephen O'Hara looked up as he finished his meal. "My God, but if I could only persuade Mags the housekeeper to cook things like this, I'd give her double pay for her troubles, and that's a fact!"

They finished their meal with three ice-cream sundaes – chocolate for Tom, caramel for Sheila and strawberry for Stephen.

Tom's head began to droop with tiredness as he licked the last of the ice cream from his spoon.

"Come on, son," said Stephen. "Time you were getting home – and maybe forty winks would be the order of the day, eh, Mammy?"

He winked at Sheila and she smiled.

"What's forty winks, Mam?" Tom enquired sleepily as they settled into the back of Stephen's car. Sheila didn't have to answer. His head fell sideways and she held him closer to her, the enormity of her situation once more rearing its ugly head as she tried to come to terms with the painful reality that now she was on her own. And if Sam did come back, what then? Could they possibly live together, as man and wife, after all that had happened?

Stephen O'Hara looked at her through his rear-view mirror and smiled reassuringly. "Keep those dark thoughts at bay for a little while, Sheila – take one day at a time – have trust in the Lord." He said the last bit with such determination that Sheila felt guilty for being so cynical, envying him his faith, his air of quiet complacency that everything would work itself out in the end.

Her faith had never really been a great force in her life. Oh, she had prayed when money was scarce, or when the children were sick, like the Christmas Deirdre was rushed to hospital with a threatened burst appendix. This time it was different. How could she pray for something as intangible as the repair of a broken marriage? Even the Lord must have His limitations, she thought bitterly.

"Do you think He'll be able to put things back together again, Father – just the way they used to be? Do you think if I have faith in the Lord, all the bad bits will be blown away on the wind and we can start again?"

"I won't insult your intelligence by parroting a few comforting platitudes, Sheila," he answered her quietly, keeping his gaze fixed on the road ahead. "But time has a great way of making the world come full circle, helps us to recognise when it's time to let go – or hold on. I think the Lord plays a major role in directing our paths, steering us in the right direction. Give Him a chance, like a good girl!"

Chapter 6

The car pulled up outside the house, and Father Stephen helped Sheila get Tom out of the car and up the path, holding him firmly while she rummaged in her bag for her keys. But before she had a chance to get the key into the lock, the door was opened slowly, and Deirdre stood there, her face tear-stained.

"Deirdre, love, what's the matter – what's happened?"

Deirdre flung herself into her mother's arms, her shoulders heaving as she tried to speak between sobs. "It's Dad – he rang – just about half an hour ago – I couldn't hear him very well – he said something about being sorry for the mess – I think he thought he was speaking to you, Mam!" She began to cry again, great pitiful sobs that tore at Sheila's heart, and for the hundredth time since he had left, she cursed Sam for doing this thing to them. Yet at the same time hope was dawning.

"Come on," said Stephen. "Let's all go into the house before the neighbours start getting nosey around here."

He gave Sheila a gentle shove and her feet moved mechanically inside the front door into the hallway. She still had her arm about Deirdre's shoulders but she felt it was more to support herself than to offer any degree of comfort to the girl.

"Mam! Deirdre said Dad rang!" Sharon was standing at the top of the stairs, her face flushed with excitement. "He was calling from someplace foreign – Deirdre said it was through a German telephone exchange! He's coming home, I just know he is!" As Sharon looked down on the group in the hall, her mind was racing. Maybe things would be back to normal soon, if Dad came home – Mam wasn't up to much on her own. Besides, there was the financial aspect . . . there was the summer tour to consider ... the class were going to the South of France this year. There was no way Mam could afford it. Not on her own. But if Dad should decide to come back ...

At fifteen, Sharon had already grasped the

fundamental art of survival.

Father Stephen looked up at the girl, saw through the concerned look on her young face and thought to himself 'A cute young one'. He looked at the pale face of Deirdre, her hands plucking distractedly at the buttons on her school uniform. The contrast between the two girls was striking. He felt sorry for the older one. With a sister like Sharon, he knew she was in for a rough ride, even without any of this hassle with their father.

"Did he say he was coming home, love?" asked Sheila, her heart pounding.

"He didn't say ..." Deirdre said dully, pushing a strand of hair back from her face.

Sharon ran down the stairs, bouncing from one step to the next. "Yes, did he say when he was coming? Maybe he's on a business trip and he couldn't tell us about it – you know how some firms swear their employees to secrecy about business and all that stuff!" Her face looked animated. He was coming home, she just knew it! And if Mam played her cards right, everything would be fine again. It must have been at least some of her fault, this break-up. Dad had always been such fun, not like Mam, always giving out about silly things, like skipping classes.

"Where was he ringing from?" Sheila asked anxiously. "A German exchange, you said?"

"I don't know, Mam. He didn't say where he was," said Deirdre, "but it sounded long distance – he was surrounded by buzzing sounds and I heard a girl speaking in German in the background. She was saying something to him – I heard him say '*Ich werde nicht lange*' – that means 'I won't be long' in German. Would he be in Germany, Mam – on business?"

Father Stephen looked at Sheila enquiringly. If he was out of the country then things might be a bit more complicated than just getting fed up with his wife and family. There was the money taken out of the bank account, money Sheila couldn't account for, money that a computer software salesman could never hope to accumulate in such a short space of time.

"I don't know, Father," she answered his unspoken enquiry tiredly. "I don't know what to think any more."

Tom was sitting quietly on the sofa in the living room. His eyes were focused on the Santa photograph perched on the mantelpiece. There was Sam's face, smiling out at him, one arm about Tom, the other holding Tom's Santa parcel. There had been a combat set inside, he remembered. All the pieces were missing now, just a small few with broken arms and legs thrown beneath his bed upstairs.

"Mam! The surprise! You never got me the

surprise – you *promised*!" He looked at Sheila reproachfully.

"Didn't we go in for Big Macs and those sundaes – wasn't that surprise enough?" Father Stephen demanded, catching Tom, swinging him high into the air and down again.

Tom stared at the big man with the powerful arms and the loud, penetrating voice. Shyness overcame him and he looked at Sheila appealingly. He had never seen a priest like this one before. They were all quiet and holy and came to visit them in the classroom to talk to them about being good and to stop committing sins, like pulling Sharon's hair, or messing up Mam's floor in the bathroom with water while he was playing canoes in the bath.

"Well? Was that a surprise or wasn't it?" Father Stephen demanded, the twinkle in his eye putting Tom at ease as he smiled shyly at him.

"Yes – I just thought Mam meant another kind of surprise – like a toy or something. I love toys," he finished stubbornly.

"We'll go into the toy shop on Saturday, I promise," Sheila said, fixing him with an encouraging smile, "and we'll have a look to see if they have a wrestler – if he's not too dear, then maybe we can get him for your collection."

Tom nodded, satisfied.

"And what about me?" Sharon glared at Sheila

angrily. "It's always Tom that gets the treats. I asked you for money the day before yesterday for the disco at the school on Friday night – and you said you hadn't got it! It's not fair!"

Sheila sat down on the old leather armchair next to the window, put her head in her hands and, to their horror, started to cry loudly, the desperation in her voice echoing about the room, her thin body almost lost in the depths of the chair as she rocked backwards and forwards, the loud cries then reduced to low, moaning noises.

"Father?" Deirdre looked at the priest helplessly. She didn't know whether to apologise for Sheila's outburst or to turn on Sharon angrily for causing the upset.

Father Stephen rapidly assessed the situation. He took Sheila by the arm, then beckoned to Deirdre to take her upstairs. "She's worn out, needs a good rest, that's all that's wrong with your mother – and a little bit of cooperation mightn't go astray." He looked at Sharon pointedly, but she turned away from him.

Priest or not, he was a busybody in her estimation. And Mam was an embarrassment, breaking down like that.

"You, young lady, go into the kitchen and make your mother a cup of tea with plenty of sugar in it," he commanded her. For a moment, he thought she was about to refuse, but then one look at his face and she obviously thought better of it.

"Tom – you do your homework, like a good lad, and let your mother sleep for a bit – when she wakes up she'll be more fun than she is now."

Tom nodded solemnly. If a rest was going to put Mam into a better mood, then he'd stay as quiet as a mouse – provided Sharon didn't start at him. She was always giving out to him. He took out his English reader and began to read slowly: *"Barry and Anne are in the shop."*

* * *

"What am I going to do, Father? I've no money – what will we live on?" Sheila lay on the bed, her back propped up against the pillow Deirdre had placed behind her. The cup of tea lay untouched on the bedside table.

Stephen O'Hara looked down at her, and made a sudden decision. "I'm going to loan you a bit." He put up his hand to stop her as she began to protest. "No, listen to me – there's more than you in this parish that needs a little financial assistance at some stage in their lives – and, if you like, I'll make it a genuine loan, with interest – until you get on your feet."

"You're very good, Father, but I really don't think –"

"I just want to see you out of this trouble and strong enough to look after your family downstairs." He nodded his head in the direction of the living room where they could hear the television blaring. "First thing in the morning, we'll go back to the gardai and tell them about the phone call."

Sheila looked at him, frightened. "What if he's in some kind of trouble, Father? I wouldn't want to get him into more of a mess than he's already in right now."

"And what about the mess he's left you in?" The priest looked at her in exasperation. "Have sense, like a good woman – he has to be found, to give you support for the children. It's his duty to look after you all, and the sooner he starts doing that, the better. The marriage might be over, but he can't run out on his responsibilities."

Chapter 7

"When was this phone call?" The young garda behind the desk was writing busily in the book opened in front of him. He had sympathy for the woman, but these things were happening every day, men running out on their responsibilities. He didn't like saying it to her but if the man was out of the country, it could take them months, even years to trace him. She could be in very bad circumstances by then, financially, unless she had the resources to keep her and the children.

"He telephoned yesterday afternoon, when the eldest girl was home from school," said Stephen.

Sheila sat, white-faced, holding the edge of the desk, her knuckles white with tension as she bit her lip, trying to remain calm.

"She thought he was speaking through a German exchange," Stephen continued.

The garda wrote rapidly, the expression on his face unaltered.

"Do you think you could put a trace on him?" Stephen leaned forward determinedly, his quiet air of authority making the young man appear more alert, forcing him to shed some of the official impartiality.

"Look, we'll do what we can, but I can't promise you anything. We'll look into the matter of the missing money, certainly, and if there's been anything shady going on, then that will speed things up a bit. He can't hide forever." He looked across at Sheila enquiringly. "What company did your husband work for, Mrs Shaughnessy?"

"Griffith and Markham, Software Specialists," she told him.

"We'll get in touch with them right away. If company funds are involved it might be worthwhile to pursue that angle rather than just treating it as a missing person's report." He finished writing in the notebook in front of him, then stood up, closing the book decisively. "Companies who trade overseas have a network of contacts who can trace somebody faster than any effort on our part – sometimes, I'll have to admit, they even operate more efficiently." He gave Sheila a reassuring smile. "Don't worry, Mrs. Shaughnessy – we'll find your husband for you – I know it's a well-worn cliché, but try to be positive."

She nodded silently. There was nothing more to be done but wait.

* * *

"Come on – let's get out of here." Stephen O'Hara led her gently down the steps of the Garda Station and out into the pale sunshine.

The gardai had promised to contact her before the end of the week.

"Griffith and Markham," Stephen mused quietly. "Isn't that John Markham, a sandy-haired chap? I went to school with him in the Christian Brothers more years ago than I care to remember." He smiled at Sheila. "A good sport, John, with a sensible head on his shoulders – even then, he had the makings of a sound businessman – selling us marbles at ten a penny having bought them himself at ten for a halfpenny."

"Sam used to call him an old stick-in-the-mud," Sheila said quietly, sitting into the passenger seat of the car and fastening the safety belt about her. "Always too cautious about expanding the business overseas. 'You have to grasp the opportunity when it presents itself,' Sam used to say."

"Well, if Johnny Markham was slow to pursue any business venture, he had good reason to – he wasn't the type to let a good chance at making a few extra quid pass him by." Stephen manoeuvred the car through the rush-hour traffic, across the bridge and then turned right into the Strand Line, an area of the city where several new business ventures combined with the older, more established firms, giving the area an air of successful enterprise. "Let's go right now and have a talk with Johnnie Markham, okay? See what exactly Sam was doing in the company over the last years?"

Sheila thought back to when Sam had first started at Griffith and Markham. Times had been good, then. Sam had never been more loving, taking extra time off to spend time with the children, taking them for day trips to the seaside, to the zoo, swimming every weekend at the local pool. The extra bit in his salary had made them relax a little, the financial burden not quite as pressing as it had been previously, now that he had a more secure, pensionable job. And then she had got pregnant, and all hell broke loose. "We can't afford another one, Sheila – Chrissake, I'd want to be working morning to night to keep us going!" She winced involuntarily when she remembered the angry cruel words that had hurt her so much then, and still had the power to do the same. He had never had much time for Tom. A big mistake, he had called him, and she lived in fear that some day he might actually say it to Tom, make the boy feel that his presence was just one 'big mistake' in their lives.

Stephen O'Hara looked sideways at her. "Penny for them?"

She shook her head. "They're not even worth that much." She sat back in her seat, resting her head against the leather head-rest.

Sam had somebody, she knew that without a doubt. He had been seeing somebody for the last year, and she had never once voiced her resentment to him, because the last threads of their crumbling marriage hung in the balance, and she wasn't going to be the one to break them completely. There had been phone calls, late at night, when he thought they had all been asleep. Sheila had remained wide awake upstairs in the bedroom, listening to the whispers, sometimes the subdued laugh, the sound of a man speaking to somebody he thought a great deal more of than Sheila. And the expensive aftershave, wrapped in several pairs of brand-new underwear at the bottom of his kitbag, packed and ready for his ritual Monday evening swim in the pool.

"I could go with you," she had suggested timidly one evening as he was about to leave.

"You? Even the sight of water makes you frightened, not to mind stripping off and getting into a pool of it!"

"I'm taking lessons – I'm much better than I was," she had protested, and she could still see him going down the garden path, the kitbag slung over his shoulder. One turn of his head, a wave, then he was gone.

She would have been in the way, because it was his night for meeting somebody special, somebody who could swim as well as he could, who could laugh at his jokes and afterwards enjoy a pint of lager as well as any man in the cosy little pub at the end of Grattan Street. And whatever time he came home, Sheila would be lying in her bed, waiting, wondering if maybe it was all her fault that Sam had picked up with another woman – because why would a man go window-shopping if his original purchase had satisfied him?

The offices of Griffith and Markham were located at the far end of the Strand, a modern office-building complex, the result of a two-phase urban renewal scheme. Outside the office windows the bulldozers could be seen weaving a path through miniature terraced houses, products of post-war years, at the time a welcome advent in place of the over-crowded flats and tenement dwellings which had housed not only families of ten and more, but also the seeds of the festering disease, tuberculosis.

Sheila paused for a moment on the upper-floor landing, watching the bulldozer below, through the double-glazed window, grind the small dwellings into the ground in a cloud of heat-filled dust.

Father Stephen knocked on the door of the offices and a female voice called "Come in!"

Stephen beckoned to Sheila to follow him. "Do you know what's missing in all this sophisticated stream of modernisation?" he asked, looking questioningly at her as they stepped into the office.

Sheila shook her head.

"Noise – the sound of typewriters clattering and ringing, and old-fashioned copying machines wheezing and belching out half-faded photocopies so illegible that you wondered why they went to the bother of copying them in the first place!"

He gave a loud laugh and Sheila smiled at his observation, noticing the girl at the desk look up suddenly, startled at the sudden sound in the otherwise noise-free office.

The girl looked at Sheila, then turned away quickly, something in her eyes telling Sheila that maybe there was something to hide from her in this place – or, she thought desperately, maybe she was becoming paranoid, every female holding a particularly sinister portfolio – out to get her man.

Maybe this was the girl, maybe she was the one ... But no – she wasn't Sam's type. Pretty, young, but there was something missing in her that would have appealed to Sam's macho image. He always favoured the strongly built, athletic type. This girl was small, like Sheila, with cornflower blue eyes which seemed, now that Sheila was looking directly at her, to offer her sympathy instead of any confirmation that she could possibly be involved with Sam.

"Hello, Mrs Shaughnessy – we met at the Christmas party in Jury's – you remember? We both drank Baileys' with ice and you had on the most divine dress, champagne-colour with slits to the side of it – I would have killed for just a wear of it!"

Sheila smiled at the girl's directness. Definitely not Sam's type. "Could you tell Mr Markham that I would like a word with him, if it's convenient?"

"Of course – I don't think there's anybody with him at the moment."

"Tell him there's an old acquaintance of his from his school days to see him," said Stephen. "O'Hara's the name. He should remember me – well built like a wrestler, I was, in those days, until the old frame went to seed with age!"

He winked at the girl and she looked slightly taken aback for a moment, then smiled at his forwardness. She was used to men trying to chat her up, but this man was genuinely friendly – she could tell by the open, direct way he looked at her, the square face and mop of untidy hair falling across his forehead giving him an almost roguish appearance.

"Just a moment . . ." She disappeared into the office behind a forest of rubber plants and within seconds reappeared followed by a small, stoutly built man, the grin on his face stretching from ear to ear as he held out his hand.

"An imposter, that's what you are! Call yourself a priest? More like a con artist!" The two men shook hands, exchanging friendly grins. "When I think of all the things you used to get up to – and now look at you – as if butter wouldn't melt in your mouth!" He looked at Sheila then, was about to say something to her, his expression growing serious. Then he looked behind him at the girl, standing in the doorway of the office, her face bright with curiosity, and said pointedly, "You could look up that data for me now, Jean – I don't want to be disturbed for a while – I have some catching up to do with this old comrade of mine!"

She looked disappointed, but at once went back to her desk while Sheila and Stephen followed her boss into the office, and he closed the door firmly behind them.

Inside, Sheila and Stephen were drawn to the

window with its magnificent view of the Curragower Falls.

Most days, such a sight would have given Sheila a wonderful feeling of restful peace, but today her thoughts were like a cauldron of anxious question marks with no positive answers. Sam's disappearance was like a void in her life that prevented her from moving on until she knew where he was, and what terrible thing he might have done, so terrible that he had to leave his wife and children without any thought for their wellbeing.

They turned back to John Markham and he gestured to them to sit facing him across his desk.

"I was waiting for you to get in touch, Sheila." He came straight to the point, pulling out a folder of consignment slips from a drawer in his desk. He opened it, scattering the papers agitatedly about the desk, his brow creased with worry lines. "These are all orders which should have reached their destinations two weeks ago."

Stephen picked up one of the slips, examining it carefully. "Dortmund, Germany." Markham nodded in affirmation. "A good order – one that Sam got for us – it was a tremendous achievement, our first breakthrough into the German market. I asked him then if he wanted a position at the 'coalface' as it were – he could have a job in the office, communicating by network, and have more time at home with you and the kids." He looked at her with his keen grey eyes. He had known instinctively, even back then, that Sam's wandering eye was driving him further and further away from Sheila. Being a solid family man, with his main priority always being his family, John Markham thought that a nine-to-five office environment would keep Sam away from temptation.

"He never told me he was offered another job," Sheila said faintly.

Sam had never mentioned it to her. He had scorned the idea when she had suggested to him that maybe he should try for an office position, one that would give him more time at home. "Not my stroke, Sheila," he had said. "I like being out on the road, meeting new people every day, trying to break down that wall of suspicion against all things modern and in any way computer-motivated. No, an office job isn't for me!"

And now here was John Markham saying that he *had* been offered such a position, and he had turned it down – and not even a mention of it to her.

"I would have promoted him to a middle-management position," John went on, putting the folder to one side, "which, of course, would open all sorts of possibilities to him, if that was what he had wanted in a job." He looked across at Sheila, his face troubled, emphasising the word 'wanted'.

Obviously Sam hadn't wanted it. He had been after something, or someone, more exciting – and had found it, but at what cost? "He had access to clients' accounts, and I trusted him. He was able to wangle lucrative orders, especially in Germany, where he seemed to have a few contacts of his own, one in particular . . ."

There was a question mark in his voice, one that didn't go undetected by Sheila, and then Stephen asked the question that was poised on her tongue, the question she had been longing to ask Sam, the one that still remained unanswered.

"Did he have somebody else, another woman?"

Sheila gripped the sides of her chair. Another woman. Another woman. The words were jumbled in her head, the heavy stillness in the office giving them added emphasis, another woman, another . . . She thought she was going to faint as the noise in her ears grew louder. And then Stephen was standing next to her, gripping her shoulders supportively, the kindness in his face making her want to cry as the noise abated, and she looked at John Markham, waiting for his reply.

"There was someone . . . we knew here, in the office, thought it was just a fling, something that would be over and done with once the orders were confirmed in Germany." He looked at Sheila sympathetically. "She was a German girl, attractive – we didn't know exactly what sort of work she did – something in personnel with a company called Lichtsturm in Berlin."

"I didn't know – but I thought there might be somebody . . ." Sheila spoke almost in a whisper, her expression tense.

John looked relieved, glad that Sam's indiscretion was now out in the open. It was only right that Sheila should know just what kind of a man he really was. "She stayed here in Limerick for a while. She didn't like hotels so we organised it with Jean outside," he pointed in the direction of the outer office, "that she should stay with her in her flat on the South Circular."

Evening swims at the gym. Expensive aftershave. Whispered phone calls in the small hours of the morning. Sheila pieced the fragments together, the pieces fitting into place like some intricate jigsaw puzzle. The sense of relief that finally Sam's infidelity was confirmed somehow made the hurt a little more bearable – because she hadn't imagined the infidelity – something she had been frightened of in the last few weeks, thinking she was heading for a nervous breakdown.

"This German girl – if he's with her, what chance have I got? He's obviously besotted with her, otherwise why would he follow her to Germany?" She stood up, going to the window, looking down at the ribbon of late afternoon traffic winding its way along the Strand Line in the direction of the Treaty Stone. It had been one of their favourite walks. Back in the days when Sam couldn't bear to let a day pass without seeing her, before they were married . . . warm Sunday afternoons, his arm about her waist, sitting on the banks of the river, making plans, plans that had all come to nothing.

"We don't know what the situation is." John Markham spoke quietly now, afraid that any further revelations might cause her even more hurt. And she was obviously distressed, the pale face gaunt, expressionless, eyes staring unseeingly through the window, her hands hanging lifeless on either side, an air of defeat about her. "But, there is another aspect . . . Our accountant drew our attention to the fact that some money was going missing from a few of the accounts . . . not much, just a little every now and then, but enough to make us wonder – all accounts that Sam might be familiar with. Then we decided to hold an extraordinary meeting of the board. It was all arranged, everybody had been summoned, including Sam – but he didn't show . . . and I'm afraid to say it, Sheila, but . . . Sam has absconded with company funds, and it's out of our hands, now – the Fraud Squad will have to investigate it."

Stephen looked at him, puzzled. "Why did you

wait so long to contact the authorities – surely when you knew the man had absconded you were anxious to track him down – and your money?"

"Our company is on the point of expanding progressively into the European markets – already quite a few overseas firms are showing an interest in our computer packages, and we were worried if even a hint of any underhand business on the part of one of our employees got to them . . ." John Markham threw his hands in the air despairingly, "we might lose out on much more than the funds Sam Shaughnessy absconded with." He looked at Sheila apologetically. "I'm sorry, Sheila – I should have told you everything from the beginning. I thought I could resolve this mess, get a few private investigations underway without bringing the police into it –"

"And without letting me know just how involved my husband was with this German woman." Sheila looked at him coldly, accusation written all over her face.

John Markham turned away. He had let her down, had put his business before his responsibility to Sheila, as the wife of one of his employees. He should have gone to the police sooner, put her out of her misery as she waited. He could only imagine the nightmare she was going through.

"I knew nothing about all this – nothing!" Her voice rose in anguish as she faced John Markham.

"I've been to the bank myself – all the money in our joint account has been withdrawn – he's left nothing – not for me – not for the children – nothing!"

Markham glanced at Stephen, an incredulous look in his eyes. A man who left his wife and children to fend for themselves no was less than a criminal. He'd had no idea the big man with the mop of light-coloured hair, the blue eyes always confident, always smiling, the assured tone in his persuasive voice – the man he had employed just six short years ago – he'd had no idea that such a man would be capable of absconding with company funds. Of leaving his wife. His children. John Markham cursed his naivety, mentally notching up another hard lesson learnt in the school of corporate swings and roundabouts.

The telephone rang on John's desk, the sudden sound making Sheila jump nervously, and she gripped Stephen's arm with clenched fingers.

Stephen spoke to her reassuringly: "Things will be sorted, Sheila – they just take time. Don't lose heart."

Markham picked up the receiver. He spoke abruptly into the phone, his expression grim. "Thank you . . . yes . . . I'll be in to see you in the morning . . . and I think somebody from the Fraud Division should be present, Michael, don't you?"

He replaced the receiver, and when Sheila looked at him, all her worst fears were confirmed.

"It's about Sam, isn't it?"

He nodded. "That was Michael Bates – Sam's withdrawal from the account was accomplished without any investigation on the part of the bank, no questions asked. The teller was on contract employment with the bank – not much experience and obviously very impressed with the businessman, Sam Shaughnessy. She didn't even bother to ask his colleagues about the withdrawal of the money because Sam Shaughnessy presented himself as a valued client and said he had some business deals which would be better negotiated 'without the rigmarole of credit transfers and Mickey Mouse drafts'." He looked at Sheila. "His own words." He got up and walked to the window, his back to them as he spoke. "Sam was devious, Sheila – this move of his was premeditated, probably for months beforehand – he was able to clear his personal bank account and not the bat of an eyelid from that fool of a bank clerk!"

Sheila stood up. There was nothing more to say, at least not for the present. She looked at Stephen O'Hara, her face pale, her hands trembling. "I want to go home now – my children will be waiting for me . . ."

He nodded.

John Markham turned to them then, held out

his hand to Sheila. "We'll sort everything out, don't you worry – Sam will be found – I guarantee it."

She nodded miserably. She didn't know how things would be sorted out when right now things looked so black – her husband painted as a criminal, and her life in tatters because of his betrayal.

Chapter 8

Stephen O'Hara sat in the small kitchen drinking tea with Sheila. He tried not to look at the unhinged doors of the teak presses, one completely broken away, lying idle beside the fridge. The walls, he observed, could do with a lick of fresh paint, the damp patches clearly visible as they mottled the peeling paintwork with dirty, black smudges.

But Sheila noticed. "I know – the place is a mess, isn't it?" She looked at him, embarrassed. "The house wasn't Sam's top priority recently, and I'm afraid I wasn't able to do much in the line of decorating."

"All that will be seen to, as soon as you get

yourself sorted out financially," Stephen said firmly. "John Markham is meeting with the bank manager and the gardai in the morning. We should be able to get a few things straightened out after that."

"I'll have to get a job – something to keep our heads above water." Sheila sipped at the mug of tea, her face weary and tense with worry lines.

From upstairs there came the sound of raised voices, then a loud cry, and the sound of a door being slammed.

Sheila looked at the priest apologetically. "Sharon is probably having a go at Tom again – those two will never get on. How on earth will I manage, Father, on my own, without Sam around to make them behave – they take no notice of me." She stood up, called out wearily "Sharon! Tommy! Come here, please! Stop that fighting!"

Stephen put a hand on her shoulder, forcing her back into the chair. "Leave it to me – years of experience with dealing with potential delinquents." He went into the hallway and with long, determined strides he went up the stairs, two at a time.

Sharon, emerging from her bedroom, hairbrush poised as though she was about to throw it, stepped back in amazement when she saw Stephen and the expression on his face.

He held out his hand solemnly. "The brush,

please, young lady – and then I want to have a few words with *all* of you – downstairs!"

Tom crept out from behind the bedroom door, his face flushed and streaked with tears. "She hit me! Just because I took her old CD and scratched it a little bit." He signified 'a little bit' with two dirty fingers.

"My best CD! I saved for ages to buy it – and that little creep wrecked it!" Sharon went for Tommy, grabbing him by the hair until he howled in pain.

"That's enough!" Stephen grasped each of them by the arm and marched them downstairs determinedly. "Where's your sister?"

"She's in her room, studying," Sharon said, sullenly. Even if he was a priest, how dare he treat her like a bold child! Interfering old – she paused in her angry thoughts, closing her eyes, the ritual of weekly Mass-going causing her to have uncustomary pangs of conscience. She said a silent prayer for forgiveness for thinking such dark thoughts about a priest, but she couldn't help herself. Her whole life was ruined since Dad had left and it was all Mam's fault, she thought sullenly. She was sure of it!

"Deirdre – will you come down here – I want to speak to you – all of you!" Stephen shouted up the stairs, his tormented thoughts causing him to raise his voice more than he had intended to.

Deirdre appeared on the landing, her face pale and worried-looking. Stephen, not for the first time, felt sorry for the girl. It was never easy, especially for the eldest child, when a couple split up. Almost every week in recent times he had been called out to try to patch up relationships between couples who had reached crisis point in their marriages. And always there were shadows in the background, children's faces frightened and uncertain, wondering what the future would hold for them.

Deirdre and Sharon, standing now in the hallway, thought he was a force to be reckoned with.

Sheila was still in the kitchen, sitting with her head in her hands, the pounding tension headache making her feel sick inside. She didn't know what Father O'Hara was saying to them. She didn't care. She just wanted a little peace for a while, time to think, to make plans.

"You'll have to calm down a bit, you guys," said Stephen, looking at them pointedly, his expression serious. "Your mother needs looking after – give her a hand, instead of driving her completely off her head."

Deirdre nodded miserably. "I know, Father, but I don't know what to do – if Dad isn't coming back, how will Mam manage? She hasn't worked for so long, not like other women – she'd find it hard to get a job now!"

"And if she does get a job – what will *we* do?" Sharon demanded. "The house is already looking like a kip, all the clothes I put into the washbasket last week are still unwashed –"

"And what's wrong with your own hands?" Stephen interrupted her grimly. "Surely you can do a bit of washing for yourself instead of waiting for your mother to do everything? She's worn out trying to cope and all you can do is whinge about your dirty laundry – shame on you!"

His reprimand earned a fresh look of resentment from Sharon. What business was it of his, anyway?

"It's up to all of you now to pull your weight around here." He looked at Tom who had been gazing up at him with wide solemn eyes. "Even you, lad – destroying things that don't belong to you!"

Tom hung his head, shamefaced, casting an uncertain glance at Sharon.

"That's what I keep telling them – but they won't listen to me, Father." Deirdre's voice trembled emotionally, then she lowered her head and began to cry quietly, all the misery of the last few weeks overwhelming her.

Stephen's face softened as he looked at her, shoulders hunched, trying to carry the weight of responsibility against all odds. "Your mother is going to try to get a job – and if she does get one, then it's up to each one of you to help her all you can – no more being waited on hand and foot, understand?" They nodded in unison, Tom stifling a weary yawn. "Fine. Now that's settled, Deirdre, you'd better get your brother to bed fast, or he'll never be in time for school in the morning."

Deirdre took Tom's hand and called to Sheila in the kitchen. "I'm taking Tom to bed, Mam, and I'll read him his bedtime story."

"No! I want Mam to read to me!" Tom protested, his voice heavy with sleep. "Mrs Mugs, Mam, the story about Mrs Mugs, please!"

Sheila came out of the kitchen, her cup of tea gripped in both hands. "All right – I'll be up to you as soon as you're changed and in bed. Hug, Tom?" She bent down to him and he put his arms about her neck, the movement uninhibited, no embarrassment even in front of the priest.

Stephen O'Hara nodded in satisfaction. They were good kids behind all the tantrums and rows and, judging by the look on Sheila's face, the worry lines now smoothed out as she hugged the boy to her, they would be her best incentive to strike out on her own and make a new life for herself. The children would keep her going. He had seen it before: women who struggled to bring up a family single-handed were stronger for it at the end of the day.

"I'll call in the morning," he said, "and tonight

I'll make a few telephone calls to a few people who owe me favours." He grinned broadly as he opened the hall door and looked back at the woman standing in the dim light in the hallway. "There's plenty of jobs around, we only have to find them and – I'm sorry to say, but it's the truth, nonetheless – sometimes it's a question of 'who you know'." He put a finger to the side of his nose, emphasising the insinuation and Sheila nodded.

She would take any job that was available at this stage. Her typing skills were out-of-date – all computers now – and shorthand seemed to have become a thing of the past. She could wait on tables, though, maybe even do some bar work, at night. She had to do something, soon.

She watched Stephen O'Hara get into his car, saw him wave behind him recklessly as he just about managed to manoeuvre the car through the roundabout at the corner of the street. She turned back to the girls and Tom.

Deirdre looked into her eyes and felt a sudden feeling of relief as she intuitively saw a different woman to the one they had been living with for the last few weeks. There was a new light in her mother's eyes, a look of determination on her face. Maybe things were going to be fine after all, she thought hopefully, following her mother inside the house, her heart lighter than it had been for weeks now.

Chapter 9

Stephen O'Hara sat, hands clasped behind his head, one foot poised casually on the edge of Donal Sheridan's desktop.

"Do make yourself comfortable, Father," Donal commented dryly. He knew him well enough to dispense with the formality of the title 'Father', but where clerics were concerned he preferred to stick to the impersonal. Favours beget favours, Donal reckoned, and from experience a too-friendly footing with Stephen O'Hara invited all sorts of compromises, mostly on his part. Clerical clout, Stephen had called it one time, a mischievous gleam in his eye. He had been looking for a donation from Donal for the church building fund. "Bloody imposition," Donal had muttered darkly, handing over a substantial cheque to the priest. He liked to bargain competitively, but a priest's collar was an unfair advantage in his opinion.

He looked across at the priest, saw the 'do me a favour' look in the face of the man, and sighed resignedly.

"OK. Out with it – what lame dog do you want me to look after now? Wait a sec – let me get you some coffee." He leaned forward and shouted to a young girl who was busy at the self-service counter, clearly visible from his small back office, her white mesh cap tilted at an angle on her head, her face flushed as she tried to handle the busy stream of customers. "Bring some coffee! And don't forget the sugar!"

Stephen O'Hara raised a disapproving eyebrow at his attitude to one of his staff.

"I don't know how you can think that your manner will nurture any loyalty in your staff – that poor young girl must be frightened out of her wits with a boss like you!"

Donal shrugged carelessly. 'Treat them mean, keep them keen' – that's my philosophy, Father – never fails – especially when you're handing out pay packets at the end of the week!" He looked at Stephen, rubbing the side of his face thoughtfully. "I suppose I'll have to pay my debts, as it were, and return the favour – then maybe I'll be out of your clutches for good. No more favours – okay?"

His forehead puckered in annoyance as Stephen gave him a broad grin, slapping his hands together enthusiastically.

"Good man!" Stephen leaned forward confidentially, his expression serious. "And it's not a stray dog I want you to look after – it's a woman who needs a job desperately right now."

"Same thing," Donal said shortly.

The young girl knocked on the door tentatively, the tray in her hands, her expression harassed as she had to leave a queue of customers waiting while she went to make the coffee for Donal. But he was the boss. There was no hesitating when 'He Who Must Be Obeyed' called the tune.

Stephen jumped up and held the door open for her as she entered.

"Thanks – just put it down there." Donal cleared a place on his desk and she deposited the tray, her hands shaking as she saw him assess her critically, noticing her hair had come loose from the catering cap. "Tidy up your hair like a good girl – it doesn't look well with the customers. How are things outside?" Donal began to pour the coffee, at the same time throwing a glance at the busy stream of customers queuing patiently at the hot counter.

"Hectic," she answered. "The lasagne is almost gone, and they're still asking for it – we'll have to take a couple of quiches from the deep freeze to tide us over the lunch-time – Brenda is up to her eyes in work." She stood awkwardly, waiting for dismissal until he waved her away impatiently.

She turned and headed for the door, her face flushed with annoyance as she pushed back a stray hair into the tight-fitting cap. She was glad to be out of his presence. He was a boss who was a hard taskmaster, always looking for shortcomings in his staff.

He had a way of making everybody feel small, in spite of the hard work they did for him, day in, day out – and it wasn't as if their wages were very generous – just the basic rate, with no bonuses for work well done – not even a bonus for any extra time put in. She almost slammed the door behind her, but thought better of it. She needed the job. Best thing to do would be to get on with it. She hurried back to the service counter, while Brenda, the head cook, called to her urgently, asking her to take some more quiches from the freezer.

Donal looked at Stephen O'Hara. The look he saw in the priest's face irritated him, with its admonishment in the intuitive dark eyes. He gave an irritated wave of the hand. "What? You think I'm a bit offhand with the staff, do you? Well, you know nothing about my business, Father, just like I know nothing about yours – so let's keep it that way, shall we?" He took a quick gulp of coffee, then tapped his desk with the tips of his fingers. "This woman – how do I know she's any good? Has she ever worked in the catering business?"

Stephen said nothing for a moment, sipping his coffee contemplatively. Then he lifted his eyes, his gaze frank as he looked at Donal.

"Do you remember how it was, at the beginning?" he asked quietly.

Donal felt as though somebody had dealt him a blow in the stomach, his thoughts in disarray for a moment. Stephen O'Hara's punchline had come home to roost. His thoughts drifted back ...

A little corner shop, the pane of glass missing in the front door, an old-fashioned bell jingling half-heartedly above the rotting panels of wood. The owner had grown old and had retired, too tired to continue to run a business that was going downhill each day. Donal wanted that business. With his whole being, he wanted to be successful, to have some purpose in his life, try to fill the void Marie had created when she had left him.

Marie. Even to remember her name stirred up troubled thoughts inside him, his heart like a lump of stone masking his hurt, his feeling of utter betrayal. She had dumped him and gone and married a Jamaican student she had met while studying at the university. She had been doing a business degree and in the end had told him casually that it was over between them, they had nothing in common any more, and she loved the Jamaican with the dark, curling hair, the expressive coal-black eyes, and the gentle touch of his hands on her body that, she said regretfully to Donal, had never been in his impatient ones.

It seemed like a lifetime ago …

He looked at Stephen O'Hara now as his thoughts drifted back to the present. He owed the man, big time. He had been at his lowest after Marie had walked out on him. He had even considered ending it all. He had been standing at the river's edge, looking into the dark waters below, his thoughts full of self-pity and of loathing for Marie, the woman who had betrayed him, who had been carrying on behind his back with another man. He had thought how pleasant it would be, to let the river carry him along, to feel the churning current beneath him, to be dragged downwards into its depths . . . he had leaned forward …

And then Stephen O'Hara had been there, pulling him away, away from the water, his voice calling him, telling him his life wasn't over. He had lost the girl he had loved with all his being, the girl he had wanted to spend the rest of his life with, and this man was telling him everything was going to be fine, the world would go on and he would get over it – in time.

Stephen O'Hara had thrown him a lifeline when he needed it most.

Donal had a bit of money saved, not much, but enough to give him a start. Stephen had approached the Credit Union on his behalf, had asked them to give Donal a loan on the strength of his savings, and he would go guarantor for him. The loan had allowed him to purchase the rundown shop at the corner of Darcy Street, an area of the city that was being taken over by the local Council under the Compulsory Purchase Order. The purchase price had been just affordable, the loan repayments a constant headache until he had started making a few renovations, adding a delicatessen counter, sectioning off a portion of the shop for sit-down meals, some cane tables and chairs, tapestries and prints of Old Limerick adorning the cream-painted walls, patterned roller blinds contrasting elegantly with the unassuming decor.

Then he had found Brenda. She had been on the Fás register for almost a year when he had approached Stephen O'Hara, asking him if he knew of anybody who could handle a fast-food outlet, the emphasis being on 'fast' he had stressed, a ruthless smile crossing his lean handsome face.

"A good woman – widowed, with three kids, all teenagers. It's not just that she needs the income – the job would help her to get to grips with life." Stephen had volunteered no more information, but there was the insinuation that Brenda McCann had had more downs than ups in her life.

And so she had come to work for Donal, her cooking transforming the place into a 'Yuppie' eating centre, solicitors and up-and-coming young business people clamouring for second helpings of her mouthwatering lasagnes and more exotic dishes like Chicken à la Brenda – her knowing wink at the customers when they pleaded with her for the recipe causing them to shrug their shoulders in defeat, instead offering their plates for more of the same.

"My lucky mascot," Donal had admitted wryly to Stephen O'Hara when he had called round one lunch-time, battling his way through the long queue at the counter to get into Donal's office. "You did me a favour, Father – that woman is indispensable!"

And now he wondered about the other woman, the one Stephen O'Hara was plugging so strongly for. Since Marie had left him, he had built a strong, insurmountable wall of tough business acumen about him, with no room for sentimentality. He had vowed nobody would ever hurt him again as

Marie had. All his energy was utilised in building up the business, his staff fully aware of what was expected of them. 'An honest day's work for an honest day's pay' was Donal Sheridan's philosophy. If an employee couldn't do the work, he had no qualms in dismissing him or her – two weeks' notice and an extra bit put into their pay envelope making them believe, ironically, that he was actually doing them a favour.

"What can she do?" He looked at Stephen, one cynical eyebrow raised. "If she's been out of work for a while, she's going to find it hard to adjust to that kind of a situation." He waved a hand towards the ever-increasing throng of lunch-time patrons at the delicatessen counter.

Stephen stood up suddenly, staring hard at Donal. "Nobody knows more than you how tough things can be when the chips are down."

Donal averted his gaze. The man knew how to twist a knife, twist and turn and force it on its way through the tough veneer of practicality that had been Donal's mainstay through the teething process of starting his own business.

"Is she easy on the eye? And can she take the pressure of working behind a fast-food counter, eight hours a day, six days a week sometimes? If she can cope with that, Father, then send her to see me, in the morning, 9.30 sharp, OK?"

He rose then, confronting the priest, his height

matching that of the other, two pairs of determined eyes battling with each other.

Then Donal smiled suddenly, extending his hand to Stephen, who accepted it in an equally affable manner. "Truce? You have a habit of digging up old skeletons that are best left buried, Father – no successful businessman wants to be reminded of his humble beginnings."

Chapter 10

"Where are *you* going?" Deirdre had been watching her sister smearing a heavy layer of pale make-up on her young skin, outlining the big, blue eyes with dark eyeliner, looking down intently at the hand mirror as she coated her eyelashes with several careful strokes of mascara.

"Out," Sharon answered briefly.

Deirdre closed her copy of Shakespeare, putting it aside reluctantly. Another hour would have been sufficient to memorise Portia's speech for the exam tomorrow. *"Such it is as are those dulcet sounds in break of day that creep into the dreaming bridegroom's ear ..."* She mumbled the words beneath her breath, and Sharon looked at her in amusement.

"Pure rot – that's what I call it – boring old lines, all for some stupid exam that won't be any good to you in the end, anyway!" She pushed her blonde hair back from her face dramatically. "'*Dreaming bridegroom's ear!*'" she mimicked, her head thrown back, eyes closed, a derisory pained expression on her painted face. Then she strode across the room, picked up the textbook, then tossed it defiantly into Deirdre's lap. "Here – read some more of this slop! It's the most boring thing I've ever sat through in English class. Just remember, Dee . . ." She pointed an emphatic finger at her sister. "All that the dreaming bridegroom wants is sex, and lots of it – none of that romantic rubbish – and if and when I marry it will be to a millionaire with loads of money to keep me in the manner to which I shall grow very, very accustomed!" She started brushing her hair, seated in front of the mirror at the dressing-table, two bright spots of anger burning on her cheeks. "If my mother had a bit of backbone, and been more assertive, giving my father what he needed –"

"Sharon!" Dee looked at her, horrified. She hated Sharon talking about her mam like that. It just didn't seem right.

"Well, I'm right. I know I am!" She tossed her hair back from her face. "Mam should have been more sexy, more outgoing, maybe have taken some courses in computer studies so that she could go back to working, even part-time. If she'd been earning her own income all these years, my father would never have left her – money is like a magnet to men!"

"Don't be so ridiculous," Deirdre said quietly. "Mam has always been here for us – and for Dad! She isn't career-minded, and nobody should condemn her for that!"

"Oh, for heaven's sake, Dee – don't be such an old stick-in-the-mud!" The anger in Sharon's voice was frightening.

She'd wake Tom who had just gone off to sleep in the next room, thought Deirdre, and her mother who had taken a sleeping tablet just before she went to bed, her heavy breathing audible even in the girls' room.

"Stupid, stupid, lines, why do you bother to learn them? They're rubbish! All about languishing after men who couldn't care less about you, anyway, once they get tired of you!" Her eyes blazed as she stared at her reflection in the mirror. "Well, I can promise you, Dee – that won't happen to me – take them and leave them, that'll be my motto – and I'm going to keep on the lookout for a nice, rich, steady husband and I'll make sure to keep him happy – if you know what I mean." She looked at Deirdre with a meaningful glance, laughing loudly at her sister's obvious disgust. "Oh, come on, Dee – loosen up – go back to your romantic Shakespeare and dream about your knight in shining armour!"

"It's Mam's first day at her new job in the morning, Shar – let's forget all this silly talk and give her some encouragement!" Deirdre pleaded, watching her put on a black, lacy see-through blouse and black skin-tight pants.

She knew Sharon was going down to the club. All the teenagers congregated there at weekends for clandestine smokes and a few games of pool and generally to sound off about 'inconsiderate' parents who thought 11.30 curfew time was more than reasonable. Deirdre had gone there once or twice, but hadn't thought much of the crowd, her natural shyness a barrier to involving herself in any of their conversations. Sharon, with her easy wit and bubbly, outgoing personality, had all the boys flocking round her, in particular one seventeen-year-old with a gold-cross earring in his left ear and a closely cropped hairstyle that showed his protruding ears to full advantage. There was something about him that Deirdre didn't like – the way he looked at other girls while he had his arm possessively about Sharon's shoulders, the way he jerked his head at the other boys in the group, indicating that he wanted to talk to them in private – then they would exit *en masse*, outside into the paved courtyard in front of the club, huddling together in a corner.

Deirdre had followed them outside one night, and had seen the blue smoke-haze rise from inside the small circle of youths and knew it wasn't just cigarettes they were smoking. She knew a lot of the girls at school were into the drug scene. Skunk, Ecstasy and other drugs were handed round discreetly in the nightclubs, and even in the school grounds, where the drugs were passed to eager recipients in return for ten-euro notes. Deirdre hoped Sharon wasn't taking drugs, but the fact that she was broke after just getting her pocket money from their mam left her wondering, and worrying.

"Don't go out, Shar – we'll go down and make some toast and tea and bring it up to bed with us – we can play a few CDs – I just got Katie Melua's *Piece by Piece*." Deirdre knew that all the coaxing in the world would be no good. Sharon was determined to go out, and with her mother asleep and unlikely to wake until the early hours of the morning, it was the perfect opportunity.

Sharon knew Deirdre wouldn't tell on her. Dee was dull and worried like an old woman, but she wasn't a telltale.

"I'll be back well before one o'clock," she informed Deirdre firmly.

"It's too dangerous, Shar – anything could happen to you."

Sharon blew her a kiss, then picked up her boots and padded silently across the landing, pausing for a moment outside her mother's bedroom door. She listened for a moment to the heavy breathing, then smiled, satisfied. She quickly went downstairs, sat down on the bottom step to lace her feet into the boots, grabbed her jacket from the hallstand, then opened the hall door.

Deirdre watched from the top of the stairs as she closed the door silently behind her, the latch clicking ominously. She shivered, and pulled her dressing-gown about her, tying the belt with shaking fingers. As if there wasn't enough happening in their lives, and now Sharon had to start, making things even more complicated.

She went back into the bedroom and sat in the chair by the window. She wouldn't go to bed. Not until Sharon was back. She felt her eyes close tiredly, but she shook herself awake, the rustling sound in the copper beech tree in the middle of the garden making her feel apprehensive, the black clouds shifting hazily across the darkening sky sending the first spatter of raindrops beating against the window.

Oh Shar – come home soon! she prayed quietly, then sank her face into her upturned palms, the tears spilling through the slits of her fingers on to the pale blue dressing-gown.

Chapter 11

"Jesus – look at Shar – she's in a bad way!" Linda Sullivan looked at her friend's face. Sharon was rocking from side to side, her face bright with animation, her eyes dancing about the room as her feet tapped against the floor to the lively beat of the music echoing loudly in the interior of Darcy's Place. The flashing disco lights seemed to make her more excited as she raised her arms, clicking her fingers to the beat of the music, some of the boys in their company smirking as they recognised the effect of the drugs that had been handed round the club earlier unknown to Len Darcy, the owner. He usually turned a blind eye to the subterfuge but sometimes he liked to make an example of someone by throwing them out of the club, just to let them know that he wasn't a complete idiot, so they had learned the technique of passing the goods discreetly. The colourful lighting swirled and floated in a mixed array of kaleidoscopic images about Sharon's face, distorting the features, her red-painted mouth appearing almost black, the thickly pencilled eyeliner making her look grotesque and cheap.

Declan Murphy looked at Linda and shrugged his shoulders indifferently. "She wanted the stuff, we gave her some – nobody forced her."

"But she's not used to drugs – she just wanted to try something new!" Linda protested, frightened at Sharon's appearance. She tried to get her to stand up, but Sharon pushed her away, her hands and feet now moving quickly, her hair falling across her face as she rocked to the beat, beads of sweat on her forehead.

"Give over acting like my mother, Lin – do something useful – get me a drink of water, for God's sake – my mouth is as dry as sandpaper!" She looked at Linda impatiently, trying to free herself from the urgent grasp Linda had on her arm.

From across the poolroom Linda could see Len Darcy craning his fat neck to see what was going on. If he caught even the sniff of somebody doing drugs, there might be trouble. This could be one of his nights when he would make an example of somebody – maybe the police would be called in – Linda could imagine what her father would have to say if she was involved in anything like that.

"Look," she said desperately, "come on, fellas. Give me a hand!" She put a hand into her jeans' pocket and pulled out a ten-euro note. "I have just enough for a taxi – just give me a hand to get her out into the yard, and I'll get her home – please?" She looked at Declan pleadingly and he nodded, finally, reluctantly.

"OK – but if she can't know when to stop, that's not my problem!"

"What did she take? What did you give her?" Linda shouted at him above the noise of the blaring piped music.

Declan avoided her gaze, smiling knowingly at the other two boys sitting with him. They sniggered half-heartedly. Declan had already taken most of their own allowances for some skunk. They were beginning to feel the effects, but it was a nice, comforting sort of feeling, making them feel on top of everything, in control, no more thoughts of Junior Certs or Leaving Certs or confrontations with the old man when they got home.

"I said, what did she take?" Linda yelled again.

"How do I know?" Declan answered, defiantly.

"She bought a little bit of speed and some skunk – she's probably mixed them. But it was only a tiny amount."

Linda glared at him furiously. She turned and put an arm about Sharon's waist, hoisting her roughly to her feet.

Declan stood up, holding out his hand to Sharon.

She smiled up at him, taking his hand and leading him out on to the dance floor.

"Okay, Dec – I'll dance with you – I could dance all night!" She swung him out on to the dance floor.

Declan beckoned to Linda as he began to edge Sharon towards the exit, his arm about her waist, his face close to hers as he whispered in her ear and she laughed up at him, her face pale against his dark silk shirt. He pretended to be having a joke with her, but held her firmly about the waist, Linda following them close behind as they neared the exit.

Len's right-hand man was standing in the doorway, arms folded, the bow-tie about his neck incongruously gentlemanlike below the battered, unrelenting face.

"What's up with her?" he jerked a finger in Sharon's face. "I never saw her so full of beans – I wouldn't mind having a few dances with her – she'd keep any bloke on his toes!" He grinned at Declan.

Declan smiled and winked at him. "She had a few beers before we came out tonight, back at my place – then another few here – can't hold her drink at the best of times, you know what I mean, Mike?"

The man smiled a stupid conspiratorial grin at Declan. "Best get her home as fast as you can – Len doesn't hold with minors drinking – sell it to them if he got away with it, mind you – but up front likes to appear white as the lilywhite snow!"

Outside Declan looked into Linda's face, his eyes black and threatening, and she shivered. "Right – you get her home," he said. "And whatever condition she's in in the morning, don't lay it on me – she makes up her own mind how much she can take of the drugs, okay?"

"Yes – just let me get her out of here – I'll look after her." She recoiled from him as she saw the sneer on his face, then his eyes glazed over as he turned to go back inside. She didn't know what Shar saw in him. She could hear her father now as he called Declan 'a bad lot'. She had to admit he was right. She took her mobile from her pocket and dialled the taxi with shaking hands.

"Can you send a cab to Darcy's Place, please – and right away? Please – hurry!"

Sharon was hopping from one foot to the other as they waited for the cab outside the club, which luckily arrived shortly after.

Linda, trying to shove the giggling Sharon into the back of the cab, saw the expression on the driver's face in the rear-view mirror.

"OK – I know she's had a few too many – but it's not my fault!" She looked at him defiantly, but he kept staring straight ahead, the meter running while she struggled to lift Sharon into the cab, then sat in next to her.

Sharon just sat there, her eyes closed, the dark eye make-up only emphasising the deadly pallor, her dry lips muttering something that Linda thought sounded something like "Mam – I'm sorry – Mam!"

* * *

The book slipped to the floor with a heavy thud. Deirdre woke. Was that a knock on the door? She looked at her wristwatch, the hands blurred as she tried to focus on them. She had a pain in her back from sitting awkwardly in the chair and her feet were frozen. She massaged one foot against the other, trying to get some feeling back into them. There it was again. A subdued knocking on the hall door, muted enough to be barely detectable – but Deirdre, who had deliberately stayed in the chair by the window for the last three hours, heard it. She looked at her watch again – half past two o'clock in the morning! She had been sitting in that chair since eleven, dozing on and off, listening for the sound of Sharon's key in the front door. The knocking persisted. She tiptoed across the landing and down the stairs.

Two shadows were visible in the outside porch and she hesitated. What if they were intruders? How could she handle them, alone, with her mother unconscious upstairs in the back bedroom – and Tom?

"Deirdre – is that you?"

She heard the barely audible whisper as she stood, her ear close to the locked door.

"It's me – Linda – I've brought Sharon home, but she's in bad way – please let us in!"

Deirdre quickly opened the door, then stared in horror at the spectacle of Sharon leaning drunkenly against Linda, her eyes open now, a blank, uncomprehending look in their blue depths.

Linda looked at her, tear-stains on her cheeks. "It's not my fault, Dee – I told Declan she wasn't used to taking drugs – but he gave some to her anyway because she had the money to pay him. And to make it worse, she seems to have mixed them. Please, Dee – what are we going to do with her?"

Deirdre reacted quickly. "Come inside – we'll get her into the kitchen and I'll make a pot of strong coffee, then we'll get her into bed before Mam wakes up – or worse, Tom – if he wakes none of what's happened tonight will remain a secret."

They sat Sharon on a kitchen chair and Linda supported her while Deirdre put the kettle on.

Deirdre poured coffee into a large yellow mug, liberally sugared it and then held it under Sharon's mouth. "Okay, Shar – come on – drink up – this should make you feel a bit better." She put the mug to Sharon's lips and, when there was no response, forced the liquid through their parched dryness. Sharon had relaxed, her hands and feet still now, a vacant expression on her face. She stared straight ahead, a stupid smile on her face. She felt the mug against her cheek, but still her gaze remained blank, not focusing on anything in particular. She swallowed, took another sip and another, then pulled away, shaking her head.

A thought struck Linda. "Dee – no, don't!" she cried. "Not coffee! I think she's taken a little bit of speed though she's coming down now and speed is a stimulant like coffee – it might make her worse!"

Deirdre abruptly pulled the mug away. "Water, then?"

"I guess . . ."

"But, isn't water supposed to be dangerous if you've taken Ecstasy?" said Dee, desperately trying to remember the little she knew about drug use. "Did she take any Ecstasy?"

"I don't think so ... but ..."

"We'd better just get her to bed."

Deirdre went to the sink and turned on the tap, swishing the mug about under the water. Her thoughts were in turmoil. Sharon was in a bad way. She had been drugged out of her mind, and right now all she felt for her sister was revulsion and anger that she had put her in a position where Mam couldn't possibly be told about what had happened that night.

"Dee – what happened? I can't remember . . ." Sharon looked with large, frightened eyes at her sister, then at Linda. "Lin – what are you doing here – what time is it?"

"I'll tell you what time it is, Sharon," said Deirdre, turning to her sister in frustration, eyes blazing. "It's three o'clock in the morning! For God's sake, where were you?"

"At the club ..."

"It wasn't Sharon's fault – honest, Dee!" Linda looked at her, scared. If Deirdre was going to make a fuss, then her own parents would find out, and her life wouldn't be worth living after that – they would keep checks on her every minute of every day, ringing up her friends to see where she was. She'd be suffocated by them, and it was bad enough right now with Dad always on her back.

Sharon seemed to be regaining her rebellious attitude, one hand supporting her chin as she leaned heavily on the kitchen table.

"It's Mam's first day at work tomorrow," said Deirdre, glaring at Sharon's sullen face, "but you don't care! And what do you think she'll say when she sees the condition of you in the morning?"

Sharon began to giggle. "Maybe I – could stay at home – from school – please, Dee!" she begged, giggling. "You could – tell her – I have an attack of the monthlies! She always believes that – then I could sleep it off for the day – and nobody will ever know – about tonight. What do you say, Dee?"

Both girls looked at Deirdre, Linda's eyes fearful as she thought of the consequences if her father found out where she had been that night.

"All right," Deirdre sighed, "but only because I don't want to see her upset."

Linda sighed in relief. Maybe it would all blow over without anybody else having to know about it. If only Sharon would keep away from Declan, everything would be fine.

They took the stairs slowly, Deirdre urging Sharon forward, Linda bringing up the rear. Deirdre tried not to stumble as she held Sharon tightly, her sister almost a dead weight as she struggled to get her to the top.

"Be quiet, Sharon – don't wake Tom!" she

hissed angrily as every step they took was making Sharon giggle uncontrollably. "For God's sake, Sharon!" Deirdre pulled her up the last two stairs and pulled her past her mother's room. She could hear Tom stirring in his sleep and almost dragged Sharon into the bedroom, Linda following and shutting the door quietly behind them.

Linda helped Deirdre sit Sharon on the bed.

Then Sharon suddenly stiffened, not a movement out of her, her eyes staring directly ahead. Deirdre waved her hand in front of her eyes, but there was no response.

"Jesus – Deirdre – I think she's in some sort of trance!" Linda looked down at her friend in horror. "I think she needs a doctor – what will we do with her?"

"She's going to have to wait until the morning," Deirdre answered desperately. "I'm not going to frighten the daylights out of my mother at this hour, just because you two were stupid enough to go taking stuff you knew nothing about!"

Linda looked at her miserably and Deirdre's expression softened. She put out a hand and squeezed Linda's.

"I'm not blaming you, Linda – I'm just angry with Sharon." She took her sister by the shoulders and shook her hard. "Come on, Sharon – get out of it – don't frighten us like this!"

She didn't see Linda look towards the door,

didn't hear her sharp intake of breath until she heard her mother's voice behind her.

"What's going on here? Sharon – what's wrong with her?"

Sheila was across the room in an instant. She looked down at Sharon, taking her face between her hands, tilting her face up towards her. The muscles in Sharon's face relaxed, she opened her eyes and Deirdre heaved a sigh of relief. At least she was back in the land of the living again. But she didn't know what way her mother would react, and instinctively she went and stood close to Sheila as if her presence would protect her from any more trouble.

"Mam – I got a fright there," said Sharon, "must have blacked out . . . sort of feeling tired lately . . . maybe I need a tonic?"

The glib way she spoke made Deirdre wonder if maybe she had been bluffing the trance-like state that had frightened her so much.

"Where were you?" Sheila asked quietly. She wasn't a fool. The girl had taken something, she could tell by the dilated pupils, the shaky movements of the hands. Sheila had looked in the mirror several times in the past few weeks and seen the same tell-tale signs looking back at her – too many anti-depressants coupled with sleeping tablets had her feeling like a zombie at times. Only she was sure what Sharon had taken was a lot more exciting than her bottle of sleeping tablets and anti-depressants. "You were out somewhere, weren't you?"

Sharon looked at her, all wide-eyed and innocent, and Deirdre felt disgusted with her younger sister. Trying to fool Mam after waking her out of her sleep when she knew Mam was having a hard time sleeping lately – she had no consideration – she was just a selfish little cow!

"I wasn't out, Mam . . . I was here . . . all night . . . I had a bit of a nightmare when I fell asleep . . . woke everybody."

"And you, Linda," Sheila turned to Linda, "I suppose your parents know you're spending the night?"

Linda avoided looking into her eyes. Sharon's mam was nice. She didn't want to have to tell her any lies. Tears rolled down her cheeks, and she looked desperately to Sharon for support. Sharon fixed her with a cautionary look.

Linda shook her head tiredly. "No – I'm sorry, Shar – I'm not going to get into any more trouble for you." She turned to Sheila, wiping the tears from her face with the back of her hand, like a child.

Sheila felt sorry for the girl. Linda was a good kid – she hated to admit it, but her daughter wasn't the type of friend she would have chosen for the girl – 'a bad influence' was the common phrase, and in this case Sheila thought it was never more true.

"We were at the club, Mrs Shaughnessy – and Sharon has taken some drugs."

Her worst fears realised, Sheila looked at her daughter, horrified. "*Drugs?* Sharon! Is it true?"

Sharon looked at her, an absurd comical smile on her face. "Don't be such a fusspot, Mam – everybody does it!"

"My daughter doesn't do it!" Sheila was screaming at her now. She couldn't stop herself. She struck out at Sharon, the slap across her face leaving an angry-looking red mark on her cheek.

"Jesus! Leave me alone, you savage!" Sharon roared back at Sheila, leaping to her feet. "I can report you for hitting me, you know – if Dad were here, he wouldn't treat me like this!"

The two of them were standing now in the middle of the bedroom, both of them shocked, Sheila's clenched fists by her sides revealing taut knuckles beneath stretched alabaster-coloured skin.

Deirdre acted quickly. She placed herself between the two of them, and appealed to her mother. "Come on, Mam – it's late – we can talk about all of this in the morning."

"I hit her!" Sheila looked at Deirdre, the bewildered expression on her face making Deirdre want to reach out and hold her. "I never hit any of you before – I don't know what came over me."

"You won't do it again!" Sharon's angry voice was threatening. She was no longer the accused. Her mother had unwittingly turned the tables in her favour. She called the shots now. The blow across her face hadn't hurt that much. She knew by her mother's reaction that it had affected her much more. Advantage, Sharon, she thought, a smile of satisfaction spreading across her face.

Deirdre saw the look, and felt a coldness inside her, like a cold band encircling her heart, warning her that this was only the beginning of some terrible turn of events with Sharon as the central figure.

"Linda – you sleep in Sharon's bed tonight," she said quietly. "I'll fix up the camp bed for Sharon to sleep in, and in the morning I'll see what has to be done."

With Deirdre's help, she dragged out the camp bed from beside the wardrobe, then took a rolled-up sleeping bag and unfolded it on the bed. "There you go, Sharon – you get a few hours' rest, and I'll talk to you when we've all had some sleep." She hesitated for a moment, then put her arms about her daughter. The girl remained unyielding, her hands down by her sides, her eyes looking through Sheila, but not at her.

Sheila gave up. Maybe all teenagers gave the

same trouble at home – she didn't know. Deirdre was so different, though, so easy-going, with none of the rebellion that had confronted her with Sharon since she was a very small girl.

She remembered how Sharon's stubborn voice had irritated her. "*I want it now!*" had been her catchphrase. She wouldn't get what she wanted this time, though. Drugs were a completely different kettle of fish. She turned and went slowly to her bedroom. She could hear Deirdre and Linda talking in low tones and suddenly remembered something. It was the first thing she should have done, of course, but the shock of hearing about the drugs had driven everything else out of her head.

"Linda, you didn't answer me . . ." She looked into the bedroom, saw the frightened look on Linda's face as she sat up straight in the bed, hugging her knees with her hands. "Do your parents expect you home or did you tell them you'd be staying the night with Sharon?"

"They . . . expect me home," Linda answered reluctantly.

"Then I'll have to ring them, love, and let them know you're here."

"Mrs Shaughnessy – they'll kill me – Dad will, anyway – and Mam will be upset!"

"There's no other way, love – they have to know what went on tonight." She saw the whiteness of the girl's face, the tension in her body as she plucked at the sleeping bag with agitated movements. It would have been better if the girl had nothing to do with Sharon, Sheila thought tiredly. Her daughter seemed to be intent on tainting everybody with her selfish ways and indifference, her best friend included.

"All right, Mrs Shaughnessy." Linda looked at her resignedly. "Only tell Mam I'm all right – Dad will kill –" She hesitated before she went on. "He'll be angry with her if he finds out I went to the club tonight and she didn't know about it ..."

Sheila nodded. She knew Dave Sullivan, what kind of a man he was. Intimidating and threatening to his wife and children. He had been known to raise his fist to one or other of them when his frustrations got the better of him.

Still, it had to be done. She picked up the phone.

"Hello – Lily? Sheila Shaughnessy here. I'm so sorry to ring so late but I know you expected Linda home. Listen to me, you're not to worry – she's safe and sound over here with me. I'm afraid my Sharon had a little mishap tonight but she's fine – I can't explain now – I don't even know what happened – except that it was her own fault. If you could come over in the morning, after they've had a bit of sleep – maybe they can explain things better to us when they've had a rest."

Chapter 12

"Come on, Tom – Dee will take you to school –"

Tom protested loudly, pushing his bowl of cereal away from him, kicking the leg of the table obstinately with his foot. "*You* promised you'd take me – you said you were starting work today in town, and you'd drop me off before you went to your new job – you promised!" He looked at her reproachfully.

Sheila sighed. It was a pity about the job. She hadn't a hope of it now. Donal Sheridan was a businessman. He wasn't going to entertain taking on a woman who turned up late on her first day on the job. "I hope your family commitments won't interfere with working hours, Mrs Shaughnessy?"

he had cautioned her over the telephone. Something told her that Donal Sheridan wouldn't have any patience with a woman who was trying to put her life together after her husband had deserted her. She could never hope to make him understand that her teenage daughter was going through a particularly bad patch – and she could imagine the horrified look on his face if she told him that Sharon had indulged in almost an overdose of drugs. No – she could definitely forget about the job, she thought ruefully, as she forced Tom into his anorak and buckled his schoolbag on to his back.

Deirdre looked at her anxiously. "Everything will be fine, won't it, Mam?"

Sheila nodded reassuringly, although inside she felt more insecure than ever. The new job hadn't even got off the ground, and her financial situation looked bleaker than ever. Things were far from fine, but she wasn't going to burden Deirdre with any more worries. She was carrying far too much on her shoulders as it was.

"Hurry on, love – you get off to school – I've written a note for the teacher." She handed the note to Deirdre. "I've just explained that Sharon isn't feeling too well and she's staying at home today – there's no need for you to explain anything."

Deirdre put the note into the side zip of her

schoolbag, stuffing her lunch into her pocket.

"Eat your lunch, Dee – you seem to be bringing home sandwiches lately – you need to eat, love ..." She looked at her daughter worriedly. Deirdre had got thin since Sam had left them. Her appetite had never been great but lately she barely touched her food. She'd get her a tonic in the chemist, something with iron in it.

"What about Linda?" Deirdre asked.

"Linda will be fine – her mam and dad are coming over later on and we can try to sort things out – now hurry on!" She looked at the clock on the wall. "Where's Tom gone? Has he gone back up to his room?"

Upstairs, Sharon had woken. She could hear her mother's voice in the kitchen, calling to Tom that he'd be late if he didn't hurry up. Then the door opened with a loud bang as Tom ran into the bedroom, stopping in his tracks as he saw the two girls in bed still. Sharon pretended to be asleep, keeping her eyes closed. He advanced cautiously towards the camp bed, shaking her with a determined hand, while she turned away from him crossly.

"Go away, Tom! Mam is calling you for school!"

"Why aren't you going?" he demanded in injured tones. Then as realisation dawned on him, he shouted angrily "*Mam! Why can't I stay at home if Sharon is? That's not fair!"*

Deirdre came into the room and grabbed him by the arm. "Come on, Tom – we'll be late – and Sharon is staying at home today because she's sick – so is Linda." She nodded in the direction of the blonde head barely visible above the duvet.

He looked from one to the other, was about to make another protest, when Deirdre put her hand over his mouth, muffling his protests as she led him down the stairs.

Sharon could hear the front door slam behind them. She lay on her back looking up at the ceiling. She remembered the look on her mother's face last night at the very mention of the word 'drugs'. She didn't know what all the fuss was about. Drugs were very much overrated anyway. She could take them or leave them, but it was so much fun to indulge in a bit of harmless escapism. And that was the way they made her feel. She escaped from the rotten world of Dad leaving them, and Mam being frazzled and worried all the time, and the house looking like a kip – they made her feel good, and she wasn't going to stop, not for her mother, not for anyone. Besides, Sharon thought to herself dreamily, she didn't want Declan to think she was some sort of baby.

She wanted to be his girl more than anything else right now. He was the leader of the gang. All the boys idolised him, and the girls – they swarmed about him like bees to a honeypot – Declan this and Declan that, fluttering their eyelashes at him. Sharon relaxed against the pillow and closed her eyes. She would get him interested in her if only people would mind their own business and let her grow up. She could just imagine her mother going to that interfering busybody Father O'Hara again, complaining about her to him. "Oh, Father – I don't know what to do with her. She's into drugs!" She mouthed the words mockingly in the silent room.

She could hear the sound of a car pulling up outside, the slamming of the car door, the sound of footsteps then the doorbell ringing. She heaved a resigned sigh. Linda's mam had wasted no time in joining ranks with her mother.

Chapter 13

Sam stood by the open window of the upstairs flat in Friedrichstrasse. He felt restless. For the first time since he had come to Berlin with Sigrid he looked out on to the empty rain-washed street, and wished with all his heart, he had to admit, that he was back in Limerick with Sheila and the kids. It was the phone call that had intruded on his sense of adventure, had made him feel guilty about his reckless impulse to be in a position to 'do his own thing' – to have an affair with the gorgeous German woman who had excited him as Sheila had never done.

Deirdre's voice had reminded him a little of Sheila's – reserved, cautious, the timidity grating on his nerves. But it was that very familiarity that had suddenly made him long for what was past. Sigrid was a spectacular woman, every man's head turning in admiration when she walked into a room, her long blonde hair cascading about her slim shoulders, steel-grey eyes sparkling with undeniable sex appeal. He had been attracted to her ever since their first meeting in John Markham's office. He could see she was interested too, her hand resting that little bit longer than normal on his as she surveyed the computer disk catalogues with him.

It was Sam who had suggested that maybe Jean on the switchboard could put her up for the few weeks she was staying in Limerick to familiarise herself with the new computer system her firm were very interested in setting up in their own network of offices. Sigrid had been installed with Jean in her flat in Selmont Terrace. It wasn't long before Sam was finding excuses to call in the odd evening 'to discuss a few more details' about the changeover. Jean had discreetly left them alone in the flat because after a while she felt like an intruder, watching the unspoken messages passing between them.

She had bewitched him, Sam now thought wildly, his heart beating a fraction too quickly as he paced about the room. Outside, he could see the drab, rain-spattered streets of Berlin, grey buildings outlined against the insipid paleness of the early morning sky. Nothing in this place reminded him of home, and he shivered at the alien setting, so far removed from the lovely unassuming view of the Clare hills.

"*Liebling* – come back to bed – it is too early." Sigrid's sleepy voice came from the big double bed at the far side of the room. She sat up, shrugging her blonde hair back from her face, still beautiful even without make-up.

"I can't sleep," Sam answered shortly, perhaps a little too shortly, because she looked up at him sharply, her grey eyes cold and questioning.

"You are unhappy, *Liebling* – ever since you telephoned your home – I told you it was something you should not have done. You should have waited – until we had things '*in Ordnung*'." She spoke quietly, her voice caressing him from the shadowed recesses of the bed where only a few hours previously they had made love.

He went slowly across the room and sat on the side of the bed, his back turned to her. She caressed his neck slowly, tantalisingly, her hand moving across his flesh in long, languid strokes. Sam felt, to his own surprise, just a mild feeling of irritation instead of the familiar longing to hold her warm, compliant body close to his, to make love to her with a frenzy that left him pleasurably spent and longing for more.

"What is troubling you, Sam? We are quite safe, you know." She put a hand compellingly on his shoulder so that he was forced to turn towards her. Her eyes were like two hard circles of radiant steel, unyielding, cold in spite of their shining intensity. He shivered involuntarily. What had he got himself into? Only six months previously he had been riding the crest of a wave, with promotional prospects, a finger in the proverbial pie of lucrative industrial success. John Markham had set him up in the company as a shining example of what was needed to revolutionise an industry, open up gateways into Europe. He wondered now, staring at the pale-pink patterned wallpaper in Sigrid's flat, where it had all gone wrong.

He had been too greedy, and too vulnerable where a woman like Sigrid was concerned. The sweat stood in small drops of fear on his forehead, fearful of the consequences of what they had just accomplished.

"There is no need to be so afraid, *Liebling*." Sigrid threw her long shapely legs over the side of the bed, taking her dressing-gown from the coverlet.

The early morning sounds were already beginning outside, guttural German voices on their way to work, the swishing, determined sound of bicycle wheels speeding across wet cobbled stone – Friedrichstrasse, currently in the process of intense renovation, echoed with a cacophony of sound, workmen drilling into the grey cobblestone, laying the foundations of a new rail system which would modernise the city and put it on a sophisticated level equal to its EU counterparts.

"Come – we must meet Dieter at 8.30 in the Café Adler – he will cheer you up. And just think of all the money that is yet to come – we must take the iron while it is warm – is that the correct saying, *Liebling*?"

"*Strike while the iron is hot*," Sam said shortly. He wished he could turn back the clock. A quick flirtation with the lovely Sigrid and a regretful parting – that would have sufficed. But he had wanted more, and now he wasn't too sure if he could carry the rest of their plan through.

"There are opportunities for the taking in business nowadays, Sam." She sat in front of the dressing-table mirror, combing her long blonde hair, twisting it into a sophisticated roll at the back of her slender neck. "There is no room for scruples, for irritating pangs of conscience. We must look forward to the future." She assessed herself critically in the mirror, her face half turned towards him.

"What future? For God's sake, Sigrid – we'll be found out, sooner or later – and then what? I don't fancy life inside a prison cell!"

Sam paced the room, agitated, the flashing neon light above the Cafe Adler across the square casting shadows about his head, increasing his feelings of anxiety.

"Sam – *Liebling* –" She reached out to him and wrapped herself snugly into his arms, willing his tension to unwind, gratified when she felt his arms encircling her, holding her close.

"I've left everything behind – just for you, Sigrid – I want everything to come right. If this little operation doesn't work out . . ."

He was like a schoolboy, frightened and uncertain, and she silenced him with a kiss.

"The Berlin Wall may have come down, Sam, but the barriers of oblivion are still there – this is still East Berlin, no matter what reforms may have come about." Her voice was harsh and uncompromising. "There are many here who would turn a blind eye to operations such as ours. They are wary of the police and we can remain safe from the hands of the law, without fear of police intrusion, if we are *careful*!"

She emphasised the word 'careful', looking deep into his worried eyes, her look clearly indicating to him that she was a woman who had no time for a man who could be indecisive. "We planned everything together, Sam – for the last twelve months we have planned and researched every detail. Dieter will take the money to Ossie Bremmer this evening, and the consignment will be waiting for us early tomorrow morning in a small warehouse at the back of the Schauspielhaus."

Sam knew the place. He and Sigrid had been to some very 'risqué' showings at the theatre there, the audiences enthralled by the whole concept of watching a naked man parade himself seductively in front of a woman wearing only a leather purse about her neck. That particular piece of 'theatre' had lasted over two hours, the two actors not speaking, their mime leaving nothing to the imagination.

Afterwards Sam had asked Sigrid what it had been all about. She had looked at him in amazement.

"Why, it is woman's dominance over man, *Liebling* – did you not understand the message? As long as the woman holds the purse-strings, the man will keep her 'amused'." She had grown serious then, a bitter intonation in her voice. "Economically independent. Every woman is entitled to that necessity – the whole concept of the little woman staying at home, being a '*Hausfrau*' to her husband and her screaming children – it is positively degrading."

Sam had remained silent after that. Something had told him that if he displayed any sense of amusement at the comic portrayal at the theatre it would have been an insult, maybe jeopardising their relationship.

A futuristic Emily Pankhurst, he had thought, smiling to himself as he lay in bed that evening, Sigrid curled up next to him, her feminist, bra-less breasts pointing aggressively towards him.

* * *

The early morning workers had deserted the street, already seated behind office desks and in their places in factory assembly lines by the time Sam and Sigrid left the flat and crossed the square to the Café Adler.

"It's so quiet," Sam observed, looking about him in amazement. "Back home the noise of the traffic would be unbearable at this hour in the morning, car horns hooting, exhaust fumes, agitated motorists trying to jump the queues in long lines of traffic . . ." He listed the so-called annoyances almost wistfully.

Sigrid laughed. "Bicycles are far more environmentally friendly – besides being more economical. Remember, Sam, East Berliners are just slowly beginning to enjoy the benefits of Western-style living. Soon we will be just as wealthy as our neighbours – even more so ..." She tossed her hair aggressively, a sharpness in her voice sounding intimidating to Sam. "We are cautious with our spending – we know what deprivation means – we are masters of economy-style thinking! But, no doubt, in several years' time, Friedrichstrasse will be choked up with exhaust fumes and the noise level will have increased several times over." She shrugged her shoulders resignedly. "The price of freedom – such an incongruity, don't you think, my *Liebling*?"

They went into the cafe and sat in their customary window-seat looking out on to the street. The skies were steel grey, the building works going on at the corner of the street adding to the sense of decadence, Sam's depression increasing as he looked at the bulldozer demolishing a block of pre-war buildings, the walls crumbling into a mass of powdery dust and mortar. Just in front of him, with the magnificent cupolas of the German cathedral and the French cathedral outlined impressively in the background, was a small, unassuming boutique, bravely defying any ridicule of its attempts to equal the more modern ethos of the fashionable shops in the city centre. An emaciated-looking wax model, with large green-coloured plastic eyes, looked out on to the street from beneath a blue and white striped ruffled awning, her stiff body encased in a leather bodysuit.

Sigrid signalled to the waiter and ordered a pot of coffee and hot rolls.

"Dieter should be here soon – and please, Sam – cheer up – show him that you are capable of doing this job. It is the weak link in any venture that ruins everything – you understand?" She poured him a cup of the strong, black coffee, pushing the milk jug across the table to him. It was at times like this that Sam almost hated the woman he had become obsessed with. She treated him as though he was a simpleton, unable to think and move without asking first for her permission. And in a way, he thought now, as he watched the small, stocky figure of Dieter cross Friedrichstrasse, she was right. The prospect left him even more apprehensive . . . at the thought of a woman almost owning him, body and soul, changing his whole life in such a way that there was no turning back. Sweat stood out on his forehead and he wiped it away with a paper serviette which was placed beside his plate, while Sigrid smiled and waved to Dieter to join them.

* * *

Dieter Volk looked at the man sitting across from him in the Café Adler. His obviously nervous manner was off-putting, and Dieter wondered if he and Sigrid had perhaps made the wrong choice. But Sigrid had been adamant. "He will do for the purpose for which we require him, Dieter – you know how he feels about me." She had looked at Dieter with slanted eyes, a smug twist to her red-painted lips. Yes. He knew how men felt about Sigrid. There had been others, pawns she had picked up along the way each time a new venture was in the offing. They had made quite a bit of money, once the middleman had been paid and the consignment offloaded to its destination. Ireland was breaking new ground, venturing beyond the freshly opened barriers of the EU. Customs control relaxed, the drug traders had already established vantage points on the West Coast, the poisonous bags of white powder hidden beneath the creosoted boards of innocent-looking trawlers.

The money they had acquired to finance the buying and distribution of the drugs had been siphoned from the finances of little companies, such as Griffith and Markham. As Dieter looked across at the woman sitting next to Sam, putting her beautifully manicured hand on the shoulder of her accomplice, he marvelled at the way she had expertly sifted through the personnel in each company and chosen her victims. In this case it was Sam Shaughnessy, newly promoted managerial material, who was treated to her lies about the company in Germany and their interest in Griffith and Markham's software, deceiving him to the point where he was willing to do anything for her.

And then Sigrid had struck, outlining her scheme to him as they lay in bed in the flat in Selmont Terrace. Dieter smiled as he remembered her explanation of Sam's reaction.

"A man who had just made love is vulnerable, Dieter – his thoughts are still warm with the pleasures of the flesh – and when I told him that there was no such company as Lichtsturm, that our main business was dealing, not in software, but in drugs, he merely looked surprised – then asked how much money could be made in such a venture – and I knew everything would work out perfectly – because Sam Shaughnessy likes money and the power it brings him."

She had laughed aloud then, and Dieter thought of the woman Sigrid had mentioned casually, Sam's wife. They had three children. He had left them behind to be with Sigrid, a woman who had broken up several marriages before now, and who would go on to destroy several more. Such was the power that women like her possessed.

Now, Dieter addressed Sam. "It is all arranged – Ossie will be waiting at ten o'clock this evening – I am to bring him the money, and after midnight tonight the consignment will be loaded on to the cruiser and will await shipment to Bremerhaven – you need know nothing further until it has reached its destination." He looked at Sam, his eyes cold and without emotion. "You will be paid only when the operation has been completed successfully – do you understand?"

Sam nodded dumbly. He wanted out. There was no way he wanted to have anything to do with smuggling, especially drug smuggling. He had been taken in by Sigrid, bewitched by her, without regarding the consequences of their terrible operation. If they were caught – he shivered at the thought – a prison sentence, his name all over the papers, the kids disgraced – he hadn't thought of what effect it would have on Sheila. He couldn't even remember what she looked like. The only face that was with him twenty-four hours of the day, waking and sleeping, was the beautiful, bewitching face of Sigrid. All this was to please her, to make her happy.

"And what happens – afterwards?" He had planned his life only up to the point where he and Sigrid would perhaps vanish into obscurity, a tidy sum between them to get them started again, the pain of the loosened ties with home dulled by the luxury of never having to worry about shortage of money again. He wondered now if it was all worth it. Deirdre's voice still haunted him, the hurt in her words "Dad, are you coming home?", then the long pauses where he knew she had been crying quietly. He knew what type of a man he was – selfish, unfaithful, cruel to the people who loved him – and he couldn't help it. He looked across at Sigrid, her gaze directed at him, her eyes questioning, always the unspoken question – was he capable of carrying it through, without fouling up the whole operation and landing them in jail instead of some remote, idyllic paradise for the rest of their lives?

"Afterwards?" She leaned across the table and took his hand, squeezing it tightly. "We lie low, *Liebling*, until we are sure there is no possibility of discovery – then it is only a short flight from Schonefeld Airport to Sofia in Bulgaria – we will be safe, then, *Liebling*. Two years maybe and our money will be working for us in the bank in Geneva – then we can *really* start living – perhaps go to America ..." Her eyes shone with a fanatical gleam, his hand gripped in hers like a vice.

He tried to extricate it, panic increasing, his palms growing sweaty. She was still talking to him, but he could only see her lips moving, the buzzing sound in his ears preventing him from hearing. Bulgaria – like rats in hiding, a foreign country, no job to keep him occupied, to prevent him from dwelling on the terrible thing he had done to Sheila, the kids. Sitting on a stash of money he had no right to. Then America – exiled forever because of his own foolishness. He knew, with dismay, looking at the woman sitting opposite him, that there was no turning back now. She wouldn't let him go, not until she had got what she wanted from him ...

Dieter rose suddenly. "I must go. I have it arranged for tonight that the warehouse will be left open and the consignment delivered in a fruit truck." He bent down and kissed Sigrid on the cheek, his lips lingering for a moment against the soft skin.

Sam looked at the two of them and it was as though he was viewing a moving scenario of two experienced actors acting out a part, just for his benefit. Each movement seemed premeditated, Sigrid's cheek moving seductively against Dieter's lips.

Sam was an outsider. Back home in Ireland, it had been different. She'd had eyes only for him, her magnificent body moulding itself into his as they made love, her arms twined about his neck, whispered words of love, dispelling any doubts he might have felt about leaving Sheila. Now, as he looked at the two of them, silent messages passing between them, he wondered, for the hundredth time since he had come to Berlin, if he was mad to have ever got himself involved in the first place.

Chapter 14

"No! And I mean it! No more favours. I have a business to run, and I need reliable workers who'll pull their weight – not some woman who falls to bits when there's a crisis at home!"

Donal Sheridan swung his legs down from the top of his desk where he had them propped defensively and faced the priest standing in front of him.

Stephen O'Hara looked at him enquiringly. "You were only waiting for an excuse, weren't you? Anything at all so that you wouldn't have to take on another of my 'lost sheep' – isn't that it, Donal?"

The priest's voice increased in volume, and

Donal looked quickly towards the open door where he could see the inquisitive looks of two of his young waitresses. He strode across the room and closed it firmly. He was not in the best of form this morning. He had found out, just by chance as he dropped into Lowney's pub on his way home from work last evening, that a new delicatessen venture was all set to establish business almost on his own doorstep, in the run-down old barber's shop that he himself had shown interest in not so long ago. He had approached the owner, who had mumbled something about getting advice from the 'Corpo' – and Donal had been fairly satisfied that the man would give in eventually and accept his price. It now seemed that Donal had gambled and lost, all through letting things slide. He should have gone in there and bargained with the owner for a price at the very beginning, and now his opportunity had passed him by.

So when Stephen O'Hara had appeared at nine o'clock that morning, trying to persuade him to give the Shaughnessy woman a second chance, he had literally exploded.

"She didn't do it deliberately, you know," Stephen reasoned. "Her daughter had a bit of trouble the morning she was to turn up here for work."

"Yes – and I had a bit of trouble trying to ring

around, find a substitute for her, on one of our busiest mornings in a long time –"

"If you knew Sheila Shaughnessy was only starting work after twenty years, surely you realised that you should have had a back-up here, in case she couldn't cope?" Stephen O'Hara stared at him defiantly. "You're a scrooge, that's what you are, Donal – giving one of the experienced girls the morning off so that you could get Sheila to work the hours for half the amount of pay the other girls are earning – it bloody serves you right if you lost custom over your own meaness!"

Donal looked at him, startled. The expletive from the priest had surprised him. He smiled in spite of himself, and Stephen, seeing the tough veneer relax a little, took full advantage.

"Come on, man – give her another chance – say 9.30 in the morning – what about it?"

Donal sighed resignedly. "Okay. Have her come here – nine o'clock sharp. Second time lucky, eh, Father?"

* * *

Sheila thought she never again wanted to endure a week such as she had just gone through. She sat in the kitchen, the cup of coffee held tightly between her shaking hands, tears not far off as she heard the sounds of arguing coming from the girls' room upstairs. Father O'Hara had said he'd call round with news of the job, if there still was a job. There was nothing she could do about what had happened that morning.

Dave and Lily Sullivan's visit had not been very helpful. If anything, it had made a bad situation worse. Dave had been his usual lecherous self, eying Sheila with interest, his small, piglike eyes, half hidden in folds of flesh, surveying every inch of her body. If she'd had the nerve, she would have liked to slap his fleshy, overfed jaw, but she kept calm, her worry about Sharon outweighing any disgust she might have felt for Dave Sullivan. Lily had sat there, silent, passive, looking in her husband's direction every time Sheila tried to get her opinion on anything.

"Lily, did you know Linda was hanging around the club nearly every night of the week?" Sheila asked in exasperation.

"She told me she was going studying with your Sharon – she doesn't have that much pocket money to spend it in the club every night." Lily looked up at Sheila pleadingly.

Dave didn't know the half of what went on in the Sullivan home. He had a heavy hand with her when she irritated him, and Lily was afraid he'd start on the kids – so she always tried to cover up for them, especially Linda. If he ever started on

Linda, she'd have to leave him, she thought desperately. Hitting her was one thing. Hitting the kids wasn't on, not her Linda, who was a good girl at the back of it all. Just the crowd she mixed with led her astray ... Linda was sound, though.

"And Sharon told me she was studying with Linda – and you can see the condition of the two of them from all the 'studying' they did last night, can't you?" Sheila demanded, pointing to the two girls who were standing, staring intently at the pattern on the red carpet in the living room.

"What happened"? Dave Sullivan advanced threateningly towards Linda.

She shied away from him, her arm raised instinctively to protect herself and burst into tears. For a moment it looked as though he was going to strike the girl, but then Lily gave a small gasp of horror and Dave turned to her, a malevolent smile on his face as though he had found a more appropriate victim.

"Look, calm down, Dave," said Sheila. "This kind of carry-on won't do anybody any good – and like I've said before – it's all Sharon's fault she got herself into the state she was in last night – so don't blame Linda." Sheila looked at her daughter grimly. There was no expression of remorse on the girl's face, no sign that she felt even the remotest pang of guilt that she had got her best friend into such trouble. Her eyes, cold and without a trace of fear, stared now at Sheila, their outline still encircled with the severe black liner, now smudged and looking even more grotesque. Linda cowered behind her, her shoulders heaving as she sobbed bitterly, now and again looking up at her mother for some sort of moral support.

"Dope, did you say? If there's dope going round in the club, then I'm going to report that bollox Len Darcy –"

"No, Dad! Len Darcy had nothing to do with it!" Linda pleaded, tears streaming down her cheeks. "It was just the boys having a bit of fun!"

"What boys?" Dave looked at her suspiciously.

"Just friends of ours, Mr Sullivan," Sharon interrupted airily. She wasn't afraid of Dave Sullivan. She had seen his type down at the club, eying all the young ones, thinking they were in with a chance to 'pull' a few of them. Dirty old men, that's all they were. She could handle men like Dave Sullivan any time. "Look – everybody does it some time – just to see what it's like. I had a pull or two – it made me high as I wasn't used to it – and I got sick and Linda brought me home in the taxi. That's all there is to it."

"That's all!" Dave Sullivan exploded, his fat face growing redder as he looked at the calm indifference on Sharon's face. "Dope! And two young ones under age out until all hours of the morning – and nobody knowing where they were!" He glared at Lily again, accusingly. She should have seen to the girl, made sure she was in at a reasonable hour. It was all her mother's fault – Lily was a pain in the ass at the best of times.

"This Declan, Sharon?" Sheila looked at her daughter, questioningly.

"He's just a boy, Mam – we hang around together," Sharon dismissed him airily. If her mother ever knew just how she felt about Declan, she'd be grounded, not able to stir outside the door. Declan was into other things besides dope. He was 'experienced', he had told Sharon one night in the smoky, dimly lit hallway of the club. He had 'had' girls, girls the same age as Sharon, some older, he'd boasted, looking at her challengingly. She had known what he was talking about. She liked him, wanted more than anything else to be 'his' girl – and if that was the only way she could have him, then maybe it was worth a try? Every time the thought had come into her head, her mother's worried face had floated irritatingly across her conscience, not that she normally even considered that such a thing as conscience existed. So she had kept him dangling on a string, letting him wonder when she would give in. Because girls always gave in to Declan Murphy in the end. It was just a matter of time.

"I'm going to the school," Sheila said firmly, "to make a few enquiries about this stuff that's doing the rounds there."

"I'll go with you, Sheila." For the first time there was a determined tone in Lily Sullivan's voice. "Dave, you can drop myself and Sheila off at the school, then go on to work."

"Christ! A whole hour wasted with the goings-on of these two," Dave grumbled, staring angrily at Lily for a moment, then striding angrily from the room.

* * *

At 10.30 they were seated in front of the Principal in St Ita's Secondary School. "We can do nothing about it, Mrs Shaughnessy." Bernard Casey, the Principal, looked at her sympathetically. "We can only give guidelines to the pupils, warning them against using drugs, to avoid being conned by these people who peddle the stuff discreetly behind our backs. They are doing it all the time – even in the schoolyard – and we can't catch them. We don't even know who they are, although we have our suspicions."

He stood up and went to the window, looking out on to the schoolyard where groups of teenagers stood round at their mid-morning break, their shrieks of laughter reaching Sheila and Lily as they sat silently in the office.

"Times are changing, you know – the teachers

haven't the same authority they held in the past. I'm sorry to say but it's up to you, the parents, to see that they don't get involved in anything that will get them into trouble. There's very little I can do, except keep my eyes and ears open for the ringleaders."

Sheila nodded tiredly. "I know – it's just that we wanted you to know what's going on. There's one boy in particular who seems to have some uncanny influence over the others – and he's able to get his hands on the drugs."

Bernard Casey nodded. "I know the boy you're speaking about – but nobody has any proof. I've never found him with any drugs on him. He's good at his schoolwork, I would say better than average even, and doesn't give any trouble in class – so what can I do, in the circumstances?"

* * *

They got the bus at the end of William Street.

"At least we know where we stand now, Sheila," said Lily, "and I'll keep an eye on Linda – she gets pocket money from me every week, but definitely not enough for her to be frequenting the club every night – and sometimes she tells me she's with Sharon, studying in your house, so I never question it. Maybe between us we can put them back on the right track . . ." Lily looked at Sheila anxiously. She didn't want any more trouble with Dave. It was in her own interest too to make sure Linda didn't cause him any more aggravation. She shivered suddenly, thinking of the pain he had inflicted on her as she bore the brunt of his anger in the past. "We'll do our best, anyway." She almost whispered the words, desperately.

Sheila looked at her and saw the lines of worry on her forehead. She wouldn't be in Lily Sullivan's shoes for anything. Whatever trouble she had now with Sharon, at least she hadn't a lunatic of a man to contend with also.

Chapter 15

Sheila put down the mug suddenly on the kitchen table, a thought too awful to contemplate coming into her head. What if Sharon was doing something underhand, just to get her hands on some quick money – where else could she possibly get enough to buy drugs? Sheila knew nothing about drugs, she had to confess, feeling guilty that this was an area of parenting that she had sorely neglected, mostly because she believed none of her children would be so stupid as to get into that scene, but she did know that it was an expensive habit, and one that Sharon could ill afford on her meagre allowance. Just how far had Sharon gone to finance her drug-taking?

Suddenly there was an explosion of noise and raised voices from the bedroom above her, the lampshade on the kitchen ceiling shuddering with the impact of some object landing on the floor above.

"Sharon! Deirdre! For pity's sake! What's wrong with the two of you?" She stood up angrily, pushing her chair back from the table.

Halfway up the stairs, she heard the doorbell ring and she paused, looking towards the closed bedroom door on the landing above where the sound of angry voices was to be clearly heard.

Tom poked his head out of his room, his eyes big and frightened-looking.

"Mam – they're at it again – they're fighting, and they won't stop!"

The doorbell rang, this time more determinedly, and she went down to open it, her face showing her irritation as she faced Stephen O'Hara who was standing on the doorstep.

"A fine welcome, I must say – it sounds like a bedlam asylum upstairs, and you look like a very harassed warder, trying to keep the peace without much success!"

He strode past her while she stood there, mouth open, her eyes following him as he went up the stairs, two at a time, then banged loudly on the bedroom door.

There was a sudden silence, then Sheila heard

Deirdre's voice, muffled, tearful, call out, "Who is it?" while Sharon's angry voice shushed her in the background.

"Oh, shut up, Sharon," said Deirdre. "Just leave me alone!"

"Come out of there, the two of you, before I break down the door!"

Stephen's voice sounded intimidating even to Sheila, as she waited for the girls' reaction. If only Sam were here, there would be none of this hassle. Maybe he had been right – she was a wimp after all. Even the girls took no notice of her, and when Tom got older, maybe he'd turn out the same. Her life was going to be one long misery, and just for a second she imagined how peaceful it would be, to just lie down with a few extra sleeping tablets, let the muzzy feeling wash over her, forget everything, as if this torment had never been.

The two girls were standing at the top of the stairs. She hadn't heard them come out of their room, but now she saw Deirdre looking at Sharon with such contempt that she hurried up the stairs and stood next to Stephen. Then she recoiled in horror at the angry red bruise on the side of Deirdre's face.

Sharon looked at her mother, then gave Stephen a cold stare, the beautiful eyes dull and ugly-looking with the black, heavy eyeliner accentuating whatever torment was eating away at her inside.

"What's happened?" Sheila spoke quietly, her mind in turmoil. Keep your head, she told herself firmly, whatever is wrong can be sorted out. A teenage quarrel, nothing more, nothing to get worked up about.

Father O'Hara looked at the girls intently, then pointed to the stairs. "OK. Come on – down to the kitchen, and your mother will make us a pot of tea – there are things to be sorted out! Tom, you get ready for bed, there's a good boy – your mam will come up to tuck you in soon."

Downstairs again, Sheila put on the kettle, taking the mugs from the mug rack mechanically, slicing thick slices of fruitcake, buttering them the way Tom and the girls liked it.

"Do you like butter, Father?" she asked him, telling herself it was a stupid question, almost laughing out loud at her flippant enquiry when the situation was so tense in the room.

"Lovely, Sheila!" He beamed at her, ignoring the tension in the silent faces of the two girls sitting opposite one another. Sharon slouched in her chair, posture defiant, pink-tipped fingernails tapping the tabletop agitatedly.

"Sharon – take those mugs from your mother and bring them to the table. Deirdre – get your brother a glass of milk and take it up to him with some of that cake."

Deirdre was back and Stephen had the situation well in hand by the time Sheila sat down.

She looked at the red mark on Deirdre's face, then at Sharon, the unspoken question communicating itself to the younger girl.

"It was an accident," Sharon said sulkily.

Deirdre looked up quickly, opened her mouth as if to protest, then closed it again. Mam was upset enough, no point in making a bad situation worse.

"If it was an accident," said Sheila, "then you'd better have a pretty good explanation, my lady!"

Deirdre saw the anger in her mother's face. She shook her head tearfully, rubbing at the painful mark on her face. She didn't want to get Sharon into any more trouble.

"No, Mam – forget about it – we'll sort things out between ourselves – please – just leave it!"

"Your mother can't leave it, Deirdre, because the same thing will probably happen again and again," Stephen said carefully, "and whatever is eating you two will fester and turn into something bigger than you both can handle – so out with it now!" He reached for a slice of fruitcake as he watched from the corner of his eye for the girls' reaction.

Deirdre hesitated, then spoke hesitantly. "We had an argument – that's all."

"About what?" Sheila looked at them, puzzled. An argument was one thing – the girls were always arguing over something or another – but for Sharon to strike out like she did it must have been something more serious than just the usual who borrowed what, and whose turn it was to tidy the room.

"I hit her, okay – satisfied? I hit her because she bugged me!" Sharon's voice rose hysterically.

Sheila had never seen her so agitated, the muscles in her body twitching nervously, fingers plucking at the tablecloth, eyes protruding, looking through Sheila, focusing on nothing in particular.

"She bugged you," Sheila repeated, mystified at the explanation.

"She took something belonging to me," Deirdre said, her bottom lip quivering as she tried to hold back the tears. "I asked her for it back and she refused."

"A lousy ten euro – and I was going to pay you back –"

"Please! Not in front of Father!" Sheila was embarrassed at the rough language of Sharon.

"I don't care – he shouldn't be here anyway, poking his nose in where it doesn't concern him!" Sharon looked at Stephen coldly. He was an irritating intrusion on their family. Why didn't he just mind his own bloody business and do his good works somewhere else instead of bothering them?

Sheila looked at her in horror.

Stephen turned to the girl, his gaze intent as he spoke quietly, emphasising each word. "Something is troubling you, Sharon – let us in on it, okay? We're only trying to help. If you took money from Deirdre, what did you need it for? Was it so important that you had to actually *steal* it?"

"I didn't steal it!" Sharon shouted angrily. "I was going to pay it back!"

Sheila went and stood in front of her daughter. The jigsaw was beginning to slot into place. The money Sharon had for her fun, Deirdre's vague replies every time she had asked her why she wasn't going out with Sharon – too tired, too much studying to do – the answer was beginning to dawn on Sheila. A conspiracy of silence between the two of them, covering for Sharon. Deirdre had always been the martyr, the one who hated making trouble.

"If you took money, what did you spend it on?" Sheila waited while Sharon looked at her sullenly. "What did you spend it on?" she repeated, the angry undercurrent evident in her voice.

Sharon thought of Declan's handsome face, the way it had lit up with pleasure when she had produced the money for the drugs. "There's plenty more where that came from," she had boasted airily. Her own pocket money and Deirdre's combined bought her Declan's admiration every time – a girl with the readies for the drug on the spot – it made her look so sophisticated, in Declan's eyes. "I gave it – to a friend!" she said defiantly, looking from Stephen O'Hara to her mother.

"You bought drugs that made you sick the night Linda brought you home, didn't you?" Sheila was shouting now, the fear rising in the pit of her stomach. Jesus! As if she didn't have enough on her plate, her daughter was taking drugs, just for the fun of it! Where was it all going to end?

"She's been taking my pocket money," Deirdre said. Her voice sounded tired, defeated. She was sick of covering up for Sharon, giving her some of her pocket money, sometimes even all of it, making excuses to Mam why she wasn't going out with her friends, like Sharon did. She hadn't the money. It was that simple. Sharon wheedled the money out of her each week, promising faithfully to pay back every penny of it. She never did, and Deirdre was finished playing the silly game of hiding the truth from her mother.

"You took Deirdre's money, bought drugs with it – and you stand there as if you've done nothing wrong! Oh, Sharon! What's come over you? Can't you even see how much you've hurt everybody?"

Sharon looked at her mother's face. She knew she had hurt her, at a time when she needed all the support she could get. She had tormented her with all the lies, with her bullying in the house, because taking the money from Deirdre was nothing short of bullying – she knew all this, and still she resented the reprimands. And Father O'Hara sitting there, with his holier-than-thou attitude! Angrily she kicked the leg of the table, slouching defiantly in her chair.

"Mam?" Tom had appeared in the doorway, his sleepy small face flushed, blonde curls falling over his forehead. "Mammy, I want to go to bed – *I'm tired*!"

"I'll take care of him for you, Mam – sit down and finish your tea." Deirdre took the small boy expertly into her arms, lifting him effortlessly, his head lolling on her shoulder as she carried him up the stairs.

When they had left the kitchen, Sheila sat down in her chair, not looking at Sharon, the mug of tea remaining untouched on the table.

Stephen O'Hara looked at the sullen face of the girl sitting opposite him, and suddenly felt afraid for the woman who was trying to handle a bad situation alone. The girl needed help, and soon, if things weren't to get worse. It was the wrong time to suggest counselling. The girl would be defiant, refusing to see that she had any problem, and Sheila was too preoccupied with trying to put her own life in order to persuade Sharon to go to see anyone about her problem. And she had a problem.

Stephen looked at the bulging pupils of the eyes, the restless hands plucking awkwardly at her clothes, running impatiently across the table, drumming a tattoo on the tablecloth.

"You had better go to bed, Sharon," said Sheila. "I'll speak to you again in the morning – when I feel a little more able to cope."

Sharon rose, upsetting the mug of tea in front of her, the brown liquid dripping slowly on to the tiled floor. Sheila said nothing. Sharon was beyond reasoning with at this stage. If Stephen O'Hara hadn't been there, she would have taken an extra dose of sleeping tablets, and gone to bed, hoping that she would never wake up. She had never felt so low since Sam had left her. Curse you, Sam, she thought wildly, the terror inside her making her feel physically sick, knots of tension winding themselves like a vicious band about her head.

Sharon slammed the kitchen door, pounded up the stairs, and they heard the bedroom door open and slam shut behind her.

A thought suddenly occurred to Sheila. She

looked at Stephen. “If Sharon is taking money from Deirdre, maybe she’s getting it from some place else as well – and where did Linda get the money to keep her company every night at the club?” She looked at her watch. Almost ten o’clock. She rose to her feet. She’d give Lily Sullivan a ring, ask her just one question. One question was all that was necessary to find out the answer to the terrible thing she had been thinking, about her own daughter, her own Sharon, the little girl she had taught, ever since she had been able to walk, that stealing was a bad thing, good people didn’t steal things.

“Where are you going?” Stephen followed her into the hallway.

She picked up the receiver, not looking at him, her trembling finger dialling Lily Sullivan’s number. He watched her as she paused for a moment, her eyes closed, then spoke into the mouthpiece, her voice almost a whisper.

“Hello, Lily? Can you tell me – I know it’s a terrible thing to ask you – but have you any money missing – you know, money around the house, money you might have put away for bills, in a special place – do you know what I’m saying, Lily? I can’t think of any other way the girls would have got their hands on that much money.” She waited.

Stephen knew Lily had gone to check. Surely

the girls wouldn't go that far? He waited with Sheila, standing in the doorway of the kitchen, his mug of tea held in one hand, the loud ticking of the hall clock counting the seconds with them, waiting, waiting for Lily's answer. Sheila's grip on the receiver tightened, her face almost the colour of the pale, white-painted background.

"Yes – right – how much, Lily? Fifty, maybe more. Don't go upsetting yourself – our first priority is to get the girls sorted out before they get into real trouble – and Lily – don't tell Dave – things would only get worse."

She replaced the receiver and turned to the priest, tears streaming down her face. "There's the electricity money missing – fifty euro of it – and the awful thing is, Father, I'm afraid to confront my own daughter about it. I'm afraid of her, Father, because she's like a stranger to me – and there doesn't seem to be anything I can do to make things right again!"

She sat on the bottom stair and put her head in her hands, sobbing quietly. A picture of Sam came into her head. Sam, with his laughing eyes, the mocking sneer as he looked at her, his voice drumming into her subconscious: "You're just a wimp, Sheila – just look at you! Come up against a crisis and you fall to pieces – just like I knew you would!"

She straightened up, wiping away the tears

angrily. She'd show him who was a wimp! Crying wasn't going to get her anywhere.

Stephen saw the determined light in her eyes and grew hopeful. He had persuaded Donal to give her another chance. If he saw her in this condition, she hadn't a hope of getting a job from him – a job she needed badly right now, if only for her own sake. Something to occupy herself, keep the dark thoughts at bay. She hadn't been far from the edge tonight. It only needed a slight push in the wrong direction to send her completely over. Suicide was a word that came into his head, and he pushed it aside. Donal would see to it that she was kept busy. Stephen had to smile at the thought of Donal Sheridan playing the Good Samaritan to anyone. The man hadn't a compassionate bone in his body. But if he gave Sheila this chance, then there was hope that she would come out of this mess with a bit of dignity on her side – and her sanity intact.

"You're to go to see Donal in the morning, Sheila," he said, going to sit on the stairs next to her.

She looked up at him disbelievingly. "You don't mean it! After the last time – he still wants to give me a chance?"

Stephen crossed his fingers behind his back and said a mental prayer for the white lie he was about to tell. "He told me these things happen –

everybody has a family crisis to cope with at some stage – usually at the wrong time – so he asked me would you be still interested in the job. Do you think you could still manage it, Sheila?"

He looked at her anxiously, then smiled with relief. Sheila's face was bright with enthusiasm, her hand reaching out to clasp his. She nodded adamantly.

"I'll be there – before he opens in the morning, I'll be outside the shop, in my brand-new spotted pinny! Maybe things aren't that bad after all, Father – if I can just keep calm, take a day at a time, maybe things will sort themselves out for the best."

Chapter 16

True to her word, Sheila was waiting outside Tasty Bits at nine o'clock the following morning. She felt nervous and elated at the same time, her heart racing madly, her mouth so dry that she could hardly swallow. She hadn't had time for even a cup of tea, trying to get Tom ready for school, stuffing lunches into schoolbags, almost dragging Sharon from her bed under a hail of angry protests. But she had managed it, and now here she was, dressed in a simple black short skirt and white blouse, her cream swing coat that she had purchased at the sales just after Christmas lending a touch of chic to the outfit.

The new short hairstyle suited her, little wispy

pieces curling attractively on to her forehead and cheeks, and she got more than just one admiring glance from a few male passers by. A black Audi pulled up at the kerbside and Donal Sheridan emerged dressed in a casual jacket and jeans, open-necked shirt revealing tanned skin, conveying the impression to Sheila that here was a man who enjoyed the finer things in life. As he approached her, she could smell the masculine scent of aftershave, nostalgic, bittersweet, and she bit her lip to hold back the tears. It was the same aftershave Sam used to wear and she turned away for a moment from Donal Sheridan's direct gaze, horrified that she was going to let herself down by crying all over him.

He greeted her and she followed him into the shop, then stood back as he motioned her to wait until he had the burglar alarm disconnected.

"The noise of that thing once it goes off is deafening at this time in the morning – don't want the neighbours complaining." He nodded wryly in the direction of the shop next door which was in the process of renovation. "Competition there, one of these days – on second thoughts, maybe the odd burglar alarm going off early in the morning might put them off buying the place!" He went past the self-service counter to the office at the back, then held the door open for Sheila to follow him.

She was lingering, looking about her, impressed. He certainly had taste, she thought admiringly as she surveyed the intimate nooks strategically placed so as to allow privacy to the clients as well as a restful view of the magnificent stretch of river flowing east to west parallel to the rear of Baker Street.

"Mrs Shaughnessy?"

He waited patiently while she reddened visibly, then hurried after him into the small office, annoyed with herself for her gaucheness, like a child looking around a sweet shop.

"I'm glad the place seems to impress you," he said. "Of course, it's a different matter altogether working here, as I'm sure Father O'Hara must already have explained to you." He watched for her reaction, some doubt crossing her features, maybe, a hesitation for just a fraction of a second that would give him some excuse for suggesting that maybe she wasn't suitable for the work. But there was no uncertainty in the beautiful eyes gazing up at him, unflinching, and the determined thrust to her chin. A good-looking woman for her age, he thought chauvinistically. A bit too thin, maybe, but attractive, just the same – and those eyes – he could see more than one emotion behind their dark-blue depths, could see the sadness that had given her worry creases before her time – and immediately wanted to put her out of her misery.

"Okay. This is how it is: I'll be wanting you here three days a week, from 8.30 in the morning until 2.30 in the afternoon – with thirty minutes' break at eleven before the lunch-time activity starts – and you'll have to work the odd late night, because we open until 9.30 on a Friday night – there are a lot of workers living in apartment-land around this area and they all want a hot meal without the bother of cooking for themselves before they head off for their drinking sessions and night clubs."

He outlined every detail precisely, now and then looking at her for confirmation, and she nodded each time. Sheila would have agreed to any terms of employment at this stage. She needed to be independent, to have some money coming into the house without having to go to Social Services. She would only go for some state assistance if she had hit rock bottom. She had been brought up with the philosophy that you worked for what you needed, her mother an example of being independent, looking for nothing from nobody, taking on three part-time jobs to keep them while at the same time making sure that Sheila wasn't neglected, a shining example of battling against the odds. The thought of standing in a line of people all waiting for some hand-out left her feeling like a failure.

She couldn't bear to have to tell strangers her life story, to have to tell them that Sam had left her …

"How are you fixed at home?" He looked at her sharply.

This was the question she had been expecting from him, and her answer might be the perfect excuse he needed to tell her she wasn't suitable for the position. She squared her shoulders determinedly, looking him firmly in the eyes. The thoughts galloped through her brain in the few seconds it took her to answer him. Deirdre would collect Tom from school on the days she was working, and she could prepare some sandwiches and have some soup ready in a flask for them until she got home to cook a proper dinner …

She smiled at him positively. "That's fine – there'll be no problems at home." She closed her eyes as he bent down to get her an Employees' Tax Form from the desk, and prayed with all her heart that she was telling the truth …

* * *

By the time eleven o'clock came, Sheila felt as though she had just run a marathon. Her legs were aching, her arms rigid from carrying trays to and from tables. Her mind was in a whirl from trying to remember all the orders that were fired at her from all sides as she stood behind the self-service counter.

"Two coffees, one with cream, one tea – three of your fruit scones – you might lightly heat them up, love ..." The elderly woman with the tangerine-coloured lipstick and pink-rouged cheeks, daring honey-coloured streaks in her grey hair, smiled at her encouragingly. "Your first day, is it, love? Never mind, you'll get into the swing of things in no time ... just take your time. We're in no hurry. Our time is our own!" She nodded in the direction of her two friends, a tall thin woman with a brightly flowered scarf knotted loosely about her neck. The other woman, more conservatively dressed in a black-and-white check skirt, the pattern only serving to emphasise the generous curves of the wearer, waved a friendly hand in Sheila's direction. They all looked encouragingly at Sheila and she felt immediately better.

The woman in the check skirt reminded her of her mother. She wondered, with a lump in her throat, what she would have made of her daughter's situation now, if she was still alive? She had died only three years previously, a slow, painful death, her body riddled with cancer. Sheila missed her so much, especially now when she could have done with a mother's comforting arm about her. Tears pricked her eyelids and she forced them back, pushing the plate of scones into the microwave. If only she had a sister to talk to – but her father had died just after Sheila was born, and there had just been herself and Mam. She had always been shy as a child, hard for her to make friends, the legacy of being an only child, living most of her time in a make-believe world of dolls and later as a teenager listening to her music and reading, never really bothering to break out of her shell, even with her mother's gentle persuasion.

Sam had been the one to draw her out of herself, to make her laugh at his teasing. She had met him at a rugby club dance, and had no eyes for anybody else since that moment. It had been a whirlwind romance, Sam putting the engagement ring on her finger even before she could catch her breath, drawing her into a marriage that was to end so miserably. Sheila wondered how she could have been so naive. Even when they were engaged, Sam had been surveying the 'talent' around at the week-end rugby club dances. She had ignored it because she had loved him with all her heart, and the fear of losing him was much more unbearable than any degree of unfaithfulness on his part. Her mother had known though. She had tried to warn her, told Sheila to take her time, to look around before she ventured into any marriage with Sam.

It had been no use. Sam had been her hero –

he could do no wrong in her eyes.

"Are those scones ready, Sheila?" Donal appeared behind her and she jumped nervously. "I'm sorry – I just wanted to know if you were managing all right – didn't mean to startle you. Is Brenda showing you the ropes?"

He felt something for the woman he hadn't felt for a long time. Pity. He had felt pity for himself when the girl he loved had ditched him and now he could see the same kind of despair that had driven him to the edge shining out at him from Sheila's large, beautiful eyes.

Brenda was taking a batch of freshly baked rolls from the oven in the baking alcove to the right of the self-service, her face flushed, the small white cap askew on her mop of frizzy dark hair.

"Sheila's doing just fine, Donal," she said. "I haven't even time to look around me this morning and she's managing pretty much on her own but there're no problems!" She looked up at him with a cheeky grin. "So stop worrying and get back to your sums in the office and let us work in peace!"

He smiled at her directness, saw her wink at Sheila. Things seemed to be working out. As long as he got no aggravation from them or the customers, then he was satisfied. He nodded and went back to the office.

Father O'Hara had been right. He had been lucky with his employees – at least some of them, he thought darkly, giving his head an irritated shake as he dismissed some mental pictures from his mind. All water under the bridge, time to move on ... He had left his office door open and he had a full view of the deli area outside. He watched as Sheila opened the door of the microwave, taking out the scones carefully, pleased with the way she used the plastic hygiene gloves before she handled the confectionery. He watched as she arranged the tea-tray daintily for the elderly ladies, even to the finishing touch of placing serviettes beneath each plate. He couldn't stop looking at her. He didn't know what was wrong with him, he thought irritably. He seemed to be noticing every little thing about her, the way she walked, the shy smile as she spoke to the customers, the way her hair curled about her face, cheeks flushed with nervous tension. He must be having a mid-life crisis, he thought wryly.

After all, there was nothing spectacular about the woman. He had gone out with several women since Marie, all beautiful, much more beautiful than Sheila Shaughnessy – yet there was something about her that made him turn and look at her every time he heard her voice. There was a thoughtful look on his tanned face as he looked indifferently at the pile of account books on his desk, which remained unopened for a long while as he gazed, his thoughts far away.

Chapter 17

"Those school days, the happiest days of our lives, eh, John?" Stephen O'Hara was sitting in John Markham's office smiling across at his school friend.

John Markham nodded and smiled. "Do you remember the way you used to cadge a ride on the dray horses coming up the dock from the coal-yard – a right delinquent you were – the one who could hang on the longest – and look at you now!"

Behind the humour, Stephen could detect the concern in John Markham's voice.

Markham shuffled papers in front of him, clearing his throat as he looked up at Stephen, the expression on his face now grim.

"Do you know what that guy has done? Dipped his sticky fingers into the assets of some major shareholders in the company – accounts thrown wide open for him – a right cute shot – and do you know what's even more ludicrous?" He waved a telex message under Stephen's nose, his face growing red with agitation. "This! From the Industrial Fraud Squad in Dublin – no such company as Lichsturm Inc! No such German woman interested in a major software changeover. Do you know something, Stephen? If you called me a fool this minute, I wouldn't contradict you!"

Stephen O'Hara took the telex message and glanced at it, then placed it carefully back on the desk. Things were even worse than he had imagined. Sheila would have to be told, and God knows what effect it would have on her, just as she was beginning to pull herself out of the nightmare.

* * *

"I never touched your money! Why are you blaming *me*?" Sharon's angry voice rang out in the hallway as Deirdre came in the door from school.

She threw her schoolbag behind the hallstand

and followed the sound of angry voices into the kitchen. Sheila was sitting at the table, a brown envelope opened in front of her. She picked up three twenty-euro notes and held them up for inspection in front of Sharon's face.

"The bill money – I scraped it together over the last four weeks out of my wages. Where do you think we're going to get free electricity, free telephone calls – even the food we put into our mouths – how is it all going to be paid for? There are two ten-euro notes missing, Sharon – I want some explanations!"

The sudden silence in the room resounded with bitter acrimony between mother and daughter. Sharon turned defiantly towards the window, her back to her mother and Deirdre.

Sheila went across the room and took the girl firmly by the shoulders. "Please, Sharon, speak to me – what did you do with the money?"

"Take your hands off me – if you dare hit me, I'll report you, do you hear?" Sharon spat out the words, the hatred boiling up inside her, her eyes bright with anger. Sheila stepped back from her. She couldn't handle the girl any more. She was a stranger to her now and she wondered, if this thing hadn't happened between herself and Sam, would Sharon have been a different person? The guilt that haunted every minute of her day now pressed itself on her unrelentingly.

It was all my fault that Sam grew cold, indifferent, she thought. Everything he said about me was true! I was a wimp, a whiner, a torment to him with my old-fashioned lovemaking, never trying anything different, never pleasing him in bed because of my inhibitions . . . everything, everything was my fault . . . the voice drummed into her brain, Sam's voice, mocking, arguing, the psychological bruising still hurting so much.

"Mam – stop crying, please stop – don't say those things! It wasn't your fault, don't blame yourself – please stop!"

Sheila looked up, startled. She hadn't been aware she had been voicing her anguish aloud, with such conviction that the two girls were shocked by it. Sharon stood by the window, her eyes wide and frightened. Deirdre was grasping her arm, trying to get her to sit down. Her knees felt suddenly fragile, unable to support her trembling body.

"I took the money and I'll pay you back," Sharon whispered.

Deirdre looked at Sharon with such contempt that she turned away, feeling ashamed.

"I don't know how I'll manage," said Sheila, making a huge effort to pull herself together. "Money is tight enough as it is without this happening." She picked up the notes on the table, stuffing them back inside the envelope. "What happened with Linda, Sharon? What did her mother say to her when she found out about the missing money? Did she get away with it – stealing just to finance your fun down at the club? How low can you get?" Sheila looked at Sharon and the girl returned her angry look with an indifferent shrug of her shoulders.

"Her father stopped her pocket money for a month – and he said she'll have to pay back every penny of it." Sharon began to look nervous, her hands shaking uncontrollably. "But she'll never manage to pay that back out of her pocket money – so she says she'll have to do some baby-sitting maybe – or part-time work in a shop." She looked at her mother suspiciously, the old rebellion showing in her eyes once more. "And don't you get any ideas about me working – I couldn't take a job in a shop – I'm only sixteen – and I have my studies –"

"Right!" Sheila went to the drawer beside the sink and took out a notepad and a pen. "Here – you write, and I'll dictate!"

"What –?" Sharon looked confused as she took the notepad from her.

"Baby-sitter available," said Sheila, "very reliable, experienced with children –"

"I have no experience with children! Oh, Mam, for heaven's sake!"

Sheila stabbed the notepad with her finger.

"*Write!* You're experienced in looking after Tom, aren't you? If you're big and capable enough to be out until all hours with your friends at the club, then you're big enough to have a baby-sitting job. Now start writing, and I'll stick it up in the shop window when I go in to work in the morning."

Chapter 18

Michael Bates sat behind his desk, one hand stroking his chin thoughtfully. The fellow Shaughnessy had really taken him for a sucker – and he could blame nobody but himself for being so unprofessional. Usually he checked every client thoroughly before any transactions, but this time – maybe it was because he was worried about Shirley and the baby, maybe it was because Sam Shaughnessy appeared so affable, his salesman's smile intimating the fullest reassurance that his intentions were strictly bona fide. There was going to be hell to pay at the Directors' Meeting in three days' time, and he would be sitting in the hot seat awaiting execution.

The man had been smart, withdrawing the amounts at regular intervals. "The price of living beyond our means," he had offered by way of explanation to the teller. "My wife and I have an agreement – I deposit the money, I withdraw the money, she spends it – it seems to work very well for her – and as for me –" he had raised his hands resignedly, offering the girl a charm-ridden smile, "I just keep earning the precious stuff!" He had gone to the same girl each time, and Michael Bates could just imagine him, waving all those behind him in the queue forward until 'his' girl became available. Then a smile and a wink and a quick compliment "My, we're looking good today" and the shy blush of the teller as she handed over the money – the glib explanation – "A few business deals abroad – got to keep on top of things in this new European economy – nothing as urgent though as my wife's trip to Tenerife with her golfing friends – I don't know who this joint account benefits most – her or me!" These were Sam's words as narrated by the tearful girl whose banking career was forever tainted by the dishonesty of an unscrupulous man.

Well, it was out of his hands, now. The police and the Fraud Squad had their investigations underway, and it was just a matter of waiting for the outcome. There was a knock on the door, and he called out impatiently, "Come in!"

Muriel's expertly made-up face looked round the door at him, her expression sympathetic. "A cup of coffee, Mr Bates? I have it just made."

"Thank you, Muriel – that would be nice."

He smiled at her and she disappeared for a minute, coming back with a freshly brewed cup of decaffeinated and a chocolate biscuit.

"Just to keep your strength up," she offered when he looked at the biscuit enquiringly. He liked the way she fussed over him. If he was honest with himself, he liked the way she looked, too. Magnificent figure, the light silk blouse clinging to the curves of her shapely breasts – he felt shocked at his assessment. He had never looked at another woman since his marriage to Shirley.

True, she hadn't been very amorous lately, and her reluctance to make love left him feeling frustrated and irritable. It was her condition, of course, as well as the fact that she resented Michael's obvious delight at the forthcoming event.

"Barefoot and pregnant," she had said cynically one evening watching him prepare for a business dinner with a client. "I could be the one dressing up and going out for a meal with a valuable client this evening, instead of sitting here like this!" She had looked down at her growing bulge resentfully. "Barefoot and pregnant," she repeated. "If men had their way, that's the way women would be seen for the course of their productive years – my God – productive!" She had laughed aloud then. "Such a misconception, literally – productive in body, maybe, but definitely not in mind. If I'm not careful I could turn into a vegetable, sitting here, brooding over the 'happy event'."

Michael sipped his coffee and watched Muriel as she tidied up his desk, filing away papers in the filing cabinet by the window, her deft movements, the faint scent of her perfume, soothing him. She looked at him, a smile curving her full, pink-tinted lips.

"Is there anything else I can do for you, Mr Bates?" The insinuation was there, as bold and challenging as any invitation he had experienced in the past from female companions. She was interested, if he was, her eyes conveyed the message to him. The sooner Shirley had this baby the better – get their relationship back on an even keel, stop him from making a fool of himself with a girl who was only too ready to hop into bed with him.

He finished his coffee, then turned to her, his manner businesslike. "Muriel, I'm going to lunch today at Tasty Bits – I've heard the food there is pretty good, so I'll give it a try." The truth was, he didn't want to lunch at any of his usual haunts, didn't want to meet any of his business colleagues who would look at him, and sympathise with him for not being 'on the ball' where Shaughnessy was concerned. The grapevine had been busy – people who were only too pleased to see him taken down a peg. Michael Bates' promotion to seniority had been climactic, his insatiable appetite for work not going unnoticed by his superiors. As he left the office, he could see ten pairs of eyes follow him through the swing-doors and down the steps of the bank, tellers and colleagues exchanging knowing looks – was Bates' job in the balance? Some brushed the lapels of their jackets and straightened their shoulders determinedly. Promotion might be in the offing – best to be prepared.

* * *

"I'll have the lasagne, please – a double portion – it's just delicious!" The man in front of Michael Bates smacked his lips appreciatively.

Sheila was standing behind the steaming container of fresh vegetable soup, her face flushed, little strands of her hair escaping from her white frilled cap. She turned and took a large slice of the lasagne from the microwave, decorating it with some chopped parsley. "Here you go, sir – just pay at the cash desk – next please?" She didn't see him for a moment until she heard him call her name.

"Mrs Shaughnessy?"

Then she looked up, a quick smile on her face. "Mr Bates – I haven't seen you here before – what can I get you?"

The queue behind was growing impatient, so he pushed his tray along the counter, talking to her as he took a plate of salad from the cold section. "I wonder – could I have some of that lasagne also, please – I've heard it's very good."

She nodded pleasantly. "Of course! There you are – freshly made this morning – one of Brenda's specialities!" She pointed across at Brenda who was busy taking some more vegetarian pizzas from the oven.

"How are you, Mrs Shaughnessy – I must admire you – you seem to be coping very well here. Has there been any news?" He left his enquiry vague, the customers behind too close for any personal conversation.

"If you take the table near the window," she indicated the table set into the narrow alcove in the corner, "I'll be able to talk to you shortly." She looked at her watch. "I can take five minutes – I'll join you over there."

He nodded and took the tray across to the table, pushing his chair back to sit down. When he looked up, she was standing there, a spotless white apron covering her navy and white uniform. She had changed, he thought, since their last meeting. Something about her made her seem stronger, more in control. The woman with the sad face and the tearful voice who had confronted him in his office was no longer there, changed overnight into a confident, capable person, her gaze direct, none of the frightening morbidity about her which had made him doubt her ability to cope on the previous occasion.

"Do you like the work?' he asked. It was a ridiculous question, he knew that immediately after he had spoken, but it broke the ice and she laughed softly.

"Like? That isn't quite the right word, Mr Bates – but it's a question of survival, and I count myself very lucky to have any sort of work at all." She looked behind her at the half-open office door where Donal Sheridan sat behind his desk, now and then glancing up to see how things were going outside. "He's a slave-driver – I've never worked so hard in my whole life! And do you know something? It's been like therapy, just what I needed to pull me back from the edge." She spoke calmly, and he wondered what had happened to the little wimp of a woman who had turned into this strong, self-possessed woman almost overnight?

Maybe Shirley was right. Confinement to the

home, looking after kids, wasn't every woman's cup of tea. The proof of that theory was staring him in the face now, Sheila's confidence radiant, the worry lines across her forehead almost non-existent. The job meant a lot to her, he could see.

"If I could get my family sorted out now, I'd be on top of the world – well, not quite – things will never be the same again – but maybe everything happens in life for a reason." She smiled suddenly then, and he could see the strength in her blue eyes.

"If there's anything I can do for you, just tell me – please, Mrs Shaughnessy – I want to help you – *I owe you*!" His voice was almost pleading. He felt responsible for the situation the woman found herself in, and if he could help in any way, then he was more than willing.

She shook her head. "Thank you, Mr Bates – but I'm managing quite well now." With a smile, she turned and went back to the counter. Just before she went back into the hot-counter section he saw her fix a small square sign on the side window of the dining area. When he had finished his meal, he passed it as he made his way to the front door. He paused and read it with interest. He looked round for Sheila, but she was nowhere to be seen and he made a mental note to give her a ring as soon as he got back to the office. This was one area where he might be able to assist her, ease some of the helplessness he felt with regard to helping her out.

* * *

It was nearly time for Sheila to go and pick Tom up from the school. She had made an arrangement with Brenda that she would cut out her break in the morning, and take the time instead after the lunches, so that she could get the 2.30 bus from the city centre to the school, collect Tom, take him home, and get his lunch – then Deirdre would take over when she came in from school.

She had told Donal Sheridan about the arrangement, and to make up for any inconvenience, she had told him, she'd come back in the afternoon from four to five, when the place got busy with shoppers popping in for afternoon tea. "If Brenda has no objections, then it's fine with me," had been his comment. He had watched her at work, cleaning out the large food containers with Brenda, holding over her break until two o'clock when she took a quick cup of coffee and a hot scone, then grabbed her coat to catch the bus for the school. Precisely at four o'clock she reappeared, not even bothering to go to the ladies' room to fix her hair or make-up, her small, neat figure scurrying between the tables, clearing places for customers, her friendly smile always welcoming.

"Sheila, there's a telephone call for you!" Brenda called to her from the back kitchen and Sheila hurried to answer it.

"Sheila – it's me – Michael Bates – I noticed you put a sign in the window of the restaurant – would I be right in assuming you have somebody looking for baby-sitting work?"

Sheila flushed bright red as she grasped the receiver. She didn't want anybody to think she was forcing her children into work because of their financial situation. She felt horrified that Michael Bates might think such a thing. Her voice was shaking as she answered him. "It's my daughter, Sharon – she thought a little baby-sitting might earn her some extra pocket-money – teenagers need so much these days to keep abreast with their friends." She bit her lip, a deep frown outlined on her forehead.

Michael Bates knew from the tone in her voice that there was something else behind the innocent explanation of a teenager looking for a bit 'extra'. Something that troubled Sheila Shaughnessy quite a bit, judging from the sound of her voice.

"Well, I'd like to help."

She listened to the kindness in his voice, his obvious concern, and wanted to tell him then the whole story, the way Sharon had been behaving since Sam left, the missing money, the verbal abuse from the girl which hurt her more than anything else that Sharon could have done. But she remained silent. If word got round that Sharon was that 'type' then she wouldn't stand a chance of reforming, getting back to her old self. The old Sharon was hidden somewhere beneath the anger and the insults – it was just a matter of time.

"Look," said Michael, "I have a few friends who'd be glad of somebody reliable to look after their small ones for an evening – it's hard to get somebody you can trust. I'll ask around, and if something comes up, I'll get in touch."

Sheila hated herself for the sudden dark thought that came into her head. If Sharon should let her down, in front of Michael Bates and his friends, she'd never live it down, never get over the embarrassment. The night she had come home from the club, pupils dilated, the incoherent stare as she seemed to look through them – supposing she did the same thing, in a strange house? Supposing she took drugs, while she was looking after children – could she have it on her conscience if her daughter couldn't be trusted to take care of vulnerable children?

"Please – don't trouble yourself –" she began faintly, but Michael Bates spoke determinedly.

"No trouble – I'll have a few people queuing

up for Sharon's services by next weekend. Just wait and see!"

She put down the receiver and hurried to collect Tom from school, her thoughts full of misgivings as she wondered if she had done the right thing by placing the advertisement in the window. Would Sharon let her down, just when she was trying to make everything normal again?

Chapter 19

"Father – say that again – and slowly, please – I just can't believe what you're saying." Sheila looked at Stephen O'Hara incredulously. "Not Sam – he was never dishonest. For as long as we were married, he never did a thing out of the way where his business was concerned!"

He was sitting opposite her in his cosy little parlour. He had asked her to call in to see him on her way home from work, and now as she sat looking at him with such disbelief on her thin face he wished that he could take some of the terrible burden from her inadequate shoulders.

"It's true, Sheila – he seems to have disappeared into thin air – the Fraud Squad in Dublin are putting out tracers in Germany – but there was no such company as Lichsturm Inc and as for the woman . . ." he looked at her anxiously, afraid of her reaction to any reference to the woman who had so cleverly lured Sam Shaughnessy away from his family, "there's no trace of her – the police believe there's more to it than just a white-collar crime."

"All that money Sam is supposed to have taken – where is it? What could he possibly do with it?" Sheila asked, her hands moving nervously on her lap.

"The bank traced it to a relatively small banking outlet in Geneva – and that's where the investigations apparently came to a dead end." He poured her a cup of tea, handing it to her with one hand, the milk jug in the other. She nodded as he poured the milk into her cup.

"That's fine, Father – thank you – what do you mean, a dead end?"

"It's been 'moved' from there." Stephen O'Hara's face was grim. "They're obviously keeping it for a purpose – they must be going to do something with it, and soon, if they've taken it out of the Geneva bank."

"Is he setting up his own business – in some foreign country, maybe using the money as his security?" All sorts of possibilities entered Sheila's head, the Sam she had married obliterated by the stranger he had become. Her Sam – his only weakness being the glad eye he had for the women – harmless, fun-loving Sam, now involved in some scam which, she felt sure, was way above his head. "Do you think they're still together, Father? The woman and Sam? Sometimes life has a way of turning the tables when you least expect it – when trouble appears, that's the real test – if people really love each other."

Stephen stood up and went to the writing desk by the window, its drawers overflowing untidily with bits and pieces of memoranda, church collection envelopes, an assortment of items that Stephen presumed 'would come in useful at some stage'. He took a small brown envelope from its depths and handed it to Sheila. "I want you to take this – until you're on your feet, and you can pay me back at your own pace."

She began to protest, but he shoved it into her unwilling hand.

"Donal Sheridan isn't the worst of employers, but he isn't reputed for paying his employees over and above the basic minimum rate. You must be finding it hard going, until your affairs are sorted out."

Sheila nodded, unable to speak, the lump in her throat growing bigger as she tried to thank him. It was true – her wages from Tasty Bits were just about keeping their heads above water and she had been forced to go to the unemployment office.

It had been a bitter pill to swallow.

She had felt utterly humiliated, sitting, waiting her turn to speak to the tired-looking girl at hatch F.

The girl had asked in a singsong voice if Sheila was working.

"Yes – part-time."

"How many hours?" the girl asked, not looking up at her, as though she was reading from a well-rehearsed script.

Sheila tried to keep her voice as low as possible while she answered questions which seemed embarrassing to her, and yet, looking furtively over her shoulder at the line of people waiting patiently behind, she saw that none of them was taking the slightest notice of the interrogation. Most of those women and men, their unsmiling faces devoid of expression, were maybe in the same position as herself. The heavy weight seemed to lift from her shoulders and, in spite of the not-very-encouraging response from the girl, she was in a more optimistic frame of mind.

"Fill in the form and get your employer to sign it – then send it off to this address – "

The girl had written a hastily scrawled address

on the back of a blank piece of paper, and shoved it beneath the glass window with the form.

Sheila's hand had shaken visibly when, in the privacy of her bedroom after everybody had gone to bed, under '*Marital Status*' she had written '*Separated*'.

She had posted it the following day on her way home from work, Donal Sheridan having filled in the necessary information with some irritation.

She knew that was why he kept his staff to a minimum. Too much red tape, too much dealing with employment issues and employees' 'rights'. Better to pay them out of his back pocket and keep everything 'off the record'. Only that wasn't on any more – not with Unfair Dismissal Acts, and Equality Acts, and discrimination cases.

So he had filled in everything, and signed his name to it, no doubt hoping that was the end of Sheila Shaughnessy's claims for Social Welfare.

So Sheila was waiting for the Social Welfare assessment of her situation. They lived on sausages and chips for the latter part of every week, the chicken for Sunday dinner lasting until Wednesday's curry with rice.

So now the envelope from Stephen O'Hara was literally a godsend. Tom needed new shoes and Deirdre needed a new English schoolbook that would set her back twenty euro.

Stephen accompanied her to the door, a

contemplative look on his face.

"Did you ever think of going in to Gingerbread, Sheila – the Lone Parent Organization? If nothing else, it would be healthy therapy for you, get to hear from people in the same position as yourself, see how they're coping with things ... they're a very worthwhile little group ..."

Sheila shook her head vigorously. "I'm not in that category yet, Father, Sam might still . . ." Her voice shook and she faced him, the expression on her face hopeful, begging him not to destroy her illusions.

He spoke gently, afraid that if he pushed too hard she might turn against him, resent him for interfering, just like Sharon. "You are a single parent, Sheila, and like it or not, you *are* trying to cope on your own." He watched her face cloud over as she listened reluctantly. "Just give it a try – just the one visit, you needn't go any more if it does nothing for you – you never know, it might just be the help you need right now. Some people coming together for a cup of tea and a custard-cream biscuit, people like you, on their own, trying to bring up their families alone!"

"I'm not in the mood, Father, for that carry-on!" She shook her head wearily as he opened the hall door for her.

From the doorway they could see the corner of the street, and she noticed two young people standing at the pedestrian crossing, their arms about each other. Her heart missed a beat. The girl looked very familiar, though she couldn't be sure because her back was turned to her. The same hairstyle, the school bag with the same yellow and black stripes down the side. It was Sharon, she knew it was, with a boy who had his arms about her waist, pulling her to him, bending down and kissing her. They had eyes only for each other, and a few young schoolchildren near them giggled in amusement.

"Father ... "

He followed her gaze to where the two teenagers were now almost holding each other up, slouched against the postbox near the traffic lights.

"It's Sharon. I'll go and get her," she said.

She walked purposefully past St Finbarr's. The girl turned towards her as she heard the click of her heels, the boy looking up as she approached, an insolent look on his face.

"Sharon! What are you doing here – why aren't you at home? I left your dinner in the oven – it must be burnt to a crisp by now!"

She ignored the boy. Now that she was standing next to him, she didn't like his arrogant expression, the sneering droop to his lips. It was an insolence she found repulsive.

"For God's sake, Mam, I'm on my way home

– will you stop being so paranoid? And it's not as if you have a gourmet dinner waiting for me!"

"Are you going to introduce me to your friend?" Sheila tried to calm the anger inside her while she looked at the boy, his eyes bright with amusement. He was a cheeky young fellow, she thought, irritated. He was obviously laughing at her, his arm still about Sharon possessively.

"This is Declan – we're in the same class together," she said, smiling up at him.

Sheila could have smacked her across the face, with her condescending air as though her mother was some sort of angst-ridden woman, trying to spoil her fun.

"Well, Declan – you won't mind if my daughter comes with me now, will you?" Sheila forced a smile.

"Sure – see you, Shar – at school tomorrow!"

He winked at Sharon and she was about to protest until she saw the look on Sheila's face. Best to go quietly. By the look on her mother's face, it wouldn't take much to cause an explosion, and she didn't want any more trouble, not from her or that busybody priest.

They walked back towards Stephen's house, where he stood waiting expectantly at the door.

"Will you come in to see Father Stephen with me, Sharon, please?" Sheila put her hand on Sharon's arm.

Sharon began to shake her head, but then thought it would be stupid to walk away now, especially as Declan had gone home and she had just missed the bus and they might just get a lift home from Stephen O'Hara. So she said nothing but followed Sheila up the steps and into the hallway of the priest's house.

* * *

They had spoken to her for almost an hour. She had stood over by the window, arms folded, her back to them, not uttering a word. The only feature that moved were her eyes, sick and restless, darting about the busy street outside, the noise of the traffic increasing the restlessness that seemed to increase each day, her anger at the most trivial thing exploding unexpectedly, sometimes even frightening Sharon herself.

"Are you taking anything, Sharon? You know what I mean – trying out anything that's making you so angry with – everybody?" Sheila stopped herself from saying 'with me'. It would have probably brought on another tirade of vindictiveness. Any reference to Sheila seemed to incense her lately, as though her mother was the cause of all her misery.

"I'm not taking drugs, if that's what you're talking about." The lie slipped quickly, glibly, from her tongue. Declan had given her a few 'twists' of some new stuff that he had recently got hold of. "You're my special girl, so you can have it on 'tick' – until you get some cash together for me." He had held her close, nuzzling his face against her cheek, his touch sending beautiful sensations through her body. She knew by the way he looked at her, sizing up her body hungrily every time they met, that it wouldn't be long before he wanted her to go the whole way – and she wouldn't refuse him.

She looked at her mother and Father O'Hara – judge and jury, that's what they were. She had a sudden picture of her mother dressed in one of those long black cloaks and white fuzzy wigs and giggled hysterically. She couldn't stop her from doing what she wanted with Declan. Couldn't stop her from going the whole way, if that's what he wanted. She was in control now – nobody was going to dictate to her. She looked at Father O'Hara insolently.

"Is your duty-talk done yet, Father? Because I think I have a plate of dried-up sausages and chips waiting at home for me – if you'll excuse me." She walked past them, out into the hallway, and they heard the slam of the door as she let herself out.

Sheila looked at the priest, her cheeks stained with fresh tears.

"What night is it on – this Gingerbread meeting, Father?"

"Wednesdays – eight thirty." He scribbled the address on a piece of notepaper lying on top of his desk.

She took the piece of paper from him silently and put it into her handbag. "Thank you, Father– I think I'll try it – I'd try anything at this stage – maybe somebody can give me advice on how to cope with a teenager who hates me with every bone in her body!"

* * *

Michael Bates called the following evening. Sheila was having a shower when she heard the telephone ring.

"Sharon – Deirdre – will one of you get that, please?" she called loudly. She heard the bedroom door open, then the silence as the receiver was picked up. She had just finished drying herself when there was a tap on the door. She wrapped her towelling robe about her, her hair still wet against the collar. She opened the door and Sharon stood there, her eyes blazing.

"Why do you have to keep interfering? Do you know who that was? Michael bloody Bates!" She mimicked Michael Bates' voice angrily. "'Hello – I wonder could I speak to Sharon? Oh, it's you, Sharon – your mum told me you were interested in baby-sitting – could you make it tonight? A friend of mine – they're going to a business dinner and have two small children, three and five.'"

She broke off breathlessly, and Sheila wondered if she had made a terrible mistake in putting the postcard in the window of the shop. Once Sharon got into one of her moods, she was impossible to deal with.

"Well, it's a bit of pocket money, isn't it?" Sheila tried to remain calm. She towel-dried her hair nervously as the girl followed her into her bedroom.

"I wanted to go out tonight!"

"With Declan?" Sheila asked, not looking at her, continuing to dry her hair, afraid to stop the exercise in case her show of indifference would be seen by Sharon for what it was: a cover-up for the knot of anxiety that was twisting itself inside her stomach, making her feel physically sick. She had to remain in control, show the girl that she was the boss, beyond manipulation.

"Mam, can't you ring him, make some excuse?" Sharon wheedled, her voice now quietly reasonable.

"Why didn't *you* make your own excuses – you had the opportunity – he spoke to you – all you had to say was that you couldn't make it this evening." Sheila dropped the wet towel on the bed and looked steadily at her daughter, and when Sharon's gaze fell first, she knew, with relief, that she had won. Behind all the rebellion, Sharon wasn't a fool. It was beneficial to keep in with business people like Michael Bates. People with contacts. Like her father, Sheila thought wryly, one foot always trying for the next rung on the ladder. She was easy to impress, and the distinguished, polished voice of Michael Bates must have appealed to her sense of class value. Of course she could baby-sit. No problem. Sheila wondered if other people suffered the same insolence from Sharon as she did, but as she heard the front door bang shut and the crunch of Sharon's feet down the gravelled drive, she knew instinctively that she was the punching-bag her daughter took out all her frustration on. An angel to outsiders. If Sharon had been disagreeable at school she knew she would have been called in to have a meeting with Bernard Casey.

She was worried about her. The dark circles beneath her eyes were a permanent feature lately, the nervous tick in her left eye more pronounced. When she spoke to her it was as though the girl was about to explode, the very sound of Sheila's voice making her scowl angrily, so that Sheila remained silent most of the time, hoping that it was just a phase she was going through. Maybe a visit to the doctor might be in order, she thought worriedly, as she went downstairs to make a cup of tea.

Tom was sleeping soundly. Deirdre was studying in her bedroom. It was the only time in the day that Sheila could really call her own. When the kettle boiled, she put a tea bag into the mug, pouring the hot water on top. She stirred it lethargically, adding a little milk, then went into the living room, relaxing into the leather couch, propping her legs up on the coffee table. She closed her eyes, listening for a moment to the silence. The road outside was quiet, just the odd spurt of laughter as young people passed, the occasional sound of a car coming or going.

She remained there, without turning on the television, savouring the peace of the moment. She'd had a tiring day at Tasty Bits, having to work three hours' overtime because Brenda had to go home with a tummy bug.

There had been no news from the police of Sam, and at this stage she was beginning to lose hope. They had made their 'enquiries', as the young garda with an air of officialdom had told her politely. They had nothing much to go on, but their investigations were 'ongoing'. The catch-phrases would have appeared amusing to Sheila, if they weren't so depressingly obscure. Sam could be anywhere, and the woman too. The shadows in the room lengthened, and as it grew dark Sheila's anxiety increased. It was in the lonely hours, when she had too much time to think, that the worry of her situation seemed to press itself on her even more forcefully. What if Sam *was* found? The only thing ahead of him now was prison – absconding with company funds was no petty crime.

"Mam – why don't you turn on the light? It's dark in here."

Deirdre had opened the door quietly, her small face in the light of the street lamp worried as she looked at Sheila lying on the sofa, eyes closed., cup of tea, now cold, placed on the coffee table.

"In a minute, love – leave it off for a while – it's so peaceful."

Deirdre crossed the room and sat next to her. "You're worrying about Dad, aren't you – is there any news? Have the police found out where he is?" She started to tremble, her whole body shaking as she tried to hold back the tears. Sheila pulled her close, although what words of reassurance she could give her she honestly didn't know, because things had never looked so bad.

"Don't worry, love – everything will be fine – you wait and see . . ." She had five euro in her purse until Saturday morning, and this was only Tuesday. The Social Welfare people had written to her, saying they were reviewing her case, and for the moment she would receive an interim payment from them until she was officially categorised as a 'Lone Parent'.

When Sheila had seen the amount allocated she had been devastated. There was so much to be paid: the mortgage, electricity, telephone, school expenses, and without Stephen O'Hara's contribution she would be in dire circumstances. Thank God the mortgage was nearly paid off. Another six months and the house would be paid for – maybe things might get a little easier then, and at least they had the security of a roof over their heads.

"Come on, love – I've made a few chocolate brownies – I hid them from Sharon – you know what a glutton she is for chocolate!" Sheila took Deirdre's hand and led her towards the kitchen. "We'll have some hot chocolate and hot chocolate brownies – how about that for a feast of chocolate delight?"

Deirdre smiled back reluctantly. Things were never so bad when she saw her mother smile. Her spirits lifted as she went to put on the kettle.

"We'll polish them off between us – I think we deserve a little treat, don't you?" Sheila gave her a reassuring wink.

Deirdre relaxed. The black cloud constantly drifting above her head was beginning to fade, if only a little. Hot chocolate mightn't solve everything, but it was a start.

Chapter 20

"I want you to read me a story – Mammy always reads me a story before I go to sleep!"

The plaintive little voice grated on Sharon's nerves, and her headache was beginning to get worse. If the little monster kept up his tirade for much longer, she'd be ready to explode. The Mickey Mouse pattern on the bedroom wallpaper was beginning to swim before her eyes. She could see the little boy sitting up in his bed, his big brown eyes surveying her solemnly. In the pink cot in the corner the baby slept, one thumb stuck between the baby-pink lips, completely oblivious to the tension between Sharon and her little brother.

"Okay, kid, cool it – I'll tell you a story – but it's to be a short one, right?" Sharon looked at him crossly. It was almost 10.30. Declan had said he'd call about ten. The Holmes were due back any time after midnight. Mrs Holmes had been pleasant but with an air of authority that suggested to Sharon that she was somebody accustomed to telling people how to do things her way.

"I would much rather stay home tonight – the children can be wearing some days and today has been particularly so, with the baby teething." She brushed a blonde hair back into its sophisticated up-style behind her neck and gave herself a critical once-over in the hall mirror. "However, Sharon – business is business and, as Leonard says, contacts are extremely important!"

Sharon knew exactly what Leonard Holmes meant. Get in with the right people, and you were made for life.

In spite of her obsession with Declan right now, Sharon was sharp enough to believe intuitively that he wouldn't last the course with her. Ultimately, she had better things in mind – a well-paid job, maybe in France, away from all the hassle at home. She could visualise herself sharing a little apartment overlooking the Left Bank, her companion a dark and distinguished-looking man, not a boy . . . as a matter of fact, Sharon thought dreamily, not unlike Mr Holmes . . . dinner by candlelight each evening, the best wine, his eyes sending messages across the table to her, messages Declan was sending to her right now.

She knew what Declan was after. The other girls in their group had succumbed to their boyfriends' demands before now – Sharon was the only one who had held out. Until now.

She finished the story hurriedly, ignoring the little boy's protests that she hadn't finished it off properly.

"You left the best bits out – Mummy always tells it better!" His small voice rose aggressively. "I don't want you to baby-sit any more!"

Sharon cursed under her breath. She could hear the ring of the doorbell and tucked the boy into bed firmly, leaving the night-light glowing as she closed the door after her. She ran down the stairs, and looked at herself in the mirror, her face flushed with excitement, before she opened the door for Declan.

He stood there, an insolent grin on his face. "Hi, Shar – you really pick classy joints for your baby-sitting – what a joint!"

He looked about him admiringly. Expensive, ornately framed pictures hung on the damask-patterned wallpaper, the rich Persian carpet beneath his feet literally rippling with expense as his feet sunk into the pile. Two heavy stone urns stood elegantly at either side of the wrought-iron staircase, each overflowing with a display of exotic-looking plants. From the hallway he could see into the living room, French doors opening out into the elegant patio, the wrought-iron garden set complemented elegantly by a large black and white parasol. In the living room, extending from one end of the far wall to the other, decorated in sophisticated shades of cream and cool green, a large television screen showing the latest new release beamed impressively into the palatial setting afforded by the Holmes' affluence.

"What a set-up!" Declan whistled appreciatively, his greedy eyes taking in everything. "Think of what you could knock off here, Shar – it'd keep us in clover for a while, that's for certain!"

Sharon looked at him sharply. She knew what he was thinking, but that wasn't part of the plan. She had just wanted to show him the house, to impress him with its luxury, bring him upstairs to the master bedroom, just to show him the giant-sized, silk-clad bed, pale-blue satin sheets shimmering seductively in the moonlight coming through the French frosted windows . . .

"Dec – you mustn't touch anything – you hear? Otherwise you'll blow it for us! Besides the pocket money, it'll be a good place to be alone – you understand?"

He looked at her then, realisation dawning on him. Tonight was his night. He had hinted and waited for her far longer than he had with other girls. He smiled at her in the half-light, and she couldn't see his features, just a shadowed outline of his face, still and strangely disturbing, his silence like a question mark.

"Do you mean what I think you mean, Shar?" he whispered at last.

She nodded, even though she knew her slight affirmation was pulling her deeper into a situation that at times seemed suffocating. She adored Declan. Wanted more than anything to be his, his special girl. He had given her her first taste of speed, and she had taken it because she didn't want him to think she was a wimp. And now she was hooked on it, and the feeling of dependency frightened her, because if anything should happen between herself and Declan, if they should have a row, if he put his eye on some other girl, her lifeline to the stuff would be severed for good – and then what would she do?

She woke at night sometimes, bathed in sweat, the very thought of a bust-up between them frightening her into such an obedience to Declan that it even amazed herself. She couldn't let him get tired of her – she needed him, for the present. Later on, it would be different. She could get off the stuff, find somebody with a lot of money and he would fall in love with her and that would be that. She could cut her ties with home – there was nothing to hold her there any more. Dad had adored her, called her his little angel, indulged her any time she looked at him with her big pleading eyes – 'Please, Dad, I *need* that dress!" And whatever she asked would be given to her, his eyes twinkling indulgently.

Those times were gone. Her mother was different, could see through her so much that Sharon resented her with a viciousness that ate into her, coming to the surface every time her mother even looked at her.

No – Declan was the bottom rung of the ladder, but she was on her way up, and he was a wonderful place to start. She went to him now, twining her arms about his neck, her body swaying from side to side, curving her hips into his.

He watched her, fascinated. Maybe he had misjudged this one. The urgent pressing of her body against his excited him. He had taken a little speed before he had come out, just enough to give him an edge, and now he was feeling in top form, his sexual urges intensified as Sharon's softness seemed to burn into his skin, her body moulded into his. He took her hand, leading her towards the stairs, their bodies floating upwards, towards the large bedroom at the top of the stairs.

"I have something for you, Shar," he whispered softly. He pulled a small packet from his jeans pocket, and held it in front of her, tantalising her with it, her eyes never leaving the packet as she followed him into the bedroom, watching as he threw it on the bed.

He went across the room and drew the heavy curtains.

She looked at his back and for a moment her thoughts were muddled, wondering what she was doing here, with a faceless boy who promised her a little bit of heaven. She sank down on the bed, holding her head between her hands, then she felt the pressure of his hands on her shoulders, his voice coming softly through a haze of uncertainty as she tried to focus on what was happening.

"Come on, Shar – relax – everything will be fine, and I'll look after you – you don't have to worry – I'm taking precautions!" He showed her the packet of condoms he had taken from his pocket.

She relaxed and smiled. Everything was falling into place. Declan would take care of her, the stuff in the packet would help her get her thoughts in order. She would show everyone that she wasn't a child. Declan wanted her, like a man wanted a woman. She wondered what it would be like.

Some of the girls in school had told her it hurt the first time, but right now, all she could feel was the awful gnawing feeling inside her, the feeling she had been experiencing on and off for the last few months, telling her it was time for some more of the skunk Declan had given her. Declan was lying on top of her now, his body moving up and down, slowly, then more urgently, against her body. She tried to breathe, then began to panic, his weight suffocating her as she tried to struggle against him, tried to shift his body from her.

"Declan – no – please – I don't want to!" She began to cry. Tears were suddenly running down her cheeks as she tried to push him away – his mouth was clamped firmly on hers, his tongue struggling to force its way through her unyielding lips.

"I'll tell Mummy – Mummy wouldn't like it if she knew there was a bold boy like that in the house!"

The small voice penetrated through her panic. Declan turned suddenly towards the door, and at the same time, Sharon used all her strength to push against him so that he fell sideways, rolling off the bed and on to the floor. He gave a muttered oath, then stood up suddenly, advancing towards the little boy standing in the open doorway. When Sharon saw the look on his face she darted quickly across the room, placing herself in front of the child.

"Declan – please – I think you'd better go!"

"What in the world is going on here?"

Ellen Holmes was standing at the top of the stairs looking, horrified, into the bedroom. She called the child to her and he turned, his eyes big and frightened, running into her arms, burying his face into her as she knelt to hold him.

"I think you'd better leave." Ellen Holmes looked at Declan coldly.

He was about to say something, then shrugged his shoulders. "OK. No big deal – see you, Shar!" He barely gave her a backward glance as he descended the stairs quickly, then the bang of the front door and he was gone.

Sharon waited, Ellen Holmes still holding her son close to her.

"I came home early, I told Leonard I was worried about the children – Clodagh had an attack of the snuffles all day – and Liam didn't seem to take to you. I was uneasy and concerned – and with justification, so it would seem!" She picked up the boy and carried him into the bedroom, leaving the door open as she came out again. "Go to sleep, Liam, there's a good boy. Mummy will be here – I'm not going anywhere tonight!" she finished grimly, looking at Sharon as she sat on the bed, a stubborn look on her flushed guilty face.

Ellen Holmes looked about the bedroom, then

went to draw back the curtains, the light from the full moon sending milk-white shadows about the elegant room. Sharon could just tell what she was thinking. Her bedroom had been defiled, used for a purpose she had never envisaged, the baby-sitter and her boyfriend making the most of an opportunity that she, unwittingly, had handed to them.

"I'll call you a taxi to take you home – and I don't think it will be necessary to mention this incident to your mother – from what I gather from Michael Bates, she has enough to trouble her besides this –" she paused in mid-sentence, searching for a word that would convey the message clearly to Sharon, "this complete betrayal of trust. My God! I hate to think what might have happened if I hadn't come home!."

Sharon looked at the pale, angry face confronting her, the beautiful blonde hair pinned in a French pleat at the nape of her elegant neck, the mint-green silk dress clinging to her slim body. The woman was all that she wanted to be in a couple of years' time, and she felt humiliated because this female perfection had found her and Declan in such a compromising situation.

"I'm sorry," she said feebly. The words were trite, unnecessary.

Ellen Holmes went downstairs without a word, and Sharon could hear her on the telephone, then the receiver being put down firmly.

"Sharon – the taxi will be here to collect you in five minutes – make sure you have all your things – don't leave anything behind."

The meaning behind the blunt statement was not lost on Sharon. Leave nothing behind, because you won't be coming back. She and Declan had blown it. She didn't know how she was going to explain the evening to her mother, how she was going to tell her that her baby-sitting job was cancelled. She pulled on her jacket, feeling suddenly cold, her hands both numb and clammy at the same time. She had trouble doing up her buttons, and she knew, if Ellen Holmes hadn't arrived when she did, Declan would have given her what she needed, in the brown packet he had thrown so carelessly on the bed ... the packet!

She hurried back up the stairs and into the bedroom. There was no sign of the packet. She began to search frantically. It was wedged between the wall and the bed, and she pulled vigorously until it was firmly in her grasp. Drops of sweat stood out on her forehead, but she smiled with satisfaction. Maybe the night hadn't been a total write-off after all. She'd have to give it back to Declan, of course, but not before she had taken just a little, just enough to stop the shakes in her hands and the awful tight feeling in her head as though she was about to explode.

[illegible]

[illegible] to the packet.

She went back [illegible] turn the [illegible] There was no [illegible] in the packet. She [illegible] between the [illegible] and the [illegible] Maybe he [illegible]

[illegible]

Chapter 21

"You're home early – I wasn't expecting you until much later." Sheila looked up, surprised, as she turned down the volume on the television with the remote control. Deirdre had gone to her room to study, and Tom was playing with his wrestlers on the sofa, every now and then giving an exaggerated roar as the favourite wrestler won his 'match' against his opponent. "Didn't they want you after all or . . . ?"

Sheila's voice trailed off questioningly as she watched the expression on her daughter's face change from irritation to obvious anger.

"Look, Mam – they just changed their minds about going to a nightclub after the meal, so they came home – they ordered me a taxi – they'd had a few glasses of wine with their meal, so neither of them was driving." Sharon offered her explanation curtly.

The explanation made Sheila nod her head in relief. Of course. A taxi was the obvious choice, if the Holmes had been drinking.

"Do you want something to eat? I could make some toasted sandwiches if you're hungry?" Sheila got up to go into the kitchen, but Sharon shook her head. All she wanted was to get away from her mother's probing. She didn't want anything to eat, she didn't want to talk to anybody, she just wanted to crawl into bed and put her head under the duvet and blot out the whole bloody mess of a world that had been her lot ever since Dad had left . . .

"I'm going to bed – I don't want anything." Sharon climbed the stairs slowly. Her body was shaking, every muscle felt as if it was on stand-by, waiting for some physical assault, her brain filled with thoughts of Declan, and Mrs Holmes, and the accusing stare of the little boy when he discovered them in the bedroom. The muzzy feeling in her head made her lose her balance momentarily and she staggered against the wall.

Sheila, coming up behind her, looked at her daughter sharply. If she didn't know better, she would swear that Sharon had been drinking, but there was no smell of alcohol from her, and she felt sure that the Holmes weren't the type to tolerate such behaviour.

"Sharon – are you all right, love?"

The girl nodded, not turning round, then opened the door of her bedroom and went inside quickly, closing the door behind her.

Sheila stood outside for a moment, about to enter, then thought better of it. She could sense a row brewing, and it would have been a pointless exercise to start a full-scale shouting match at this hour of the night. Something was wrong. She could sense it, just as she had sensed any kind of trouble between Sam and herself in the past.

Like father, like daughter. The words floated about her subconscious as she lay in bed, staring unseeingly at the shadow of the moon behind the flower-patterned curtains. She wouldn't sleep. Another of those nights when all sorts of worries tormented her: Sam, the children, money, her own future – a woman on her own with just a halfpenny job to support her. Her last thought, before she dozed restlessly, was that she would have to work a full day tomorrow, because Brenda's ulcer was acting up again, and Donal Sheridan had observed, with businesslike acumen, that Sheila was just as skilful as Brenda at cooking the house speciality.

"Double time – I'll pay you double time if you

can cope with the orders," he had told her. It wasn't a request, more of an 'or else' – and Sheila had said it would be no problem, a smile on her face to hide any anxiety she was feeling. It would mean the kids would have no hot meal until the evening, because she hadn't a microwave – another of her silly assumptions that a meal from a microwave wasn't a proper meal – but that was back in the days when Sam had been the breadwinner and she had time to cook meals on demand. If she prepared something beforehand, it would be unappetising by the time they got home from school to dish it up. She saw Donal Sheridan's face, floating in and out of her subconscious, challenging her to refuse, his cynical smile irritating.

She lay in bed, waking and sleeping, until the first light appeared in the room, then got up and tiptoed to the bathroom before anyone else woke. She stood under the lukewarm shower, closing her eyes against the spray of tepid water. She'd cope. There was no other way. And Sharon would be sorted out – she'd make an appointment to see the doctor with her for some afternoon after school. A picture of Sam came into her mind and she closed her eyes and let the water run over her face. She was missing him like a deep ache inside her. A physical hurt. Missing his touch, missing his presence in the bed next to her at night, missing his breath on her face as he fell into a deep sleep after their lovemaking. This period she was going through now was like a punishment for taking so much for granted. She didn't think she could face years of this misery, of Sam's absence from her life, missing years, when they could be so close, and grow old together, and love each other until death parted them . . .

She didn't know she had been crying until she stood in front of the bathroom mirror and saw the angry red blotches beneath her eyes.

* * *

"I'll bring home some lasagne, and we can have it with chips for tea, all right?" She pulled Tom to her, hugging him as he threw his arms about her neck.

"I don't want you to go to work, Mam – I miss you – and Sharon is so cross when you're not home – she hits me!"

He spoke aggrievedly and she looked up at Sharon leaving the house, her schoolbag still standing next to the fridge.

"Sharon – don't forget your books – and what's this about hitting Tom?" Sheila looked at Sharon sharply and Sharon pulled a face at her brother.

"Little telltale! I don't know what he's talking

about but if he acts up when you're not here, then I'm going to thump him one – he's not going to get away with anything while I'm around, just because he's Mummy's pet!"

Sheila was about to reply angrily, but Sharon was already gone, the schoolbag still propped against the fridge.

Deirdre kissed her, a half-eaten slice of toast still in her hand. "I'd better get going, Mam – I've a French test this morning – I'll take Tom into school for you so that you won't be late at the restaurant."

Sheila smiled at her gratefully. "Thanks, love, and I'll collect Tom at three and bring him home – you'll be back from school by quarter to four, won't you? I can get the 3.50 bus back into town then."

Deirdre nodded. "Don't worry – and I'll keep an eye on Sharon – see that she doesn't bully him."

Sheila watched them as they went up the road, hand in hand, Deirdre pulling a reluctant Tom behind her. If she could only get through this day without a hitch, she felt she could cope with anything. Fifteen lasagnes and about the same amount of quiches by lunch-time. She took a deep breath, letting it out slowly. This was her biggest test since she had gone to work at Tasty Bits. She hoped she wouldn't fail it, because if anything should happen to the job she knew it would be really difficult to get another one, a woman in her position, and at her age. She took one last look in the mirror over the kitchen sink, pulled on her coat, and almost tripped over Sharon's schoolbag as she hurried towards the door. She kicked it aside in frustration and Sharon's books spilled out over the kitchen floor, covers torn and childish graffiti decorating the pages. She paused, her eyes focusing on a small square paper packet, held together with Sellotape. She didn't stop to look at the time as she bent slowly to pick it up.

Her fingers pulled at the paper, tearing it open, the off-white substance in the little inner plastic bag exposed to her puzzled eyes. She didn't know what it was, but if it was wrapped and Sellotaped so carefully, obviously double-wrapped judging from the paper around it, it must be something very important to Sharon – or somebody else ... She didn't want to open the plastic bag. The substance felt soft, like powder, as her fingers ran over the surface of the plastic. A word came into her head, a small word that refused to go away, but nagged at her, willing her to think it, to say it, a word that would devastate her. Drugs. What if it was the drug that had been doing the rounds in the schoolyards, distributed secretly, one teenage hand to another, stuffed into jeans' pockets and down the fronts of innocent-looking school uniforms? The hands on the clock in the kitchen moved slowly. She counted the ticking dispassionately. Ticking away the seconds, while she stood there, undecided as to what she should do next. If she didn't get a move on she would be late for work. She could imagine Donal Sheridan sitting behind his desk, fuming angrily as he looked at his watch. But nothing seemed to matter any more. So many terrible things had happened to her, and this was the climax of the horrors she had gone through this past six months.

The episode in the club wasn't a one-off incident. Sharon was on drugs. It was clear from her sore eyes, often blood-shot, especially in the mornings, her excuse that her eye make-up was irritating them, making them sensitive, her irritability, her sudden bursts of temper, and in contrast those quiet periods when she appeared in some kind of world of her own, gazing into the distance, oblivious of what was being said, or what was going on around her. It was obvious. Sheila felt she must have been in denial up to now. She went to the drawer in the kitchen and got some Sellotape, with trembling fingers sealing the packet once more and slipping it into her handbag, then she opened the back door and stepped outside to put the key under the geranium plant. She always left a key outside in case of emergency. She had only been doing it for the last few months, and it suddenly struck her that maybe she had been unconsciously leaving it out for Sam, in case he should come home and find nobody at home, his key mislaid somewhere, just the way it had always been.

"Mother of God, help me!" She whispered the prayer as she went down the path, her eyes blinded with tears.

She didn't notice Esther Looney standing on the footpath, about to get into her little red Micra.

Esther looked curiously at Sheila, then smiled brightly, showing all her perfectly crowned white teeth. "Sheila, can I give you a lift somewhere? I'm going into town – an appointment with my hairdresser."

Sheila looked at her, all the misery she felt inside showing in her face, making Esther feel a bit guilty with her talk of hairdressers when she knew Sheila had obviously more on her mind than hair appointments. Sam's disappearance was local knowledge by this time, and she felt great pity for the woman with the pinched white face, traces of tears on her cheeks, who stood before her now.

"Come on," she said quietly. She opened the passenger door and took Sheila firmly by the arm, steering her into the seat. "The restaurant, isn't it? I'll have you there in a jiffy – just relax and let Esther play road-hog!"

The early-morning traffic had lessened as

Esther drove swiftly but carefully through the roundabout and onto the dual carriageway leading to the city. She didn't speak until she reached the traffic-lights at the corner of Baker Place, then while the lights were red she turned to Sheila, concern on her face.

"Things are bad for you, I know, Sheila – at the moment everything must be looking pretty horrible – but the wheel always turns – an old saying, but true." She looked down at her wedding ring ruefully, the thin gold band slipping easily around her thin finger. "Things aren't always what they seem – my marriage isn't a bed of roses either – men can be bloody cruel!" She spat out the words, then looked across at Sheila, horrified at her outburst.

Sheila forgot her own worries momentarily as she saw Esther was genuinely upset. She put a hand on her arm tentatively. She had never known Esther Looney to be so vulnerable, her sudden admission that anything might be amiss with her 'perfect' life completely out of character. Even perfect women like Esther Looney had problems with their men, she thought wryly. She wondered if a man could ever be pleased, or if he was constantly seeking greener pastures. "Thanks, Esther – for the lift – and the sympathy."

Esther nodded, unable to speak. The lights turned to green, she released the clutch and the car jerked forward.

Reaching Tasty Bits, she slowly pulled in to the kerb.

Sheila could see Donal Sheridan standing inside the doorway, the expression on his face indecipherable.

"Good luck, Sheila!" Esther nodded her head wryly in Donal's direction and Sheila smiled.

"Thanks, Esther, you too."

The two women looked at each other, an unspoken understanding between them. Sheila watched the red car disappear from view as she stood on the pavement, uncertain of her welcome inside Tasty Bits. Should she go inside and face Donal Sheridan's wrath, suffer the humiliation of being fired in front of the whole restaurant, busy now with breakfast-time trade? Or should she just cut her losses and walk away, register with the employment agency for another job? Before she had time to make up her mind, he was standing in front of her, his handsome face surveying hers indifferently.

"Well? Are we to be honoured with your presence today, Sheila? Or has your new position as sous-chef of Tasty Bits gone to your head?"

His tone, for him, was quite genial and she looked at him, bewildered by his attitude. She had expected a torrent of abuse, then to be given two weeks' notice and told to look for some other position as soon as possible. And now here he was, Donal Sheridan, noted for his cut-throat attitude with business people and his less-than-merciful approach to his employees, actually beckoning her to come inside and resume her duties as soon as possible. She looked at her watch. Almost ten o'clock. She was an hour and a half late for work. The two young waitresses eyed her curiously as she followed Donal through the restaurant and into his office.

When the door had closed behind them, he turned towards her, and with a sinking feeling inside, she realized that his genial reception outside the restaurant had been merely a charade, a cover-up for what he really felt – anger at her lateness. Her heart sank when she saw the unyielding look on his face.

"I don't have time for employees who take time out whenever they feel like it – especially on a day like today when I'm short-staffed. Take a look outside – the place is filling up already for breakfasts – imagine what it will be like at lunch-time!" He spoke quietly, but with a sting of accusation in his voice that brought tears to her eyes.

How dare he? She had worked hard for him, had organised her lunch breaks around the time she had taken off to bring Tom home from school. Her work in the restaurant had been complimented by customers, people who frequented Tasty Bits almost every day. "A touch of class," she had heard one man comment admiringly to his business companion after she had served them their lunch, and now, here was the Almighty Donal verbally chastising her for being late, without even giving her the courtesy of allowing her to explain!

She drew herself up to her full height and took a deep breath before replying politely. "If you've quite finished, Mr Sheridan – I'll gladly work the day for you, get the lasagnes and quiches ready on time, serve in between in the restaurant, even help with the clearing up at the end of the day!" Her eyes met his in equal combat. "Then you can give me my marching orders and dismiss me. To tell you the truth, Mr Sheridan, you pay your employees very badly. I know a restaurant off O'Connell Street where I can get much more than the going rate, plus tips – and not work half as hard as here!" She finished defiantly, not taking her eyes from his face as he stood in front of her, his expression admitting nothing of what he might be feeling or thinking.

She swung round, opening the door with a flourish, her legs beginning to feel a little unsteady beneath her. Outside the door, she steadied herself for a moment, closing her eyes, horrified at what she had just done. She could forget references from him, she thought hysterically. He'd probably go to Stephen O'Hara, and tell him all about the episode, and then her one and only friend would be gone from her life as well. The feeling of desolation was too much. She wiped her eyes with the back of her hand, and went into the cooking area at the back, hanging up her coat behind the door.

"Are you all right, Sheila?" Orla, the young waitress, eyed her anxiously.

Sheila nodded, giving her a watery smile. "I'll be fine – just as soon as I have that first batch of lasagne in the oven."

She took her apron from the closet where the catering uniforms were kept, her hands shaking as she tied it firmly behind her back.

"Now – let's get a move on – I've a feeling this day is going to be my swansong!" The girl looked at her, startled, but Sheila just smiled back. "Never mind – I'm in a funny mood today – I'll survive!"

She worked without a break until midday, the sweat trickling down her back and running between her breasts as she struggled to meet her target. There was a determined look in her eyes as she covered the lasagnes with the rich, creamy cheese sauce Brenda had taught her to make. She had a pot of the mixture left over so she decided that a few vol-au-vents wouldn't go astray – old skinflint Donal should give her a medal, she thought sarcastically as she prepared the vol-au-vent cases, filling each with her own recipe of diced mushrooms and bacon, some chopped chives for decoration and, as an afterthought, adding her own particular touch to the sauce, a tiny dash of cider vinegar and brown sugar, a sweet and sour piquancy that the children loved when she added it to various dishes at home – not that she had experimented much lately, she thought wryly, as she shoved the baking tray laden with vol-au-vents into the oven. Beans and chips and sausages didn't cry out for imaginative sauces.

She looked towards the office door, but she hadn't seen Donal since this morning's confrontation and now, having calmed down considerably, her energies absorbed by the amount of work she had got through in the last couple of hours, she could only wish that if he did appear, he would have the discretion not to say anything until they had a private moment together.

She stuck her head round the door of his office. "I have to go – to collect my son from school."

He looked up, his pen poised over a set of figures he was trying to put into some semblance of satisfactory profit margins for the accountant who was calling later on in the day. They weren't all that promising, competition dogging him relentlessly, and his expression when he looked at her sent a sinking feeling through her.

"Fine – you'll be back by four?" he asked curtly, his brow furrowed in irritation.

"We've just cleared the lunchtime rush – there's not one lasagne left – and the vol-au-vents went like hot cakes – pardon the pun." She smiled then, her face flushed, with tiny tendrils of blonde curls framing it attractively.

His face relaxed, giving her an unexpected smile. "I'm sorry about this morning – I've a few business problems – nothing that can't be solved, but I tend to take it out on everybody else. Accept my apologies – and congratulations for a job well done."

The speech had been unexpected and she began to see her boss in a new light, somebody who could admit to a mistake and apologise subsequently. It was a Donal Sheridan she had never imagined, hidden beneath layers of business-like cynicism, and for a moment she almost sympathised with him for whatever problems he was trying to deal with.

"So I still have my job?" she asked hesitantly.

He nodded. "There was never any question of firing you – you're a good employee and apart, from the morning you started, time-keeping was never a problem until now – I'm sure you must have had a good reason for it."

Sheila thought of the packet filled with the powdery substance. She still had it in her handbag, uncertain what to do with it. "I had a problem at home – but it won't happen again, I promise you. All right, then, I'll be off."

He stood up suddenly and followed her out of the office into the kitchen.

"Okay, girls – it seems to be quietening down for a bit – take an extra ten minutes for break."

"That's great, Mr – I mean Donal!" Orla's face lit up with pleasure. The boss was in a good mood. So far her day was going fairly well. She had a date with a gorgeous bloke tonight after work – he was taking her out for a meal and afterwards they were going bowling – and tomorrow was her day off, time to recover, because hopefully she'd bring him back to the house she shared with three of her mates tonight, and . . . Her imagination conjured up delicious images in her head of making love to him, his blond hair close to hers . . . She smiled involuntarily. Yes, it had been a good day for her, and the best, she hoped, was yet to come!

She looked at Donal Sheridan's face, and she could even detect a smile on those handsome features. He was a changed man since Sheila had come to work in the restaurant. Sometimes Orla saw him looking at Sheila when he knew she was preoccupied with serving at the tables, watching her every movement as she skilfully made her way from table to table, her small neat figure never faltering, a friendly smile never far from her lips. Maybe he fancies her, Orla thought dreamily. They'd get together and live happily ever after, just like in those true romance magazines she was always reading.

His voice suddenly broke through her daydreaming, sharp and authoritative.

"Get a move on, Orla, for God's sake – or you'll be the only one staying behind tonight to clean up!"

She looked up at his irritated expression and her thoughts of romance between Sheila and Donal Sheridan dissipated as quickly as they had come. No woman could put up with such mood swings. Her imagination had got the better of her.

"Yes, Donal – Mr Sheridan," she answered him, disappointedly. Prince Charming had turned back into the Beast.

But there was still Eric, her fabulous date for tonight, she thought happily, and she sang softly under her breath as she went to pick up the order for table three.

* * *

"Mam – a policeman rang while you were at work." Deirdre met her in the hallway, her face anxious. "He said he'd call you back – I think it's something to do with Dad. He didn't say what he wanted, just that he'd call back. What do you think he wants?"

Sheila looked troubled, her thoughts negative as she put her arm about Deirdre and led her into the kitchen. Maybe they had contacted Sam. Had something happened to him? Was he injured somewhere, lying in some hospital bed? She knew she was thinking the worst, but she could think of nothing positive at the moment.

"I don't know, Dee – we'll have to wait and see. I don't have time to deal with it now – I can't be late again for work. Tom – come on, son – get off your uniform and get into your tracksuit. Here, Dee –" She unwrapped the large pizza and put it on the table. "Heat it in the oven for a few minutes and I'll make the chips – Sharon shouldn't be long more – we can leave hers in the oven for her ..."

She had made light of the telephone call, but her head was starting to pound with the tension of the day, and now the call from the police. Would the nightmare never end?

* * *

"If somebody calls while I'm at work, Dee, tell them I'll be home by 6.30 and take a message."

She bent and kissed the top of Tom's blond head, as he sat, legs crossed, on the mat in front of the TV.

"I'll be good, Mam!" he mumbled, his eyes glued to the wrestling match on the screen.

She'd call in to see Stephen O'Hara on her way home from work. She'd show him the packet she had found in Sharon's schoolbag and maybe he'd advise her what to do ... She couldn't afford to dwell on Sam's whereabouts. Whatever about him, Sharon was her priority at the moment. She ran towards the bus stop, the bus already pulling away from the pavement. If she was late a second time, she would never have the courage to show her face in Tasty Bits again – no job was worth the humiliation of having to face Donal Sheridan in one of his dark moods ...

Chapter 22

"Ossie has been paid – the consignment has been left in the warehouse – now all we have to deal with is the safe shipment of a half a million dollars' worth of heroin to the west coast of Ireland." Dieter looked at Sam speculatively.

They were sitting in Sigrid's apartment, the sound of steak sizzling coming from the miniscule kitchenette behind the plastic curtain, Sigrid's off-key voice humming the latest pop song on Berlin radio. Everything was so alien to Sam's sense of homeliness – even the smell of food cooking was different to home, spices and garlic replacing the familiar aroma of fried onions and gravy.

"Our man is reliable – the trawler will remain

outside Irish waters and the consignment will be transferred to a small yacht waiting at the Head –" He looked at Sam quizzically. "Hag's Head, that is the place."

"Hag's Head?" Sam repeated slowly.

Everything was going too fast – he was on a fast-moving carousel, and he wanted to get off, but there was no way out now, he had to carry it through to the bitter end.

They had been on holiday at Lahinch, their yearly pilgrimage to the West Coast. It had been the best week of that summer, sweltering heat and the sea water like a lukewarm bath. He remembered splashing in and out of the great breakers renowned on that part of the coast. Sheila hadn't been able to swim, and he smiled wistfully now as he remembered the terror on her face each time a wave broke over her tense body. The best of times, and the worst of times . . . She had irritated him with her clinging ways, her hand gripping his wet arm as he tried to pull her further into the water. He had suggested a drive along the coast afterwards, just as the red ball of fire sank gloriously beneath the horizon and they had all bundled into the old Fiat. He had driven to Ennistymon, then on to Liscannor, hiring out a pleasure launch in Liscannor Bay to take them out to the Sound.

"There you go!" The boatman had pointed a

mahogany-brown finger to the large expanse of rock jutting out from the mainland. "Hag's Head – and a bitch of a one, I might tell you – fishermen steer clear of her, if they know what's good for them – she has fangs that'd cut through iron beneath that innocent head of hers.".

Looking back, despite his irritation with Sheila, Sam thought that it had been the best holiday they had ever spent together. Where had things gone wrong?

He looked at the cold, staring eyes of Sigrid, and wondered how a woman like that could have such a hold over him.

"Half a million – where in the hell did we get the money to finance that amount of stuff?" He was angry now as he looked from Dieter to Sigrid, their smug expressions making him feel like a simpleton, an outsider they had barely tolerated, because he was 'convenient' for the time being.

"We have our reserves," Sigrid said abruptly. "Griffith and Markham just added the finishing touches, you know?"

She smiled then, and it was as though the whole purpose of the operation had been erased from his mind, the subterfuge and the deception, the milking of funds from long-standing accounts – it was all obliterated by the dazzling, hypnotic smile on Sigrid's magnificent face, her eyes telling him the things that had attracted him to her in the first place. He relaxed.

"There – eat your steak – like a good little boy," she coaxed him, tantalising him as she bent over, her hair touching his cheek, her breasts rubbing against his shoulder, pleasurable, inviting. If Dieter hadn't been there, he would have taken her then, rolling her on to the colourful woven mat in the middle of the floor, their lovemaking prolonged and satisfying. He could see Dieter smiling across the table at him. The man even knew what he was thinking, Sam thought angrily. He knew, because he had shared the same intimacy with Sigrid – every look between them was a giveaway. Sam was just the surrogate lover, the man she had chosen out of maybe a dozen others to play the game with them.

He finished eating, the meat tasting like sawdust in his mouth. He drank heavily, the bottles of wine on the table emptying rapidly as Dieter and Sigrid sat back and watched – and waited – until he was half asleep, slumped in his chair, the glass tilted on its side on the pink-and-white-striped tablecloth . . .

Chapter 23

The rain had been falling steadily for almost three days, the coastline almost obliterated by the veil of dense mist, like a ribbon of grey and white smoke expanding rapidly from the horizon. The unmarked garda car was discreet, half hidden in a twist of road that led downwards to the bay, front and back right-hand wheels tilted at an angle in the water-logged ditch.

Sergeant Jim Mallen sat at the wheel, settling himself more comfortably in his seat, giving his companion a cynical look as he watched him light a cigarette, then quench it again, stubbing it out impatiently on the dashboard.

"OK! You can take that look off your face, Mr

Perfect No-smoking No-drinking Saint!" Lexi Fulham grinned at his partner. "That's why I hate stake-outs like this – just waiting for something to happen – what's a man to do except smoke his brains out from boredom?"

Jim Mallen closed his eyes, his head lolling against the steamed-up window of the car. It was a bitch of a night. He hated doing surveillance work, especially in this God-forsaken part of the country. The drug haul was expected to be in the region of half a million euro, a tip-off from the Belgian police. Since the EU barriers had come down, the drug barons were having a ball, and this particular consignment had been pinpointed by the Drug Squad ever since it had left Bremerhaven in Germany.

The Iron Curtain had never been demolished, he thought tiredly. Just taken down and ironed out and put back up again to screen the drugs coming in from Eastern Europe. He yawned loudly, his eyes heavy with sleep.

If tonight were the night, as soon as they sighted anything suspicious they would call for back-up – and pray God the local lads, supposedly on high alert, got down here quickly. Otherwise he and Lexi would have to beat a swift retreat – they could hardly take on a gang of drug-smugglers themselves.

He sighed deeply.

Lexi Fulham looked at his companion quizzically. "You have strong views about this drug culture, don't you, Jim? It goes beyond the boundaries of your job . . ."

"The drugs are pouring in from all parts – Turkey, South America, the Caribbean Islands – and the dealers are multiplying like bloody vultures – dirty hands itching to get the stuff on the open market. Ireland is a prime target for them, especially with all these bloody coastal places where they can pull in and be off before they're discovered ..." He clenched his hands on the steering wheel, his face white with anger. "Young kids, no more than eleven years old, I've seen them, Lexi, out of their minds because of some bastard who makes his living from poisoning children!"

"I know, Jim. I know."

Silence descended until, some time after, Jim muttered, "Lexi, I can't keep my eyes open . . . Wake me in five minutes if I drift off . . ."

Lexi nodded. Even five minutes' sleep could work wonders in levels of alertness. Jim sank his chin on to his chest, closing his eyes once more.

Lexi sat there, the silence in the car increasing his sense of awareness of his surroundings. He could hear Jim's heavy breathing above the drumming of the rain against the roof of the car, could smell the pungent saltiness of the sea, its pure scent incongruously harmless, a sweet cover-up for the cargo of destruction making its way towards them.

"Do you know what I had on for tonight, Jim? A red-hot date with a fantastic blonde . . ."

His words went unnoticed by the other man who was snoring softly in the humid warmth of the police car. Lexi looked at the heavy jowls resting on the broad expanse of chest, and smiled. The smile was still on his face when he turned once more to look through the window at the bay below, the expression in his eyes changing to one of incredulity as he looked down the barrel of a sawn-off shotgun. The shot met its target head-on, fragments of glass piercing the rough skin of Sergeant Mallen as he opened his eyes – then closed them again as the bullet hit him in the chest, the blood spattering the lifeless body of Lexi Fulham . . .

* * *

It hit the news headlines the following morning. Sheila, trying to hurry Tom into eating his breakfast, stood still for a moment in the kitchen, the announcer's voice solemn as he described the brutal killing of two detectives on surveillance duty near Hag's Head in County Clare.

"Hag's Head," she repeated slowly.

"Mammy, what have I for lunch?"

She was only half-listening to Tom as she stuffed his lunch box into the schoolbag. She remembered the holiday they had spent on the West Coast that summer. The boat trip from Liscannor Bay, the great mass of corroded rock rising from the sea, its dark bulk frighteningly predatory. She shivered suddenly.

"Mam, there's a call for you." Deirdre appeared in the kitchen, her voice sounding agitated. "I think it's the policeman who called the last time." She pointed to the telephone, the receiver turned downwards on the hall table.

Sheila nodded. "All right, love – you go ahead with Tom – I'll be home at the usual time – make a pot of soup and have some bread rolls – I'll fix us a proper dinner later on this evening."

Deirdre looked anxious. "Mam – I don't like all these phone calls – try and find out what's happening with Dad – the police won't tell me anything." She had tears of frustration in her eyes and Sheila hugged her close.

"Come on now, love – chin up – I'll find out everything and let you know exactly what's happening. Now, take Tom to school for me, like a good girl."

She waited until she saw the two of them walk down the path and out the front gate, then she turned back into the hallway, her hand shaking a little as she picked up the receiver.

"Hello?" Her voice was hardly a whisper.

She heard the male voice, loud and impatient, at the other end.

"Mrs Shaughnessy? This is Paul Roche, Glen Street Garda Station."

"What's happened – is it Sam? You have some news for me?"

"Sam? No, Mrs Shaughnessy – it's about your daughter. A young girl took an overdose last night and had to be admitted to hospital – she told us that your daughter had given the stuff to her – I wonder would it be possible for you and your daughter to come down and see us today?" Despite the polite phrasing, his voice was insistent.

Sheila felt the blood drain from her body, her knees buckling as she sat down heavily on the stairs. "Yes – of course – I'll have to pick her up from school – I'll come as soon as I can –"

She replaced the receiver and put her head between her knees, the hall beginning to spin round and round, her head throbbing as the pain came in waves, nerves strained with tension. "Holy Mother of God – will this nightmare ever end?" she whispered, dragging herself up, holding on to the bannister for support. She would have to go to the school and collect Sharon . . . she should really phone Donal Sheridan to let him know that she would be late ... again ...

She laughed hysterically, the sound vibrating incongruously in the empty hallway.

"Dear God, he'll show me the door this time – and I wouldn't blame him one bit! If I was in his position, I'd do the very same thing!"

But what could she tell him? The truth?

She couldn't deal with phoning him now – especially as she wouldn't even be able to tell him when she *would* make it in to the restaurant.

She picked up her handbag, looking inside for her keys, then suddenly thought of the packet she still had tucked away in the bottom of her bag. If she showed it to the police, Sharon would be in even more trouble than she was in right now – and if she didn't . . .? She should have gone to Stephen O'Hara on her way home from work the previous evening, but she had decided against it, reluctant to get Sharon into even more trouble. She knew Stephen didn't think much of the girl as it was.

She turned the key in the lock of the door, then ran down the path as she saw the bus draw up at the bus stop. It was just about to pull away when she made one final spurt. Her breath was coming in short, panting gasps as she handed the driver the money.

"Have to get fit, love – then you can run a marathon, no bother to you!" The driver winked at her, and she smiled back half-heartedly.

The bus stopped right outside the gates of the school, and she quickly went inside the reception hall, past the door marked '*Staff Room*', to the Principal's office at the end of the long corridor.

She knocked once, and a voice called out, "Yes?"

When she opened the door, she saw Sharon sitting slumped in a chair by the window, Bernard Casey sitting behind his desk, his expression grim.

"Mr Casey – I have to take Sharon down to the Garda Station – they need to ask her some questions." Sheila's mouth felt dry, her voice faltering as she saw the unrelenting hard look on Sharon's face.

"I know all about it, Mrs Shaughnessy." He looked at Sheila, concern on his face. "It's that young girl, Linda Sullivan – seems she took an accidental drug overdose – had some serious side-effects. She's in hospital, looks like she'll be there for a few days."

He looked across at Sharon and she returned his look, her gaze unflinching.

"Look," she said, "if Linda took something she knew nothing about, it's not my fault – I didn't force her to do anything she didn't want to do herself." She finished on a defiant note, tossing her hair back from her face.

Sheila's heart sank. This wasn't going to be

easy. Poor Linda, quiet Linda, with that shy smile and the protective way she looked after Sharon, trying to keep her out of trouble, defending her every time she landed in it. Sharon didn't deserve a friend like her. Sheila had to admit reluctantly that Sharon wasn't the kind of companion any mother would like for her daughter.

"You told me you were sleeping overnight in Sullivans' last night! What in God's name happened, Sharon? And I want no lies, just the truth, please."

Sharon turned her eyes heavenwards, her hands clasped together behind her head.

"We just had a bit of fun, that's all. Declan got his hands on some new stuff – I might as well tell you now, because you'll only find out sooner or later."

She sneered derisively at Bernard Casey and Sheila could have slapped her then, slapped her until all the badness was out of her, until she had her own little girl back again, the one she could identify with, not this sullen, arrogant girl who seemed to have no regard for authority, no respect for Sheila's concern or the life of her friend. She thought of the packet of stuff in her handbag. She couldn't hold on to it – it would have to be handed over to the authorities. She sweated uncomfortably, the silence in Bernard Casey's office oppressive as her mind worked frantically.

Sheila looked at Bernard Casey enquiringly. "Do you think I could make a phone call? There's somebody I need to ask the advice of." She would ring Stephen O'Hara. She could talk to him – he'd know what to do.

The Principal nodded towards the phone. "Of course."

"Thank you." Sheila picked up the receiver and punched out the number.

"Hello – Father O'Hara – I'm at St Ita's School – yes – I'm afraid so." She looked across at Sharon. "I'd really appreciate it, Father, if you could come down here – please?" She replaced the receiver and nodded to Bernard Casey. "A friend of mine, Father O'Hara – he'll give us a drive down to the Garda Station. But he won't be free for another hour or so . . . "

Bernard Casey looked at her sympathetically. "Stay here in the office if you wish until he gets here – I won't be here – there's a lecture this morning. I'll let my secretary know you're staying here. Now, I have to ring the bell for assembly." He looked across at Sharon pointedly. "Maybe you remember what the lecture is about, Sharon? The Dangers of Drug-taking. Makes you wonder, doesn't it – is there any point in breaking our backs to try to get through to a group of know-it-all juveniles?" He left the office quickly, and Sheila could hear the staccato sound of his shoes on the polished corridor as he made his way towards the assembly hall.

Time dragged slowly past, Sheila trying to read some magazines, Sharon dozing, and eventually Stephen O'Hara arrived.

He entered the office, grim-faced. His eyes focused on Sharon as she turned her face away from him, concentrating on the empty schoolyard outside.

"Let's go – and I hope for your sake the girl comes out of this in one piece, Sharon. Her mother is in a terrible state." He went and stood in front of Sharon, but she kept her face averted, her fingers tapping impatiently on the side of the chair. "She took the money from her mother's purse." He looked at Sheila's worried face, hating to pile all this trouble on her, but she had to be told. "Then herself and this lady here –" he pointed at Sharon accusingly, "they both did a runner late last night – down to the club. News was out – a 'friend' of theirs had got his hands on some crazy stuff – 'snowballs', they call them." He emphasized the word sarcastically, all the time looking for some semblance of remorse on Sharon's face, but all he saw was the hard, unresponsive shell of indifference, and he wondered where in God's name did a woman as reserved and as sensitive as Sheila Shaughnessy get such a daughter? "The effects of these so-called snowballs are like those of Ecstasy but they are twenty times stronger and twenty times more lethal." He turned away. "Come on – the car's outside – the sooner we get this interview over with the better!"

* * *

"Where did you get the pills, Sharon?" Sergeant Paul Roche asked again, looking at the girl kindly. He had seen a few like her in his time with the drug unit. A hardness that seemed impenetrable, and yet – he lived in hope for all of them. It was easy to get involved with the wrong set – easier still to get hooked on a problem that would eventually destroy them if they didn't do something about it.

"I told you – I got them from a friend." Sharon's air of hostility was beginning to wilt a little, the officious atmosphere in the police station intimidating, although she would never admit it. Sharon Shaughnessy was afraid of nothing, and nobody. That was why Declan liked her so much – she was on for anything, no inhibitions, 'a great crack' her friends called her.

Linda was a fool to take so many of the snowballs. They had divided them between them in Linda's bedroom, had made jokes as Sharon put the little piles of round white pills on separate pieces of foolscap paper – "One for you, one for me!" Counting like a child distributing sweets at a party. Afterwards, when they had been equally divided, she had indicated one of the little piles to Linda.

"Okay – that's your lot. I'll take some of mine now, and keep the rest for later – Declan says you get a far better kick out of it if you take it at intervals." She had looked eagerly at Linda. "Just wait until you feel the buzz it gives you, Lin – you'll never want it to stop – it's just crazy!"

And now Linda was lying unconscious in the hospital, hooked to a drip that fed fixes of nutrition into her rather than a lethal dose of snowballs.

"I think you had better tell us who this 'friend' is," Paul Roche said quietly, his head bent over a sheet of paper in front of him. He knew who it was. All he needed was verification from the girl, a name – that was all he needed to try and clamp down on the pushers ...

* * *

It was after three o'clock when they left the Garda Station. Sharon looked dazed as she followed Sheila and Stephen O'Hara down the steps and across to the carpark. Declan would never look at her again. She had snitched on him, and in their gang that was the worst kind of betrayal. Once the guards had their finger on you, you were branded forever as a suspect whenever anything went wrong – break-ins, muggings. The word was out that Declan was a pusher – he didn't stand a chance.

"Why, just *why* did you insist that I give them Declan's name?" she demanded. She sat in the back seat of the car, her breathing close to Sheila's ear as she bent forward, almost threateningly, so that Sheila moved away from her in her seat.

"There was no alternative unless you wanted to end up in the Juvenile Court in the morning – as it is, you got off lightly, young lady – a bit of voluntary community work won't do you any harm." Sheila spoke harshly, but inside she could feel a mixture of emotions battling with each other, her heart frozen into a hard lump of ice. She had to pretend indifference, to hide any anxiety that threatened to surface at any time. That wasn't the way to handle Sharon. '*Loving but detached*' – she had that motto etched in her memory from a newspaper cutting she had kept in her dressing-table about teenage drug-taking.

She glanced sideways at Father O'Hara and he smiled approvingly. She was going the right way about things, he thought, no screaming matches, just a touch of the *laissez-faire* and gradually, maybe, he thought hopefully, the girl would come round.

"No more communication from Sam?" he asked quietly. He glanced in the rear-view mirror, but Sharon had sat back, her eyes closed, arms folded defiantly across her chest.

"No – I had a quick word with them before I left – that sergeant is nice, but all he could say was that the file had been sent to the Fraud Squad in Dublin and still no trace of him."

He waited for some kind of emotional reaction but there was none, Sheila's face pale but composed as they travelled slowly in the line of built-up traffic coming from the factories in the industrial estate.

The car eventually pulled up outside Tasty Bits.

"Well, I'd better face the music." She laughed ruefully as she pictured the expression on Donal Sheridan's face when she had to give him her latest excuse for not turning up for work.

"I'll go in with you, if you like?"

She shook her head emphatically. "If you could just keep an eye on Sharon, Father, will you?" She glanced back at the girl, now sleeping soundly, her head resting against the window.

"Okay. Off you go."

Sheila got out slowly, taking a deep breath before she braced herself and opened the front door of the restaurant.

Brenda was winding her way through the

narrow spaces between the tables, her frilled cap sitting lopsided on her hair, face flushed as she tried to balance two dishes of lasagne in her hands. She hurried up to Sheila. "Jesus, Sheila, where were you? We were up the walls all day!" she muttered. "Two of the waitresses rang in sick – that old tummy bug that's doing the rounds – and I've had to help out at tables as well as doing my stint in the kitchen!"

"I'm sorry, Brenda – I really couldn't help it."

"Donal's in his office." Brenda nodded her head in the direction of the office, just as the door opened and he appeared, his face expressionless as he looked at Sheila.

She went towards him, and had to almost force her way past his unyielding figure as he stood in the doorway.

"If you have anything to say to me, Mr Sheridan," she said pointedly, going inside and turning to him, her gaze steady. "I would prefer if you said it in private, please. I think I'm entitled to that much – no splendid scene in front of the other employees or customers, okay?"

He nodded, closing the door with a loud bang and walking across to stand in front of her.

He had been angry. He had cursed his own stupidity more than once that day in hiring a woman who had come to him only on some goody-goody priest's recommendation. He'd have to pay Brenda and the other girls double time for the amount of work they had put in, and with the new snack-and-delicatessen bar opening next door, he could ill-afford to pay anyone more than was necessary. His profits would plummet if the new place took on, and by all appearances the new owner was sparing no expense in making his new acquisition as enticing to the general public as was possible. Plush green velvet seating and rolls of top quality carpeting were being delivered every day – not your common industrial stuff, Donal thought angrily, oh no, it had to be the best for Leonard Holmes, one of the up-and-coming yuppie businessmen in the city.

"Well – what was it this time, Sheila?" He stood, his tall frame looking down at her.

"I had a bit of a family crisis." She bit her lip, reluctant to let him know just what had happened, but there was no way out. If she was to hold on to her job, she had to tell him the truth. And maybe, when he heard the truth, she thought miserably, he wouldn't want to keep her on, anyway. She took a deep breath, looking him in the eyes as she explained quietly. "My daughter has been dabbling in drugs – like a lot of her contemporaries, looking for some excitement – and a friend of hers ended up in hospital – some side-effects she hadn't bargained for."

He stared silently, then went and sat at his desk.

"Look, I know you've had to put up with a lot from me, and I'm sorry – but I'm trying to cope on my own, with a teenager who obviously has some issues that have to be resolved." She looked at him, desperately trying to make him understand. "It couldn't be helped – I suppose there's no use in asking you to give me another chance." She waited, looking at his long, bronzed fingers clasped pyramid-style in front of him, the gold signet ring on the third finger of his right hand glinting expensively as the last of the afternoon sunshine invaded the small room, casting mellow shards of milky light about the cream-painted walls.

"You're obviously going through a bad patch. I've had a few bad episodes myself in my life, but nothing that couldn't be overcome." He looked at her with his dark eyes, his expression neither sympathetic nor accusatory. "I was wondering – would you care to come out with me – this evening – for dinner?"

The invitation was so unexpected that she looked at him for a moment, wondering if he had spoken at all.

"I beg your pardon," she said faintly.

"I said, I was wondering if you'd care to come out with me tonight," he said impatiently, drumming his fingers against the table top. "You obviously need a little lift in that turbulent life of yours – a break away from your troubles for at least one evening."

He watched the expression on her face change from surprise to puzzlement. The woman fascinated him in some ridiculous sort of way. Not since he had broken up with Marie had he felt this spark of interest in a member of the opposite sex, and his rule of 'love them and leave them' wouldn't be thrown aside in this instance either.

He was going to fire Sheila Shaughnessy. There was no doubt in his mind. But she was vulnerable at the moment, her job was on the line, and a woman in her circumstances might just be willing to chance a compromise . . . If the evening didn't go according to plan, Donal's plan, then there was nothing to lose – he'd fire her anyway. If things turned out the way he wanted them to, then he could string her along for a while, and still get rid of her whenever and however he pleased, citing the obvious fact of an employer-employee relationship being in jeopardy when a 'personal' element came into the equation.

He smiled at her, his most charming, man-about-town smile, and Sheila stood, speechless, wondering if maybe Donal Sheridan was going a little bit crazy in the head.

She had come in, expecting to be fired, and all she had received was an invitation to dinner, the crucial matter of her absence from work all day seemingly ignored ...

"I don't know what to say ..."

"Yes or no – are you free tonight?" He eyed her speculatively.

"I suppose so – but what about the job – am I fired or what?" She looked at him, bewildered.

His eyes took in the neat, curvaceous figure beneath her regulatory uniform, the long slim legs beneath the modest black skirt. It was certainly worth a try, he decided idly. He was in the mood for a little light diversion with business pressures mounting on him by the day ... Besides, it would get that nuisance of a priest off his back for good. He couldn't envisage Stephen O'Hara sending any more of his female waifs to look for employment from Donal if he knew he had 'tried it on' with one of them. He laughed outright, and Sheila began to wonder if her conclusions about him had been justified. There was something strange about the man . . . but a dinner invitation would surely be harmless enough ...

"We can discuss where we're going in that respect over dinner, okay, Sheila?" He smiled enigmatically and she nodded dumbly. He stood up then, striding past her and out into the restaurant.

She waited for a few seconds in the office, uncertain of what to do next. Had that been a dismissal – or did he intend that she should stay on and work until closing time? No. She needed to go home – she couldn't leave Sharon now.

She smiled at Brenda as she went past the kitchen. Brenda nodded, giving her a rueful grin, then mouthing 'See you in the morning' across the sea of customers, then quickly turned back to dishing out portions of cheesecake to a young couple, the man tapping his fingers impatiently against the glass front of the serving counter.

"Service here is deplorable," he muttered to the girl. "Think we'll try the place next door the next time."

Donal Sheridan, overhearing the comment, frowned darkly, cursing Leonard Holmes for encroaching on his territory . . .

* * *

"He wants me to go out to dinner with him – said nothing about firing me – I don't understand the man, Father – I really don't!"

Stephen O'Hara gripped the steering wheel tightly as he drove. He glanced at her, his face perplexed. "An invitation to dinner – that guy will never cease to amaze me!"

He could have said more, but thought it best to give Donal the benefit of the doubt. Maybe he was genuinely interested in taking Sheila to dinner, an innocent invitation, to make up for his intolerant attitude . . . maybe . . . but Stephen somehow didn't think so.

But, as he drew up to the kerbside outside Sheila's house and stopped with a grating jerk of the gears, he decided he had to give her at least a word of warning.

"Sheila – be careful."

The tone of his voice made her look at him in surprise. "What do you mean, be careful? I know he can be a bit chauvinistic at times, but – what exactly are you trying to say, Father?"

Stephen O'Hara remembered the girl with the long flowing blonde hair who had come to him in tears – how long ago was it now? It was about a year and a half. She had got herself into 'trouble', she told Stephen, her eyes wide and frightened-looking.

"Do you know who's the father?" he had enquired gently, and she had nodded, a desolate look on her face. He had seen it too many times before on the faces of other young women who had tried to finish the nightmare once and for all.

"He's my employer – I don't know should I give you his name . . ."

"Tell me – it won't go any further than this room."

"Donal Sheridan. I was desperate for a job, and he took me on, without references – he said my dedication to my work would be reference enough." She had laughed hysterically then, and Stephen had spent the rest of the evening advising her, giving her an address where she could contact some people who would help her to find a place to stay until the baby was born.

And he had gone to Donal Sheridan. He had lashed out at the man with all the strength of the anger he had felt inside, but it had been like hitting against a brick wall.

"None of your business, Father – and maybe the baby isn't mine – have you thought of that possibility?"

Donal's smug grin had incensed Stephen.

"You'll look after that girl and her baby when the time comes!"

"I'll write a substantial cheque – that'll do the trick, believe me, Father – and now, if you'll excuse me, I have a business to run!"

And that had been the end of it. But Stephen had kept the memory of the girl's ravaged face in his mind. With uncharacteristic ruthlessness, he had made sure that Donal would remember something of it also, and frequently called in favours, like donations to the church, jobs for people desperate for work, like Brenda, and Sheila Shaughnessy. Things had worked out well for Brenda, and Stephen O'Hara thought the man must have learnt his lesson, because there had been no further problems with female employees, and Sheila seemed to be getting on well – until now.

As he wondered how best to answer Sheila's question, Sharon woke up, shifting herself with exaggerated slowness, pushing her elbow vehemently against the back of Stephen's seat.

He turned and looked at her sternly. "Give your mother a hand with the dinner this evening. She's going out for a little R and R for a change."

"I'll be going to bed – I don't want anything to eat – I'm too tired." Sharon stepped out of the car and went slowly into the house.

Sheila waited until she had disappeared inside the front door, then opened her handbag, taking out the small packet and handing it to Stephen. "Take a look, Father – I feel like I'm carrying a time-bomb around with me – I found it in Sharon's schoolbag this morning."

He turned the packet over slowly in his hands, then loosened the sellotape carefully, revealing a second wrapping which he carefully opened. Surveying the little plastic bag with its contents he knew exactly what it was.

"This is a substance called 'speed', Sheila. It's an amphetamine – it stimulates the nervous system. It's addictive and dangerous." There was nothing in his voice to intimate that he was unduly surprised at the contents of the packet. "A lot of the kids are into it – well, the ones who are on the look-out for something exciting to relieve their 'boring existence'!"

"What do you think I should do?" Sheila's worried expression met his and he looked at her doubtfully.

"I can only advise you to go to the gardai with this. You can't give it back to her, you know what she'll do with it – and at least the police will have proof that the boy Declan must have been handling the stuff. Where else would she get it?"

Sheila nodded miserably. "All right – I'll go down there first thing in the morning, I just want to get rid of this stuff – I feel – dirty somehow, just carrying it around in my bag ..."

the [illegible] - away [illegible] the window on the
dock, out [illegible] or something [illegible] for [illegible]
[illegible].'

'Keep [illegible] down [illegible] I should [illegible] that.' S[illegible]
[illegible] exactly [illegible] and [illegible] ed [illegible]
community.'

I can understand [illegible] going [illegible]
[illegible] just [illegible] her [illegible]
[illegible] and at [illegible] the [illegible] was [illegible]
[illegible] they [illegible] must have [illegible]
[illegible] else would [illegible]

[illegible] smiled [illegible] '[illegible]
[illegible] thing in the [illegible] I [illegible] want
to [illegible] this [illegible] - [illegible] dirty [illegible]
[illegible] a man [illegible] anything.'

Chapter 24

"What are you going to wear, Mam?" Deirdre had thrown most of Sheila's clothes out of the wardrobe and on to the bed. She was just as excited as her mother. Discarding one dress after another, shuddering at the 'old-fashioned duds', as she called them sarcastically, critically examining the few 'dressy' pieces Sheila possessed, she laid them side by side on the bed.

"Mam, you'll really have to go out and buy a few new clothes, something nice to wear – these are all positively *ancient* ..."

"Maybe if I win the Lotto I can afford to indulge myself – until then we'll just have to make do with this lot . . ." Sheila pointed to the assortment of clothes on the bed. She picked up a short black skirt from the mound. "What about this – and that pink blouse with the mandarin collar – I could wear some black beads and those crystal earrings your father ..." Her voice faltered. Sam had given her the earrings on her last birthday. She had thought then they were the most beautiful set of tiny crystals she had ever seen, their brilliance glowing expensively in the black satin box. Now she took them from the jewellery box on her dressing table, holding them close to the pink blouse, and somehow she thought their original purity had vanished, the glow not quite as overwhelming."They'll do, I suppose," she murmured tiredly. "To tell the truth, Dee – I don't feel like going out tonight."

Deirdre picked up the blouse and skirt, handing them to her determinedly. "The water is hot, go and have your shower, and put these on, for heaven's sake, Mam – you can't hibernate forever, just because Dad is gone!"

It was the first time Deirdre had mentioned Sam's disappearance without that frightened, haunted look in her eyes, and Sheila heaved a sigh of relief. Maybe things were coming round, slowly, and if Sharon could get herself sorted out, then everything would be – not perfect – it could never be that again – but endurable, yes, that was the word. Life goes on – and she was going out for a meal with a man tonight, just a brief diversion from her troubles for an evening – and where was the harm in that?

* * *

"You look wonderful, Mam – that colour really suits you."

Sheila stood in the hallway, her coat draped across her shoulders, the pink blouse with the peplum waist emphasizing her trim figure, the black skirt barely skimming the top of her knees.

"Do you really think so?" She looked down at the skirt doubtfully. "I think it's a bit too short."

"No, it's not!" Deirdre said firmly. "You have nice legs, so why not show them off – and that hairstyle really suits you – makes you look years younger!"

Sheila's blonde hair was shining with gold highlights, little wisps curling about her face, her brilliant blue eyes bright with anticipation. She looked up the stairs, to the closed door at the top of the landing. Her expression changed suddenly, the worried frown appearing once more as she looked at Deirdre apprehensively.

"You'll watch her, Dee, won't you? I'm worried about her, and if that Declan rings for her . . ."

"I know, Mam – I'll tell him she's in bed and can't come to the phone – please – just go out and have a good time – "

"Mam, will you bring me back something nice?" Tom looked up at her as he sat on the stairs, chin in hands, his eyes drooping with tiredness.

Deirdre sat next to him, putting her arm about him. "What do you want her to bring you back, Tommy? All the shops will be closed."

Sheila sighed with relief. Thank goodness she had one daughter with a bit of feeling in her, somebody she could trust.

"I don't know – something."

Sheila knelt down beside him, taking his hand in hers. "I've left some chocolate cake and lemonade in the fridge – Dee will give you some when you're in bed – a little party – all right?"

He nodded, but Sheila saw his bottom lip tremble, a tear rolling down his cheek.

"What will we do if *you* go away – maybe you won't come home any more! Who'll mind us, Mam? I don't want you to go away like Daddy!" His voice was muffled as he buried his head in her coat, and she shook her head at Deirdre.

"I can't go – not if he's thinking things like that – I'd be worried about him all evening!"

Deirdre turned Tom's face gently away from Sheila towards her. "Come on, Tommy – Mam will be back before midnight – just like Cinderella!" She looked up at Sheila and winked, her eyes bright with amusement. "We'll have our own little party, and you can even stay awake until she gets home." She looked at him persuasively. "We can watch your *Jungle Book* video."

Tom's face lit up delightedly. "You mean it, Dee – I can stay up until Mam comes home?"

She nodded. "No problem, dude! Now go up and change into your pyjamas and you can come down again!"

The doorbell rang just as Tom bounded up the stairs and Sheila looked at herself in the hall mirror, making an unnecessary adjustment to her hair. Her cheeks were flushed and her eyes glowed attractively as she opened the door to Donal Sheridan. He stood for a moment without saying a word, his eyes admiring the good-looking woman who stood before him. She was a looker, he thought speculatively. The husband must have been mad to walk out on somebody like that, no matter how itchy his feet were. Well, his loss was Donal's gain . . . he smiled at Sheila and held out a bunch of pink and white carnations. "For you – allow me –" He took a pink flower from the bunch and with a flourish produced a pin from the pocket of his coat. "Always prepared – I was a Boy Scout a long, long time ago!"

He pinned the carnation to the neck of her blouse, expertly manoeuvring the pin so that it was invisible behind the carnation. "There – just what that magnificent blouse needed to set it off!"

He had style, she had to admit. She wondered how many other flowers he had pinned to other female blouses, perhaps to other outfits far skimpier than hers. Not that it mattered to her. Donal Sheridan was nothing to her, nobody ever would be, not after Sam. A night on the town, then back to the same old humdrum existence. Dee had been right. Cinderella for an evening . . .

She turned to the girl standing in the hallway, kissed her on the cheek. "All right, love? I won't be too late – wait a moment –" She looked at Donal enquiringly.

"Where are we going – I always like to leave a telephone number at home – in case the children need to contact me." She thought a shadow of irritation appeared in his dark eyes, then thought it must have been her imagination as he smiled a brilliant smile at Deirdre.

"Do you have a piece of paper? I've a pen here someplace." He took out a pen and wrote on the notepad Deirdre handed to him. "There – it's the Silver Spoon restaurant – that new place that opened in O'Grady Square."

Sheila remembered reading about the grand opening in the local paper a few months previously. All the rich and beautiful people seemed to have come together for the evening, judging by the photographs dotted all over the society pages. She had looked at them indifferently, her mind at the time on Sharon, and how she was going to handle the girl without making an enemy out of her. *'Grand Opening of Limerick's Newest Nightspot,'* the headline ran. And tonight it was her turn to bask in the expensive ambience of the Silver Spoon. She felt a sudden feeling of trepidation. Maybe she wasn't the type to frequent such sophisticated places. She would be tongue-tied, maybe have to make conversation with friends of Donal Sheridan, people who might get the wrong impression and think that she was his 'latest' girlfriend. It wasn't too late to back down. But he was hurrying her down the driveway towards his car, and Dee was standing in the doorway behind her as if blocking her way back into the house.

She sat in the front of Donal's car, relaxing against the soft leather headrest. Just before the car pulled away from the kerb, she gave one swift look towards the bedroom window at the front of the house. She saw a girl's shadow draw back, the curtain pulled slightly to one side, and even though she couldn't see them, she could sense a pair of dazzling blue eyes on her, feel their hostility as they continued to stare from behind the net curtains, watching until the car disappeared from sight.

* * *

"Well – do you like it?"

Donal had led her to an intimate table-setting by the window, the waiter almost falling over himself as he paid attention to them, taking Sheila's coat from her, pulling the chair back for her to be seated. Donal Sheridan was well known in partying circles, and once he had established a routine for visiting a certain establishment, then it invariably followed that a strong contingency of his followers would do likewise. The owner of the Silver Spoon restaurant had warned the waiting staff to make sure that everything was satisfactory for Donal Sheridan. Satisfactory enough for him to make return visits.

Sheila looked about her admiringly. When Sam had taken her out to dinner they had never gone to very expensive places, Sam's priority lying with his stomach, and he invariably picked restaurants which were famous for their portion sizes rather than their up-market ambience. The restaurant positively oozed expense from every luxuriously carpeted, velvet-draped corner. The waiting staff looked like film stars, the men with their gelled hair and confident smiles revealing even, dazzling-white teeth, the females tall and elegant, more like models than waitresses, even the regulatory uniform of black, slim-fitting skirt and crisp white blouse not hiding their perfect figures. Obviously hand-picked, Sheila thought enviously. With females like that around, what chance had the ordinary women like Sheila got trying to find their soul mate? If she was looking for a soul mate – Sheila dismissed the ridiculous thought. She had enough problems at the moment trying to find her present husband, never mind win the attentions of another male.

Sheila cleared her throat nervously. She felt intimidated by her surroundings, the months of existing in a state of isolation, waiting for news of Sam, taking their toll on her brief period of relaxation.

"Is there something wrong?" He looked across at her, and she held her breath for a moment.

She supposed he was handsome, in a craggy sort of way, rather like a Mr Rochester type in *Jane Eyre*. She hadn't realised she had been assessing him so carefully until she saw his tanned face crease in an amused smile as he held her gaze. She blushed self-consciously. She couldn't believe that she was actually on a date with a good-looking male companion, a man who obviously thought her a fitting dinner partner judging by the unmistakable look in his eyes. She smiled back at him.

"Nothing – it's just that …" She hesitated for a brief moment, his steady gaze making her feel like a gauche schoolgirl. She was annoyed with herself for not appearing more sophisticated, more in control of a perfectly lovely evening out on the town with a handsome partner. "If you must know, I feel like a fish out of water."

He laughed aloud, covering her hand with his across the table. "Relax – just enjoy yourself – you deserve a night out."

He was meticulous in his ordering.

"A light white wine, I think – nothing too heavy or the flavour of the lobster will be spoilt."

His instructions were carried out by a smiling, dark-haired waiter who looked at Sheila with obvious admiration.

Donal winked at her. "I think you have a conquest there – and I don't blame him – you look really beautiful tonight."

His expression was serious, the sentiment obviously sincere, and Sheila blushed, glad that the subdued lighting of the restaurant hid most of her discomfiture. Nevertheless, she felt a certain degree of pleasure that he had gone to the bother of paying her a compliment. It made her feel good about herself, more confident, and maybe it was that sudden surge of self-esteem that made her say, impulsively, "Have you never had a woman of your own? Someone you would have liked to settle down with?"

She was sorry afterwards for being so outspoken. It was as though a veil had been swept across his face, and his mouth, only a few seconds previously smiling and friendly, was now set in a stern, uncompromising line.

"I had somebody, once – she married some other guy – my bad luck, eh?" His tone was one of dismissal. Sheila knew her question had been out of line, unwelcome, and for the rest of the meal she spoke only when he asked something about the children, or what she thought of the competition on his doorstep.

"You have to be prepared for that in the food industry," she answered intelligently. "Just keep your quality mark flying high at all times, and the competition won't bother you."

He nodded, well satisfied with her answer.

But after her remark about his personal life, the conversation was more on the employer-employee level, and she felt sorry that she had destroyed the more friendly, relaxed exchange of words they had enjoyed at the beginning of the meal.

* * *

"We could go for a walk by the river?" Donal suggested as he helped her into her coat, taking her elbow and guiding her down the steps of the restaurant.

Sheila closed her eyes, savouring the delicate scent of the night air fragranced with the clusters of bright spring flowers arranged in heavy ornate urns about the forecourt of the restaurant. "I'd like that – it's ages since I took a walk by the river . . ." She bit her lip, remembering times when she and Sam had strolled arm in arm along the very embankment Donal Sheridan was now guiding her towards.

His good humour had been restored, and Sheila felt relieved that he seemed to have forgotten about her insensitive question, making him recall a love affair that had obviously been a painful episode in his life. She curled her hand into his when he casually took it, and she looked at his handsome profile, starkly outlined against the night sky. A man who could break a few hearts, she thought wryly. What he was doing wasting his time with a woman like her, deserted, broke, and with three children to take care of – was a mystery. Still, it was a bit of an ego-builder, to be a Cinderella for just one evening . . .

* * *

"We'll go back to my apartment for a brandy, then I'll take you home – and I expect you to be bright and early in the morning, ready to tackle a mountain of pizzas and lasagnes – with maybe a few of your own concoctions thrown in for good measure!" His mouth curved in a thin smile as he drove slowly across the bridge and veered left into a select avenue of apartment blocks overlooking the Curragower Falls.

"You've been complimented, you know, Sheila, for your creativity – taking a simple dish and making it your own specialty by adding a few personal touches."

She felt a little dizzy, not only from the unaccustomed wine, but from the heady sense of achievement threatening to drown her as his compliments thrust her forward to a summit of success she could never have envisaged – at least, not while she had been married to Sam. One positive thing that had come from his leaving them was that she was learning to stand on her own two feet, slowly but surely taking control of her life again.

He brought the car to a halt in the paved courtyard of a discreet apartment block at the end of the avenue. She followed him tentatively up the narrow stone stairway to the left of the drive, on to a wrought-iron veranda, entwined with a profusion of green and gold-coloured creepers. When he drew her into his apartment, switching on the lamp on the mahogany coffee table inside the door, she felt as though she was entering another world, leaving all the bitterness, all the heartbreak of her life without Sam behind her. And when he handed her the glass of brandy, gently urging her to sit on the peach-coloured settee, while he settled himself quite close beside her, her dream was still intact.

She felt she was floating, high above the clouds, and Sam was whispering into her ear, he was holding her hand, so close to her, his gentle pressure familiar, inviting . . .

It was when she felt Donal Sheridan's mouth on hers, demanding, hurting her, that the dream slowly transformed itself into a nightmare. She tried to push the nightmare away from her, felt the heavy weight on top of her, and still she struggled, the blackness all round now, the previous relaxing ambience of the apartment pathetically diminished with her hoarse cries . . .

* * *

"You all right, love?" The taxi-driver looked through his rear-view mirror, his face anxious as he scanned the tormented features of his passenger.

Sheila nodded, her hands trembling uncontrollably as they lay in her lap, her blouse showing the savage tears across the front. Her hair lay in damp strands across her forehead, her eyes were bloated from crying.

Not my problem, the taxi-driver judged objectively. Best to keep my nose out of these affairs – a woman, flagging down a taxi at three in the morning, had some explaining to do to somebody – and that somebody wouldn't be him. He heard her give a low moan as she sat huddled in the rear seat, and he increased his speed, making his way through the deserted streets until he reached the address she had given him. He just wanted to be rid of the woman, didn't want any trouble from some vindictive husband – anybody who was waiting up for the woman would be in for a hell of a shock.

"There you are, love – and I'd get myself to bed, have a bit of a rest – you'll be feeling much better when you wake up."

He waited while she fumbled in her bag, taking the taxi fare from her purse. "There you are – and thank you – I don't know what I'd have done if you hadn't come along when you did . . ."

She had stumbled out on to the roadway outside Donal's apartment, the enormity of what he had done focusing her mind on just one thing: the need to get back to the children, to take hold of some semblance of normality, blot out all that happened in the apartment. A few cars had passed her, the occupants looking at her dishevelled appearance, probably thinking she was high on some sort of drug – or maybe out of her mind with drink – she had certainly been out of her mind . . .

Donal Sheridan had taken her, had raped her in his apartment, and there was nothing she could do about it. It was his word against hers, and she had gone voluntarily to his apartment, had accepted his drink, had basked in his seeming admiration, like a schoolgirl on her first date with a handsome man – and she had fallen into his trap, had been fooled by him – a gullible, stupid woman, who thought naively that such a man would be bothered with somebody like her . . .

She let herself into the house quietly, taking off her shoes in the hallway, closing the hall door with trembling hands. Not a sound could be heard, the children probably fast asleep by now, Sheila thought thankfully. Deirdre would have put Tom to bed, would be sleeping now that blissful sleep of a teenager, as yet untroubled with such perversion that Sheila had just gone through – she envied her. Only several hours ago, she had been looking forward to a pleasant evening – dinner with a seemingly nice, courteous, well-meaning escort – and now all was spoilt – including herself.

She ran up the stairs, anxious to get to the bathroom. She had to wash herself, to get rid of the smell of his skin, his skin on hers, his hands touching her, as if it was his right, just because she was alone, and vulnerable ...

The hot water splashed over her body, boiling hot, searing her skin with angry red marks, and still she tolerated it, her hands desperately massaging the soap into her hair, rooting out all the badness, the clinging scent of his aftershave that made her want to vomit, her stomach heaving as she remembered, and tried desperately to forget. Afterwards, she wrapped herself in a towel, pulling it tightly about her as she tiptoed quietly into her bedroom. She mustn't let the children know, she must pretend that she had had a lovely evening, pretend that everything was normal, and above all, try to obliterate Donal Sheridan from her thoughts.

She lay on the bed, the sleeping pills she had taken with the glass of water by her bedside beginning to take effect. She felt calmer now. She knew what she must do. Losing Sam had made her stronger, her emotions more in control, her thoughts, after the initial shock of her ordeal, more rational.

Tomorrow she would hand in her notice. She couldn't stay and work for such a man – it would feel as though she was some sort of prostitute – because, she felt certain, he would almost certainly try it again, would feel he had some hold over her, if she went back to work for him. Her eyes grew heavy with sleep and she tried to put her thoughts into some degree of order. It would be difficult to find something part-time, a job where she would have the freedom to be at home and look after the girls and Tom at certain times in the day. Maybe Father O'Hara would help her again – she had nobody she could trust, only him …

She fell asleep, her dreams making her cry out through the night, still feeling Donal Sheridan's body on hers, and when she woke, she saw Deirdre's worried face looking down into hers, sleep still heavy in her eyes.

"Mam, wake up, Mam – are you all right? You were having some kind of nightmare."

Sheila put out her arms, wrapping them tightly about the girl. "It's all right, love – just a bad dream – I'm not used to eating late at night – must have been that rich food I had for dinner."

Deirdre nodded, relieved. "Yes – that's probably it, Mam – we waited up for you but Tom got tired and cranky, so I put him to bed, and then I fell asleep, too."

"It was late when I got home – too much of a good time, love – but I'll be fine, just as soon as I have my cuppa!" She pulled herself up out of the bed, forcing herself to put a smile on her face. "What time is it? Let's have that cup of tea – before the others stir themselves. How's Sharon?" Mention of Sharon's name brought another cloud of depression on top of her.

"Sharon didn't give us any trouble, Mam – just stayed in her room – Mrs Sullivan rang to say that Linda was off the danger list – so that's good news, isn't it?" Sheila said a small silent prayer. Maybe now Sharon would see some sense, get a grip on her life. The drugs were a real worry. Declan was responsible for getting her hooked on them, and she was determined she was going to make him pay, she told herself, as she staggered painfully into the bathroom.

The only way she could put the nightmare of last night behind her was to occupy herself with other, more urgent responsibilities – and Sharon would take top priority. She looked at the dark bruising on her neck, at the white face looking back at her in the bathroom mirror. She pulled her dressing-gown collar up around the marks, trying to hide them. She couldn't let them see the results of her so-called 'night out'. She could tuck a scarf underneath the neck of her blouse, then they wouldn't know anything. She could hear Deirdre making her way downstairs to the kitchen, and she quickly went back to the bedroom, slipping into the black working skirt and white blouse, rummaging feverishly through her drawers to find a matching scarf. She found a black-and-white flowered scarf the children had bought her a couple of years ago for her birthday. She knotted it quickly, gathering it at the collar of her blouse, concealing the bruising. Then she took the torn blouse from under the bed where she had discarded it frantically the previous night, hiding it in the back of her wardrobe until she got a chance to throw it into the rubbish bin. With a final look in the mirror, she went downstairs to the kitchen.

* * *

"What kind was it, anyway? The restaurant he brought you to – was it one of those classy places where the waiters are all in bow ties and black suits?" Sharon looked at her mother enquiringly, a piece of toast halfway to her mouth.

Sheila gave a half-smile. "Yes – it was a bit up-market for my taste – I'd have preferred some place a bit more relaxing – you know, chicken and chips, and a can of Coke!"

She made an attempt to laugh, busying herself with pouring out some cereal for Tom's breakfast. Three pairs of eyes were looking at her curiously. They must guess, Sheila thought frantically, involuntarily putting her hand up to the scarf at her neck. They must guess something happened, something she didn't want to talk about. But, as she looked around the breakfast table, she realised the looks on their faces betrayed nothing more than an obligatory interest. They had their own troubles to think about – Deirdre had some important maths test this morning – and looking at Sharon's over-made-up eyes, the indifferent tilt of the chin, Sheila felt sure that her interest in the night out had been nothing more than an ice-breaker, the chance to 'test the waters' where her mother's mood was concerned And Tom – she looked at her young son stuffing his mouth with Sugar Puffs, completely absorbed in his task. They knew nothing, and for that she was glad. It would stay that way, because in future Donal Sheridan would no longer be part of their lives. She would hand in her notice that very morning, start looking around for another job.

* * *

"You're lucky I didn't report you to the police."

Sheila stood in front of him in the little back office, taking care that the office door was closed against any prying ears.

Donal Sheridan shrugged his shoulders, never looking up at her as he surveyed the sheet of accounts before him on the desk. "It was just a bit of fun – and you had a good meal – expensive too, I might add – and a nice bottle of wine, congenial company – so what are you complaining about? I'd say for a separated, run-of-the-mill woman, the night could be classed as a total success."

Sheila clenched her fists. The insult was like a blow in the face, his expression taunting as his eyes finally met hers. She couldn't bear him to look at her, memories of the previous evening still vivid. When she finally spoke, it was as if her voice was a thousand miles away, yet calm and convincing.

"I'm leaving here – the job – I'm handing in my notice."

He looked back at her, the expression on his face ambiguous. "Leaving? Surely we needn't make a personal thing of all this, Sheila?" He rose, coming round the desk to her, and she cringed back from him. "Look, you need the job, I need a good worker, so what's the hassle? You'll find it hard to get another job, I mean, you're really not trained for anything else only –"

"Only skivvying for you, you mean, is that it, Donal?" Her voice rose shakily, and she couldn't stop the trembling in her hands as she pointed an accusing finger at him. "What you did to me last night was criminal – and I could still report you – but with all the hassle I'm having at the moment, between Sam's disappearance, and Sharon ..." She bit her lip, her face taut with emotion. "I just want to forget the whole episode and start afresh – so I'm leaving. I'm sure you'll find it easy to get a 'replacement' for me!" She almost spat the words at him, anger rising inside her.

She turned then, not looking back, not daring to look about her until she was outside the door of Tasty Bits. She walked quickly, hardly noticing where she was going, until finally she ended up standing outside St Finbarr's.

So she was back to square one, she told herself wryly. Wait until Stephen O'Hara heard that she had handed in her notice. She wouldn't tell him why though – she could never tell anybody why. But what could she say to him?

She had taken a few anti-depressants for breakfast that morning, and they had dulled the memory a little. She had far more pressing worries at the minute besides feeling sorry for herself.

Squaring her shoulders, she knocked on Stephen O'Hara's front door.

Chapter 25

"Jesus! It's splashed all over the papers – two of them, shot to bits – what were you thinking of?"

The room was in semi-darkness, the curtains drawn against the street light outside. At the table in the middle of the room sat two men, busily packing the small packages of white powder into separate canvas pouches. The younger man standing in the doorway looked at them nervously, beads of sweat standing out on his forehead.

"We lost it – we were waiting near the beach for the consignment, and suddenly there was this unmarked car waiting, just waiting, with the two policemen inside – you could tell what they were waiting for . . ." He swallowed hard, remembering the feel of the trigger against his finger as he had pulled it slowly, engaging with a terrifying explosion.

"Where's Brendan now?" One of the men at the table stood up slowly, his large frame towering over Gusty, a threatening figure of evil. Gusty could almost smell the stench of the drugs from his body, and wished with all his heart he could be out of this mess – but that was impossible. Once you started running drugs with Sylvie Reddan, nobody got out – unless they were dead.

"He knows some young fella who was selling for him – he said he'd get in touch with him – try and get rid of the stuff fast – that's what you want, too, isn't it, Sylvie?"

He looked up eagerly into the man's face. He heard a snigger from the table, saw Sylvie's companion grinning malevolently in the dingy room. He felt the tight grip on his throat, the voice close to his ear, the voice that made him want to run away and hide, to disappear forever from the clutches of Sylvie Reddan . . .

"Listen to me, you dimwit – get that pal of yours and let the two of you do a runner until everything has calmed down. There's a ferry leaving at midnight tonight – once you're across lie low until I contact you – get in touch with our lads in Bristol. I don't want to see either of you until I have this lot off my hands. Jesus – talk about sending boys to do a man's job!"

Gusty heaved a sigh of relief. They were being let go, away from this mess. He nodded eagerly. "Anything you say, Sylvie – I'll get Brendan – we'll be on that boat tonight. Don't you worry."

He didn't see the look that passed between the two men.

He was halfway down the stairs of the apartment block when he remembered – what about their cut? Himself and Brendan – they were entitled to their cut, even if things had gone wrong with the shooting of the detectives, they must still have their cut …

He hesitated on the stairs, looked up at the closed door, and thought better of it. He had got out of a tricky situation; he wasn't going back again. Brendan would see to it that they got their share, one way or the other.

He disappeared into the night, a shadow passing beneath the security light, and if he had looked up, he would have seen two pairs of eyes watching him, Sylvie's expression like that of a fox tracking its victim.

* * *

"Are you on, son? There'll be something worthwhile in it for you if you can get rid of the stuff fast." Brendan looked at the youth lounging against the wall of the alley beside Darcy's Place.

Declan Murphy shrugged his shoulders indifferently. "You know you can rely on me to shift the stuff – when is it due?"

Brendan looked about him nervously. "It's here already – but we have to be careful – there was a bit of an incident, you see –"

"Yeah, so the whole country knows – talk about making a dog's dinner out of a job – 'twas you, wasn't it. Brendan? You killed the two of them?"

"Shush, for Christ's sake – keep your mouth closed!" Brendan clamped a hand over Declan's mouth, the eyes looking up at him a mixture of curiosity and contempt.

Declan shook the hand away angrily. "Hold it there – I'm not going to be manhandled by you or anybody else – I've done a good job for you up to now, and I don't want any trouble." He looked at Brendan belligerently. He wanted no trouble with the cops. That wasn't in his league. There wasn't going to be any Remand Centre for Declan Murphy – he had too many things to do, places to go, too much cop-on to be caught with his hand in the cookie jar. "I'll be around, if you want me to shift some of the stuff – you know where to find me – but I want no trouble, Brendan, mind. What happened with those policemen, that's your affair."

Brendan nodded. He was satisfied. He knew where he stood with Declan. The boy could be trusted not to grass him or Gusty. He saw Declan go back into the club, immediately surrounded by a bevy of young people. Declan was a popular guy, always in the right place at the right time, Brendan thought with satisfaction. Maybe later on he'd recommend him to Sylvie for some of the operations. He'd be a good asset to the business.

* * *

"He told me we were to get the midnight ferry from Dublin Port – lie low until things had calmed down here." Gusty spoke eagerly, throwing some jeans and underwear into the canvas hold-all.

Brendan looked at him, puzzled. "But I thought he wanted to get rid of the stuff fast? We're the only ones who know the contacts in the area – how's he going to manage without us?"

Gusty finished his packing, zipping up the bag, waiting in the doorway expectantly. "Come on, get a move on, Bren! How do *I* know what's in Sylvie's mind? Just be thankful we got out of it in one piece – you know what he's like when things go against him."

"Yeah, I know what he's like." Brendan ran a finger down the side of his face, feeling the ridge of the scar, remembering – remembering Sylvie's cold expression as he flicked the knife against his skin. He had been holding out on him – a rookie. New to the business, he'd thought he could hold back some of the stash for himself. He had been a fool in those days. The knife wound had been the initiation into Sylvie's world. He knew he was a man not to be trifled with.

Brendan looked at Gusty. He felt uneasy. Sylvie had let them off too easily. He had some kind of plan, and himself and Gusty had some part in it. A cold shiver ran down his spine. The sooner they were out of the place, the better. They could hide themselves in Britain, hopefully some place where even Sylvie couldn't find them. He watched the broad smile of relief on Gusty's face, and felt sorry for him. Poor sucker – he hadn't realised yet – it wasn't only the police they were running from – Sylvie was coming after them in a big way.

As he locked the door of the apartment, following Gusty out to the waiting cab that would take them to the bus station, he almost wished the police would get to them first.

Chapter 26

"How are you feeling?" Sharon sat uneasily on the side of the hospital bed. She had never seen so many tubes before hanging out of one person.

Linda's pale face looked up at her, the skeletal hands resting on the counterpane.

"I'm sorry, Lin – you know you're my best friend, and I'm sorry for getting you into this." She turned her head away, ashamed of the sudden tears that rolled down her cheeks. She felt Linda's hand on hers.

"It's all right, Shar – nobody forced me to take the drugs – but sometimes it's hard being your friend. You're so strong and sure of yourself, I feel a bit of a wimp if I don't go along with everything you want." She looked at her friend intently. "I have to tell you, Shar – I can't do this any more – no more sampling Declan's speed or Ecstasy or skunk or snowballs, or whatever else he happens to lay his hands on." She touched Sharon's arm tentatively. "You understand, don't you, Shar? I don't want to get into any more trouble. My mother has enough on her plate with my dad – it's not fair on her. I realised that when I landed myself in here. I didn't mean to take so much of it, you know – I could have killed myself – so I'm not messing around any more, Shar – even if it means losing you as a friend." She looked up anxiously at Sharon's face. This was make-or-break time. The test of a real friendship.

"Who said anything about breaking up our friendship," Sharon muttered, holding Linda's hand for just a fraction of a second, then quickly withdrawing it. "It's your choice – just get well so that we can go down to the club again and have a few laughs."

She looked up as the nurse came into the room, gesturing that it was time to leave. She rose thankfully. The hospital gave her the shakes. She hated the smell, the sound of muted footsteps padding along the corridors, the suffocating feeling in the clinical atmosphere. It could have been her who was lying in that bed. But she couldn't give Declan up, she wouldn't, and all the pressure in the world from her mother would be no good. She hurried towards the exit.

She ran out into the night, the heavy rain soaking her fleece, her eyes focused grimly on the road ahead. It would take her fifteen minutes to get to Declan's house. His mam would be on the evening shift at her factory, and his dad would probably be heading for the pub. They would have the house to themselves. She smiled, a small, secret smile, the thought of what he might have for her making her forget everything, except that she needed a fix.

* * *

"Father – I want to tell you something – in the seal of the confessional – please?" Sheila looked up into his enquiring face.

She was seated in his cluttered living room, a mug of coffee in front of her.

Stephen O'Hara continued to stir his coffee cup, absent-mindedly putting in three more teaspoonfuls of sugar. "What is it, Sheila – what's troubling you? Is there news of Sam?"

She shook her head miserably. "Not as far as I know – the police would have been in touch with me. But I need to tell you something, Father – and it must have the seal of the confessional."

He nodded.

Sheila knelt slowly, her face in her hands. "Bless me, Father," she began, the tears now running unchecked down her cheeks. She didn't lift her eyes until she was finished, her pale face streaked with tears.

Stephen said nothing until he had raised his hand in absolution, completing the formalities of the confessional.

Then he spoke, trying to stem the anger rising inside him. "Sheila – you must report this to the police – he can't get away with it!" He closed his eyes, conscious of his personal guilt. He had known what Donal Sheridan was like – Sheila had been vulnerable – it was his fault she had been attacked, and now she couldn't go back to the job, and he felt as though he had been playing with her life.

"I can't tell anyone, Father – I just want to forget the whole mess, find a new job, get on with things – please – you have to understand." She looked up at him, her tired eyes anxious as she pleaded with him. "That's why I had to tell you like this because I know you can't divulge it to anybody – I knew you'd have to know why I left the job, and I owed you a proper explanation."

He refilled her coffee mug, indicating for her to drink it. "It's something stronger I should be putting into that for you. I know how you feel, and if you think that this is right for you, to draw a curtain on the whole affair – then I'll go along with you – but I won't rest until I see him punished!"

Sheila sat back, relieved. She had relived all the horrific events of the evening with Donal, in telling Stephen. It had been like an exorcising of all the badness of what had happened to her. She had peace of mind now, and she could get on with dealing with the rest of her problems.

* * *

"She's leaving your employment – and I think she deserves a nice big bonus in her severance pay, don't you, Donal?" Stephen spoke curtly.

There was a short pause at the other end, then a quick, nervous laugh.

"Come on now, Stephen, what do you take me for? I'm not a charity, you know!"

"You're definitely not a charity, Donal – I could think of a few things you *are* though – all not very complimentary." His voice rose, each word carefully defined. "I want to tell you – you're getting off lucky this time – but I'll be keeping my eyes on you. Nothing will escape me in the future – particularly with regard to the staff you hire!"

He put down the receiver. The nightmare for Sheila Shaughnessy seemed never-ending. If only her husband would show up, then maybe a few pieces of the jigsaw could be put back in place . . .

* * *

"There have been problems with the shipment – but that is not our problem, *Liebling*." Sigrid stroked his cheek, comforting, caressing, the scent of her perfume overpowering him as he looked from her to Dieter suspiciously.

"What kind of problems?"

He tried to shake off her hand, and she stepped back, surprised. He was the one who used to initiate touching, kissing, who couldn't keep his hands from her – and now it was as though he had grown tired of her. Lately she could almost sense the irritation in him as she held him close to her in bed. Her face hardened.

"You are too intense, Sam – forget about your home in Ireland – we are going to a new life. In a couple of years' time we will have all the wealth you have ever dreamed of!"

"People have been killed, haven't they? I can read some German, can listen to the news – anything to do with drugs will always be world news." He looked at both of them, a sneer on his face. "So you thought you could pull it off, such brains and beauty combined couldn't fail – and instead there are two policemen killed, and a consignment too hot to handle for your 'merchandisers' at home!"

Sigrid looked at him, her eyes cold and uncompromising. "You will do what we tell you, Sam. We are travelling to Bulgaria tonight – we have a flight booked to Sofia – and a safe, comfortable place to stay, until the pressure is off from the International Police." She opened a wardrobe in the bedroom, taking out his suitcase, almost throwing it across the room to him. "There! You go and pack – it is time to go – I am tired of all these arguments!"

Sam took the suitcase reluctantly. He didn't want to go any further with Sigrid. Everything he had felt for her seemed to have evaporated, as if he was coming out of a shadowy haze into stark reality. He wished now he hadn't burnt his boats with Sheila, with the kids – the kids especially. He never thought he'd miss them so much, especially the young lad, Tom. He could almost see his cheeky grin, the mop of light-coloured hair standing up in spikes after his bath . . .

He felt a lump in his throat. This forced exile wasn't for him, but he'd have to bide his time. Sigrid could be a dangerous adversary – and Dieter. He looked at the cold, complacent expression on the man's face. Dieter would do whatever was asked of him. Like Sam, he was a slave to her wishes. Dieter was a force to be reckoned with. He began to pack slowly. He would wait, and watch, and when their backs were turned, he would make his escape. He followed them out of the apartment, to the waiting taxi that would take them to Schonefeld Airport, and from there to Sofia.

Chapter 27

"I didn't know what to do at first when I found the packet – I know she's in enough trouble as it is – and I meant to come down here before now, to hand it in – but things just happened ..." Sheila bit her lip, looking to Stephen O'Hara for support. He nodded encouragingly.

Sergeant Roche rose from behind his desk, scrutinising the package, opening it to reveal its contents. He looked up at them, his eyes registering no surprise, his expression thoughtful.

"It's that young fellow – Declan Murphy – a cool character, hard to get any real evidence on him – he'd have to be in possession for us to get a warrant on him for questioning." He looked at

Sheila sympathetically. "Looks like you're having a bad time of it, Mrs Shaughnessy – and I sympathise with you. The only advice I can give you at the moment is to stay calm, and make sure you know where Sharon is every minute of the day and night. It'll only take one slip-up from the gang, and we can close in on them!"

* * *

"I know you took the packet, Shar – I left it behind me in that bitch's house when you went baby-sitting – and where is it now?"

Declan had his hand about her shoulders, squeezing them uncomfortably, while she edged away from him nervously. He had told her he had something for her, but instead he was asking about the packet that had gone missing, the packet she felt sure her mother knew more about than she was saying …

"How do I know where it is? Maybe that Mrs Holmes took a snifter herself – maybe she's into that kind of thing?" She spoke brazenly, tossing her hair back into his face, then jumping up suddenly from the couch. "Look, Declan, if you've nothing here, then I might as well go to the club – I can see you're in one of your moods tonight – " She gasped as she felt herself being pulled down suddenly on the couch, her hand twisted painfully behind her back. "You're hurting me – please, Declan – let go – your dad might be back any time!" She was frightened. She had never seen him so angry. The gnawing feeling inside her was getting worse. If she didn't get to the club soon, all the stuff would have been handed out – she couldn't go the night without something. With a final, terrified effort, she lashed out at him and ran towards the door, hearing his quick footsteps behind her.

"Come back, Sharon – you can't get away, you know – you'll need me before the week is out!" She was outside now, running towards the bus stop, putting up her hand frantically for the bus to stop. Gratefully she sat back in the seat, looking through the steaming windows at Declan's face staring back at her. She watched him as he turned away, going slowly back down the avenue, and disappearing through the front gate of his house. She knew he hadn't finished with her. She had got a short reprieve, probably because he had more important interests on his mind for the night.

The shakes wouldn't stop. She reached into her bag and pulled out a packet of cigarettes. These would have to do, a poor substitute until she got the real thing. She started to cry, great heaving sobs, and as she looked through the window she could see her reflection, pale and frightened, with streaks of black mascara staining her cheeks.

* * *

"You're a good boy, Declan – I've heard great things about you from Brendan – reliable, trustworthy, that's what he told me."

Sylvie Reddan sat in the dark room of the B&B on the Ennis Road. He had put out feelers for the boy, it had only taken a couple of days to make sure he hadn't a hotline to the garda station, and then he had reeled him in, like a fish trapped at the end of his manipulative hook …

"Yeah – and I'm not used to compliments either, so just spit it out – what do you want done?" Declan swaggered into the centre of the room. He wasn't afraid. He'd had a few close encounters with drug-pushers in the past, and knew from experience that he needed them less than they needed him. They needed somebody young, apparently innocent, and clever – and Declan knew he fulfilled all the criteria for a lucrative assignment from the leader himself, Sylvie Reddan.

"You're in with us, son, if you can pull this off." Sylvie opened the drawer beneath the small table by the window.

Declan watched, gave a sharp intake of breath as he saw the man take the piece from a rolled-up cloth. Slowly, he moved across the room, standing close to Sylvie as he displayed the gun, stroking it almost reverently with his hand.

"Things have got a bit messy, son – people have got stupid, made us sitting ducks for the cops."

Declan nodded. It had the same effect as the speed on him, the feeling of elation, his heart pounding wildly, the buzz of expectancy inside him. He knew what was being asked of him. He wondered what it would feel like, to pull his finger back slowly, calculatingly . . . He exchanged a look with Sylvie, and the man nodded, satisfied. The boy understood. All he had to do now was to issue him with his instructions.

* * *

"Mam – Sharon doesn't look too good – she's lying on the bed, and she's sweating really bad!" Deirdre came running downstairs, while Sheila looked up at her, her heart turning over and beating against her chest.

She followed Deirdre up to the bedroom.

"Sharon – are you all right, love? Can you hear me?" She looked down at the grey, puffy face, the eyes showing no recognition.

Tom stood in the doorway, frightened, looking at the still figure lying across the bed.

Sheila pulled Sharon to her feet, relieved to

hear a small cry of protest from her daughter's blue lips.

"Call an ambulance, Dee – hurry – we need to get her to the hospital. She'll be fine – once we get her some help. Then run and ask Esther if she can mind Tom . . ."

* * *

"What was she on?" The doctor in Accident and Emergency rattled off a stream of orders to a nurse as they wheeled Sharon's unconscious body to a small room curtained off from the main admittance area.

"I don't know," Sheila whispered. "I know she's been taking drugs – her friend overdosed on them recently … snowballs, they called them. But I don't know whether that was the drug she took this time – they were mixing them too – I really don't know!" Her voice rose agitatedly. She was so frightened for Sharon. She would blame herself if anything happened to her. She was her responsibility. It was her fault . . . The feeling of blame sat on her shoulders like a great weight and when she looked up at the doctor, she saw his eyes were kind, full of sympathy. He had seen a lot more young people, just like Sharon, who had taken drugs they knew very little about. This situation wasn't any different.

"She was down at the club." Sheila looked at him desperately. "Do you think they might know what she's taken?"

The doctor picked up the telephone. "What club?"

"Darcy's Place – somebody there will surely be able to tell you what happened."

Deirdre looked at her mother, taking her hand in hers. "Don't worry, Mam – everything will be fine – when she came into the bedroom, she seemed all right, and then she just collapsed on the bed – she'll be fine." She watched the doctor replace the receiver.

"The owner says he knows nothing about drugs," he said, grimly. "But off the record he can give us the information we need – great, isn't it, when you can turn a blind eye to something like this?" He nodded in Sharon's direction, the still body lying inert on the trolley, her hair an untidy mass, soaked with perspiration, about her face. "It was snowballs all right – DOB – he said they were being passed around like sweets – he wouldn't tell us who had them, but that's for the police to investigate – right now I have all the information I need." He nodded in the direction of the waiting area inside the door of the Accident and Emergency unit. "If you wait outside in the waiting area, Mrs Shaughnessy, I'll call you when we're finished – it will take a while ..."

* * *

Stephen O'Hara sat in the waiting room, his eyes trained on the swing doors as he waited for Sheila to emerge. The girl had had a near miss, but maybe, he thought wryly, it might make her see some sense.

"Well, how is she?"

Sheila nodded tiredly. "She's doing fine. The doctor says she'll be in hospital for another few days, just to keep an eye on her – but there's no lasting damage, thank God." She couldn't keep it in any longer, the tears coming quickly, while Stephen O'Hara patted her shoulder helplessly.

"You're a fighter, Sheila – you'll get through this, I promise you – a couple of months down the road, you'll be wondering what kind of a hell you went through. It'll be just a terrible episode in your life, something that you'll put behind you forever . . ."

"The doctor says she needs some counselling, needs to go to one of those rehab places, where they can help her. She can't afford to be putting these drugs into her body – the next lot might kill her, Father." She looked at him with tears in her eyes. Sharon had a lucky escape this time. It had been a warning, not just for Sharon, but for Sheila as well. She would have to watch her daughter very carefully from now on.

"It will do her the power of good – and I know just the place– I'll give them a ring in the morning. And don't worry – everything will be sorted – give it time." He felt glad that he was in control of the situation now, able to offer some concrete help, instead of trotting out the age-old cliché of prayer solving everything. Prayer was good in itself, but sometimes it needed some back-up. He'd contact Liz Kearney in the morning, a good friend of his, in charge of the Cabhair refuge for young people just like Sharon. If anybody could set the girl on the right road, it would be Liz.

"I have to do something about a job soon, Father – I need the money, more so now, with Sharon needing some counselling."

"Don't worry about the money – in cases like this you don't have to worry about the payment." Stephen O'Hara placed a comforting hand on her shoulder. "You're on your own, your daughter needs some help, and the counselling will be supplemented by voluntary funds from the counselling services."

She wiped her eyes with the crumpled handkerchief Stephen had offered her.

She'd had an idea in her head for the last few days. Leonard Holmes was forging ahead with his restaurant, and it looked near completion. He had a notice on the local paper at the weekend about the grand opening, a special half-price offer on all meals for the day. She wondered if he needed somebody reliable, somebody experienced in the business, somebody like herself?

It would be such a relief to know she had a job, independent of State aid and handouts from Father Stephen. He had been such a friend, and she appreciated all he had done for her, but she didn't want to be relying on his handouts when she was quite capable of securing a job on her own merits. She had become much more confident in herself, knew that she had a place in the catering line. Her work in Tasty Bits had proved that, together with all the positive feed-back she had received from its clientele. Her mouth took on a hard line. She remembered the way Donal had thrown her final pay packet across the self-service counter to her. It would be sweet revenge when she saw the look on his face if he discovered she was working for the opposition.

* * *

"As you can see – I'm not quite ready yet – still a bit to get through."

Leonard Holmes looked at her steadily. They'd had enough trouble with Sharon, the daughter, and he wondered if he would be thought prejudiced if he refused the mother a job. He knew, from the hungry look in the woman's eyes, that she desperately needed it – but if he hired her, he would have the wrath of Ellen to contend with. Ever since the episode with Sharon, she hardly went out at all.

"I know that I've been working for the opposition next door, Mr Holmes – and the fact that I have left there and have come to ask you for a job must seem a bit peculiar – but I can assure you there's no ulterior motive – I need a job, and you need staff, so if you think I'm suitable . . .?"

He looked at her, realisation dawning on him. Was it possible that the woman didn't even know about the episode with Ellen? He saw the frank blue eyes staring back at him, and knew instinctively than she didn't.

Sheila hoped he wouldn't ask about Sharon, ask what she was doing with herself or, worse, if she could maybe baby-sit for them. She was ashamed, the worry of the young girl in the hospital like a weight on her shoulders. She waited, silence between them.

Then he nodded his head slowly. She was a decent woman – it wasn't her fault that she had a rebellious teenager – who hadn't these days? "All right then, we'll give it a try – I need somebody who can do some plain cooking but who can also come up with something that will tempt the taste buds of our more adventurous customers." He looked at her frankly. "Do you think you'll be up to it?"

Sheila looked at him, determination written all over her face. "I'm up to it, Mr Holmes – and I'll make sure that your customers have no complaints where I'm concerned."

She thought again of what Donal Sheridan's reaction would be when he heard that she had moved over to the opposition. She would be working in close proximity to the man, too close, but until she had a bit more experience in the business, she would just have to grit her teeth and bear it. She had a few ideas running around in her head, ideas that a couple of months ago would have seemed ludicrous even to consider. She would ask Stephen O'Hara for his advice. The man had been sent to her from heaven, she thought as she shook hands with Leonard Holmes, sealing the bargain.

If she hadn't gone to the church that day, if she hadn't met the priest who had given her so much encouragement to get through this crisis … Sheila closed her eyes. She had been on the brink of a nervous breakdown, and inch by inch she was crawling back from the edge. As she passed Tasty Bits, she saw Brenda inside, cleaning out the self-service counter. Brenda looked up, saw Sheila and waved, a smile on her round, good-natured face.

Sheila waved back, her thoughts firmly focused on her future plans. Brenda was a good worker – maybe the two of them could make plans to start up their own little business – who knows, Sheila thought excitedly, with the two of them determined to make a go of things, it wouldn't be long before they'd be up there, vying with Tasty Bits and Leonard Holmes' restaurant.

As she climbed on the bus for home, Sheila felt as though her world was beginning to come together, at last, her dreams already part of her future ...

[illegible] moved [illegible] integrity [illegible]
[illegible] the [illegible] [illegible] give [illegible]
[illegible] the two [illegible] would make [illegible]
[illegible] little [illegible]
[illegible]
[illegible] of [illegible] consider [illegible]
[illegible] up [illegible] with [illegible]
[illegible]
[illegible] as [illegible]
as though the world were beginning to [illegible]
[illegible]
[illegible]

[illegible]

Chapter 28

Declan had enjoyed the sea crossing. He had been in England, once before, visiting his aunt with his mother. He had wanted to stay that time, reluctant to go back, to a house with screaming kids and a da who raised his fist to him any time he opened his mouth. He had liked the anonymity of the place – he could walk the streets without people pointing at him, saying: "There's Declan Murphy – keep away from him if you don't want any trouble visiting your house." He had lived up to his reputation, closeted in a city small enough to make him feel suffocated. The drugs thing had given him a buzz, a bit of excitement, had given him the confidence to know that he, Declan

Murphy, might one day be a name to be reckoned with in the drugs underworld. He stood now, looking back at the shoreline, at the twinkling lights on the pier. He was conscious of what he had in his hold-all, grasped close to his chest, and he could feel his heart pounding, excited at the thought of the task ahead. Sylvie had trusted him to do the business, and he wouldn't fail.

* * *

Gusty looked round the room, at the mottled paper peeling from the walls, the sound of a siren echoing in the harbour below the open window. He looked across at Brendan sitting on the single bed close to the door. He felt uneasy. He knew by Brendan's silence that he was worried. He took out a packet of cigarettes, placed one in his mouth, offered the packet to Brendan.

Brendan shook his head impatiently. "No – for God's sake, Gusty, put the fags away and try to get to grips with the predicament we're in!"

"We just have to hang out here until things die down back home – isn't that it?" Gusty looked at him with such a naive expression that Brendan almost felt sorry for him. He had no idea, no idea that Sylvie was stalking them. They had messed up good, and now they had to pay for it. A cold sweat broke out on his forehead. He licked his lips, nodding his head, more to reassure himself than Gusty. "Sure, that's it . . . we'll lie low until Sylvie gives us the word to come home."

Gusty smiled, relieved, striking the match to light his cigarette, just as the knock came to the door. He looked at Brendan enquiringly, while Brendan cautioned him with a finger to his lips.

They weren't expecting any visitors. Nobody knew they were here, except the woman who had let them into the house last evening. She had been silent, and discreet. Just pointed up the stairs, to the room at the top, and they hadn't seen her since.

The knocking continued.

"They won't go away, Brendan – we'll have to let them in!" Gusty hissed across the room.

Brendan hesitated, then went across to the door. He could hear nothing. He placed his hand on the door handle, turning it cautiously, just as the shot penetrated the wood, and when Brendan looked down at his hand, he saw that two of his fingers had been blown off, and he started to laugh, a loud, hysterical laugh, because the sight of the blood, and the maimed fingers, seemed unexplainably comical as he wrestled with the excruciating pain.

"Brendan – Jesus, man – they're going to kill us!"

Outside the door, Declan was on a high. He was still savouring the feel of the power in his fingers as he pulled the trigger. It had been so easy.

"I'd leave that gun down, if you know what's good for you!"

The voice came to him, like something in a dream, a man's voice, full of authority.

He was angry with this intruder. He had a job to finish. There was only one down, as far as he knew, because he could hear the other fellow in the room, screaming. The voice came to him again, commanding, and he felt angry. He turned, just as the policeman grabbed his arm, pinning it behind his back. He was still holding the gun, but it felt heavy now – he tried to lift it, to point it at the cop waiting in the hallway, the cop who had the gun trained on him.

"Take it easy, there's a good man."

The hold on his arm tightened. His mouth was dry, his thoughts muddled. He had given himself a 'booster' before he came to the house, just to steady his nerves. He thought maybe that was why he was feeling so tired. The gun dropped to the floor, immediately kicked out of the way by the man holding his arm.

"Let's get down to the station – we'll read you your rights. Declan Murphy, isn't it?"

He nodded silently. The sound of the man's voice was muffled in his brain as he struggled to hold on to the words – "You have the right to remain silent . . ." The English accent had penetrated the dullness.

He remembered now. He had shot one of Sylvie's men – but the other one ... He saw the door of the bedroom open cautiously, the eyes staring out at them, lips trembling as Gusty held up his shaking arms.

"Please – don't shoot me – Brendan is unconscious – his bloody hand's blown off!"

Declan moved tiredly, back down the stairs, the cop's words echoing hollowly in his brain. "Anything you say can be held as evidence against you ..." He wanted to remain silent. It was Sylvie who got him into this. He was saying nothing until the cops had talked with Sylvie.

* * *

"We've cracked them!" Sergeant Paul Roche clenched his fist in the air.

His colleagues looked at him uneasily. The man had been under a bit of a strain lately, two of their men murdered, the gang still without a conviction.

"Will you stop looking at me as if I've lost it?" He pointed to the telex message on his desk. "Just had news from the Drugs Squad across the channel – they've nabbed two of them – just in the nick of time, because they were about to be wasted by – guess who?" He picked up a print-out from the desk. "Recognise the face? Our very own Declan – taken for a mug – probably Sylvie Reddan bribed him into going across to waste the poor fools who had botched up the job in the first place."

His mouth was set in a grim line. He was the one who'd had to go to the families of Lexi and Jim. He had stood there, in their cosy little family kitchens, telling them helplessly that two fine men had been shot in the course of their duty. He still had nightmares of those interviews, the stricken faces looking back at him, the awful, low moans of anguish when they realised there would be two empty places at the table for the rest of their lives ...

"Declan is being brought home – he wounded one guy but the other one is okay – so we're one step nearer to nailing the whole gang."

Paul Roche had telephoned Sheila earlier that morning. She'd been getting ready for work. She listened as he explained the recent developments.

"What will happen to him – Declan?"

She sounded sorry for the boy. Maybe it wasn't his fault he had got himself into this mess. The home environment had a lot to do with it, and she knew, since Sam had left her, it was no easy job bringing up a family on your own. Declan had a mother and father and still things had gone wrong with him. Just an unlucky twist of fate, if children didn't quite turn out the way you expected. She breathed a sigh of relief as he explained that Declan would have to go to court, be tried for being in possession and attempted murder. He would be out of the way for a while, hopefully long enough for Sharon to get back on her feet, get Declan out of her system.

"The drugs issue will be separate – he's in big trouble, and the only way he can make things easy for himself is to give us the names of the big guys – hopefully the name of the man who had our own men killed."

His tone was resolute, and after a brief pause Sheila spoke quietly.

"Thank you for letting me know the situation – I'm grateful to you, for all your help."

"We still don't have news of your husband, Sheila – but we're in communication all the time with our overseas network – it's only a matter of time."

Her name tripped from his tongue so easily that it surprised him. He knew she had come to regard him as a good friend, somebody she could rely on, in much the same way as she could depend on Father O'Hara. He had been gentle with her about Sharon, had seen the situation was difficult, a woman trying to cope with a rebellious teenager, and at the same time come to terms with her husband's disappearance. He had assessed the situation compassionately.

He replaced the receiver, wondering why the woman's face seemed to be constantly in his mind. He gave himself a mental shake, thinking he must be getting soft in his old age. He felt sorry for the woman, that was all there was to it. He'd get on to Head Office right away, see if there was any news from Interpol on Sam Shaughnessy.

He picked up the receiver, a thoughtful look on his face as he dialled the number.

Chapter 29

"We will go to the theatre, Sam – or maybe the museum – there are some interesting contemporary paintings that I would like to see ..."

Sigrid finished brushing her hair in front of the mirror in their room in the Rodina Hotel in Sofia. Sam stood at the window, looking out at the cluster of teenagers scattered about the Southern Blvd of Vitosa below. He thought of Dee and Sharon – they would be just like those young people, jeans and T-shirts with revolutionary slogans printed on them, all laughing, pushing against each other, rucksacks open on the ground displaying an assortment of schoolbooks.

Sigrid came to stand by him, following his

gaze, her eyes suddenly hardening.

"You are growing more morose each day, Sam, and it is not good for us – it is ruining what we have, *Liebling*. Think only of the future!"

He walked away from her, his thoughts in turmoil, his heart pounding against his chest so that he almost believed he was getting a heart attack. He would have to go home. There was nothing in this strange place for him, nothing between him and Sigrid. He didn't know how it had gone so far – drug-dealing and company embezzlement was major crime, and he didn't want to spend years locked away in some prison cell – he must have been mad!

"You go to the museum, Sigrid. I'll stay here. I'm feeling tired."

She picked up her bag, all the time looking at him, her eyes searching his face. She knew, he thought desperately. She knew it was over, but she wouldn't let him go – he was part of the set-up, it had to be followed through – she wouldn't let him go so easily. He heard the door slam behind her, watched from the window as she walked through the crowd of students, her tall, slim figure attracting admiring glances. He saw her cross the street, saw the man waiting for her, the exchange of kisses, the man holding her hand just a little bit longer than necessary . . . Dieter was always there, always in the background. Their relationship, to

Sam, seemed to be erratic, and yet, they invariably came together, as if they were destined for each other.

He took his passport from his back pocket, turning it over in his hand, hesitating for a moment, then making up his mind quickly. He lifted the receiver, dialling the number of reception.

"Yes – I need a taxi – to take me to the airport – and the times of the flights to London, if possible."

He would have to hurry. Sigrid would be gone for less than an hour. He would leave her a note saying that he had gone for a walk, that she and Dieter should go to dinner, not wait for him – that would buy him time.

His hands trembled as he shoved his clothes into the suitcase. He would be home in less than twenty-four hours. He wanted to see the children, try to explain to them. He wanted to make things right again. With a final look around the room, he turned the key in the lock and hurried down to the hotel lobby.

* * *

Sam slept right through the flight. The stewardess had offered him a tray of food, but he had waved it aside. His stomach was churning, and he had taken two sleeping pills to calm him. He remembered nothing more until they were taxiing the tarmac at Heathrow Airport.

He enquired about flights to Shannon, and there was one due in forty-five minutes. He couldn't believe it had been so easy to book a seat. The right time of the year, the booking clerk told him, smiling as he handed him his ticket and boarding pass. Tourist season over, so there were plenty of available seats.

He sat in the airport lounge, taking quick gulps from the glass of brandy in front of him. He needed something to steady his nerves, prepare him for the confrontation ahead. He wanted to see the children, first, though. He hadn't thought much about Sheila, she was just a shadow in the past – the children, though, they were important to him. He finished his brandy, just as the flight to Shannon was announced.

* * *

"Tom – do you think you'll be all right until I get back from Yvonne's? You know, Yvonne Hourigan – she's in my class – she lives in the next avenue – I have to get some homework notes from her." Deirdre looked at her young brother sitting in front of the TV in the living room. She wouldn't normally leave Tom, especially when Mam was working late at Leonard Holmes' new place – but the notes were important, and she would only be ten minutes at the most.

He looked up at her. "I'll be fine, Dee. Can I have something to eat before you go?"

She nodded. "I'll get you some crisps, and you can have a slice of the flan in the fridge – that should keep you going until I get back."

She picked up her homework notebook, ran into the kitchen and took the flan from the fridge, carefully cutting a small section and putting it on a plate. She put it on the small white tray from behind the kettle, grabbed a packet of cheese-and-onion crisps, Tom's favourite, and carried the tray back into the living room.

"There you go – that should keep you going for a bit – I'll be back soon!"

She ran out the front door, banging it shut behind her and ran down the garden path. Tom would be fine. And she wouldn't be long, just long enough to get those history notes …

* * *

Tom pressed the buttons on the control pad of the TV. There was nothing much on, and Dee was taking ages. He looked around the room anxiously. He had never been in the house on his own before. He wondered if Mam would come back soon. He had eaten the flan, and the packet of crisps, and still Dee hadn't come home. He was just about to go and get a drink from the fridge, when he heard a noise in the kitchen, the sound of the back door opening, then closing gently. He heaved a sigh or relief. Dee was home.

He opened the door to the kitchen, a smile on his face. "I thought you were never coming home, Dee – you were ages –" He stopped suddenly, his expression changing, his mouth open in a great big 'O' of surprise ...

* * *

It had been easy to get inside the house. He knew where Sheila kept the spare key outside, just in case of emergency, if one of them was locked out. Not a very safe thing to do in these times, Sam thought, but a blessing right now. He hadn't wanted to go round to the front door – that nosey Esther Looney from next door would be on the phone in a flash, probably to the police, telling them that he had turned up, on his own doorstep ...

He had let himself in silently.

He looked about the kitchen. Nothing had changed, the same cream and brown tiles on the floor, the same patterned tea set on the shelves over the sink.

He saw the kitchen door open slowly, the small head peering at him from a safe distance.

Tom's eyes took in every detail of him, a silent analysis, no running to greet him, just an air of expectancy in the air between them.

"Daddy – where were you? Mammy was crying because you went away." His small voice was reproachful.

Sam held out his arms to the boy, and he came to him, almost reluctantly, as if Sam was a stranger.

And I am, Sam thought bitterly. I threw away so much for Sigrid – and what do I have left, in the end?

"I had to go away, son – on business – but I'm back now." His words echoed pathetically in his own ears. He could never be back, not the way it was, before. The police were looking for him, and they would probably put him away, for a long time, away from the kids, from Tom …

He brushed the back of his hand across his eyes. The tears were angry ones, resentful ones. He wasn't going to be separated from the kids, from Tom, his son. He looked at the boy, an idea forming in his mind.

"What about a little adventure, son? Just you and me – we'll go on a little adventure, the two of us – women can be a nuisance at times, get in the way of men's stuff." He winked conspiratorially at Tom.

The boy hesitated. "Maybe Dee will come home, Dad – she'll be worried if I'm not here ..."

Sam took his hand reassuringly. "We'll be back before she even knows you're missing, son – come on, we'll take the bus – you'd like that, wouldn't you?"

Tom looked up into his face, saw the old familiar smile of his dad, the dad he knew before he went away, before Mam had to go out to work, and before Sharon got sick. Maybe things would be back to the way they were, now that Dad was back. He smiled, nodding his head, following Sam obediently to the back door.

Sam looked up and down the deserted roadway. There was nobody about, just the Number 10 bus turning at the end of the avenue, making its way to the bus stop.

He grabbed Tom's hand. "Come on, son – we have to go to the bus station where we can get the bus that'll take us to the seaside – you like the sea, don't you, son?"

Tom couldn't reply, his breath coming in short, sharp pants as he tried to keep up with Sam's pace. Neither of them looked back, neither of them saw the blinds in the upstairs bedroom of Esther Looney's house being pulled up, Esther's eyes following them as they climbed on to the bus.

* * *

It was raining when they got there. The small town was deserted, and Tom began to whinge a little, his small face puckered, bottom lip trembling as he tried not to cry. He was frightened of this place, with the great waves pounding on the rocks close to the beach, dark thunderclouds overhead, the screeching of the seagulls making his ears hurt. He should have stayed home, waited for Dee. He looked at the man's face close to him.

Sam was looking out to sea, a faraway look in his eyes, ignoring Tom, as if he was the only person in the world, his problems, his hopes, his ambitions tossed on the waves before him.

Sam was remembering the holidays they had spent together, Sheila, himself and the kids. It was a beautiful part of West Clare, the coastline rugged and wild, the loneliness of the place at this time of year strangely comforting. It was a haven for him right now, away from the mess of a life he had made for himself. He was safe, for the present . . .

"Dad – when are we going home?" Tom enquired, his voice quivering. "I want to go home to Mam – she'll be worried about me."

Sam looked down at him, a puzzled look in his eyes. He couldn't remember where he had picked up the young fellow. His mother would be worried . . . he should be at home. Because Sam wanted to be alone. He had to put the pieces of his life in order.

"I'll take you home soon ..."

He was irritated. The child was crying openly now. He tried to focus his thoughts on the present, but he kept seeing Sigrid's face, in the hotel room in Sofia.

He got up and led the way up the town, to the small fast-food shop near the deserted amusement park. "We'll get you something to eat," he muttered. "That'll make you feel better."

* * *

"Tom! Tom! Where are you?" Deirdre ran from room to room, feeling her heart pound wildly. Tom was gone.

She had been delayed at Yvonne's. Yvonne couldn't find the notes, and then her mother had insisted she had a cold drink – and it had been just over half an hour before she hurried back to the house. The house had been deserted, the unwashed plate in the living room showing that Tom had eaten the flan. He loved fruit flans, Deirdre thought tearfully. She pictured the little face looking up at her before she had left, trusting her to come back to mind him . . .

She ran into the hallway, lifting up the receiver to telephone her mother. Tom had to be found – maybe somebody had taken him, it was happening all over the place, now, young children being abducted.

There was a knock on the front door. Dee rushed to open it.

Esther Looney stood on the doorstep, gazing at Deirdre's tear-stained face. "Dee? What's the matter?"

"I left Tom on his own, just for a little while – and when I came back he was gone!"

"Your father took him – I saw him – through the window."

"My father!"

"I'm sorry, love – I thought everything had been sorted – that your mum knew about him taking Tom."

"I have to tell Mam – she'll know what to do," Dee sobbed bitterly.

It was all her fault, she shouldn't have left him – and Dad – what was he thinking of, taking Tom without telling any of them?

Deirdre's urgent voice almost shouted down the phone. "Mam! I think you should go to the police – Tom is missing – and Dad has taken him!"

* * *

Sheila felt a wave of panic inside her, her ears sounded as if there was a fast-moving train going through them, the sweat in the palm of her hand making the telephone piece slip from her grasp. She picked it up slowly.

"Deirdre, don't worry – I'm going to get in touch with Sergeant Roche now– he'll know what to do ..."

She turned to see Leonard Holmes looking at her anxiously.

"Anything the matter, Sheila? Can I help?"

She nodded. "I have to go to the Garda Station – an urgent family matter – I'm sorry."

Leonard Holmes picked up his car keys from the counter top. "Come on – I'll drive you there – and whatever it is, don't worry. Everything will be fine."

* * *

"Can you think of where he might go with the little fellow?" Paul Roche looked at her sympathetically. Sheila's face was grey, dark shadows beneath her eyes. He wondered how much more the woman could take. He admired her for the way she was coping.

"I don't know – Sam is a stranger to me now, I don't know what might be in his head." Sheila clasped and unclasped her hands agitatedly. Sam could be anywhere with Tom, maybe he had even taken him out of the country.

"We'll check the bus stations, trains." Paul Roche had read her thoughts. "We'll find them. You go back to the house, stay there in case Tom tries to contact you – even if he has taken him, he's bound to let you know that he's safe."

Sheila nodded.

Once again in her life, there was nothing to do but wait.

Chapter 30

"You'll be going straight to the Cabhair Centre, Sharon– it's not a prison, or anything like it, just a rehabilitation treatment centre for young people like you."

Stephen O'Hara looked at the girl sitting in the chair by the window. Her face was pale, now devoid of any make-up, her eyes staring vacantly into the hospital grounds outside.

"Is Mam coming this evening?" She looked at him enquiringly. "She's late – she's usually here before now."

Stephen said a silent prayer for the lie. "She's working hard at the new restaurant – they have plenty of customers already, and the place isn't officially opened." He saw the troubled look in her eyes. "Don't worry. She'll be along before the evening is over."

He couldn't tell her that Sheila was waiting at home, her eyes never leaving the telephone in the hallway, just in case Tom would try and contact her. He couldn't tell her about her father and how he had taken Tom from the house, both of them missing now. The man was obviously not in his right mind. To take his son without leaving word to tell Sheila that they were all right wasn't the action of a rational man. But neither was abandoning his family without a word as he had already done ...

Sharon was just about hanging on by a thread to some degree of normality. He saw the thin hollows of her cheeks, the characteristic twitching of her hands signifying the inner battle she must be having to try to wean herself off the drugs which Declan had kept in ready supply for her. No – best not to tell her what was happening at the moment.

"When will I be going, Father? I just want to get out of this place – it's doing my head in!" She rose suddenly, pacing up and down the room like a caged animal.

At least there was one thing to be thankful for out of all this mess, Stephen thought – Declan Murphy would be out of her life for a long time to come. He was already going through the court process, and there was definitely a sentence pending.

"The end of the week, at the latest – I'll collect you from here and it's only an hour's drive. You'll like the place, Sharon – especially the woman in charge, Liz Kearney – you'll be right in no time."

She looked at him despondently. Not so long ago, she'd detested this man, with his pushy ways, trying to push his way into their lives, making her feel guilty for spending time with Declan. Now, she wasn't so sure. At the moment, he was like a rock in a storm, taking control of her life, and she didn't seem to mind. She wondered about Declan. She hadn't seen him for weeks and the gang at the club thought he had got himself into some kind of trouble. She closed her eyes tiredly. Her thoughts were all getting muddled again . . . she wanted to sleep, to release the tension inside her.

"I'm tired, Father." She looked at him apologetically. "I need to sleep, now – and I'll be ready when you call – ready to go to that centre."

Stephen nodded, satisfied. He knew he was watching the start of Sharon's rehabilitation. She had admitted to herself that she had a problem. It was up to Liz Kearney now.

* * *

"Hello – Paul Roche here."

"Sergeant Roche, it's Sheila Shaughnessy." Her voice sounded agitated. "I've just remembered something – we used to go to a small fishing village in Clare for the holidays – near Hag's Head – Sam always promised Tom that the two of them would go on their own, some time – a fishing trip – men only, he used to joke with him." Her voice broke tearfully at the other end of the line. "It's only a chance, but maybe they might have gone there."

"We're on to it, right away, Sheila – leave everything to us!" Paul Roche jotted down the name she had given him. He'd contact the local Garda Station there. If the boy was there, they'd have him home in a couple of hours, providing . . . He tried to dismiss the thought. The father wasn't rational; he was liable to do anything in his present state of mind. Surely he'd never hurt the boy, though? Paul Roche hurried from the room, mentally writing down the telex message. All stations in the area would have to be informed. The boy would have to be found, and quickly.

* * *

"Dad – do you think we could go fishing, even when the weather is stormy and wet?" Tom sat in the kitchen of the little cottage on the cliff top. He was cold. He wanted to be home, in his own bed, with Mam tucking him in, telling him a story . . . He waited for Sam to answer him, but all he got was a slow nodding of Sam's head, his voice low, and Tom didn't understand what he was saying because the words were all jumbled up together.

"She thought she had some hold over me, you see, Tom – she wanted to rule my life. I couldn't have that – I was too clever for them – I ran away, home, to see you, and Dee and Sharon." He looked at Tom, a puzzled frown on his forehead. "Where's Dee, son, and Sharon – where are they?"

"Dee is fine – but Sharon got sick, Dad – she was sick from taking drugs – I know, because I heard them all talking, Mam and Father O'Hara and Dee. She's in hospital, Dad, from taking the drugs, but Mam says she'll be better soon."

Sam stared at him. He was being punished, his own daughter a victim of Sigrid's and Dieter's greed – and his own. It didn't matter where the drugs came from, the drugs his daughter had taken – those drugs were all part of the terrible underworld of drug trafficking that he and Sigrid had become part of. If he hadn't got involved in the mess, if he hadn't laid open the accounts for Sigrid, there wouldn't have been any money for negotiating drugs deals.

He put his hands to his face, and then Tom heard a low, animal-like moan. "Dad – stop –

don't cry like that – I'm frightened!" He looked at the man, fear written all over his face. "I want Mam . . ."

The wind outside rattled the door of the cottage. The rain spattered against the windowpanes, and through it all Sam suddenly heard the shouting – men shouting – outside the door now, calling to him . . .

"Mr Shaughnessy! Let us in, please– we know you have your son with you – open up, please!"

Tom saw his father move to open the door, tears flowing down his face.

It was all over, Sam thought dully. He would go to prison for what he had done, and he would deserve it. He had ruined his own daughter, not deliberately, but fate had lent a mean hand. He motioned to Tom to come with him.

Tom took his hand hesitantly, just as the garda came through the door, the serious expression on his face making Tom believe that maybe Dad would have to go away again, and maybe Mam would be sad, just like the last time. He felt the young policewoman's arms about him, and he put his head on her shoulder, hiding his face so that he wouldn't see his dad being led to the police car waiting outside.

* * *

"I'll tell you anything you want to know about this gang." Sam sat in the interrogation room of the police station, while Paul Roche opened the file in front of him. "I have nothing to lose now – I've already lost my family– what else is left?"

"Do you want to see your wife? She's waiting outside ..." Paul saw the hesitant look in his eyes, then the slow nodding of his head.

"Yes – I owe her that much." He felt strangely tired. They had sent a doctor to him when he had arrived back in Limerick. He had given him an injection and it had made him feel as though he was floating above all of this, above the police, the endless rounds of questions which he tried to answer through parched lips ... he was floating on a cloud, and now he must see Sheila, try to apologise to her, for everything ...

* * *

"You shouldn't have taken him, Sam – it was wrong of you." She sat calmly in the chair in front of him, her eyes fixed steadily on him. He was amazed at the transformation. Sheila had the look of a confident woman – a new hairstyle, the casual beige trouser suit, elegant manicured hands, with one thing missing – he felt a pang of nostalgia as he noticed the wedding ring was missing from her finger. But what had he expected? He had let her down – the ring meant nothing to her any more.

"I'm sorry, Sheila – I've made a mess of things, and I'm sorry I let you and the kids down."

"I went through a rough patch, Sam." She spoke quietly, her voice calm, not a hint of emotion showing. "I think I've come through, without too many scars."

"And Sharon – how is she – will she be all right?" He saw her raise her head to him, and this time she couldn't hide the accusation.

"She'll be fine – at least, I hope she will, with the proper care. It's going to be a long, tough road – but we'll get there."

She had dismissed him as part of the family with that 'we'. He thought of Sigrid, of her beautiful body, exciting him every time she brushed against him. Then he looked at the woman sitting across from him, Sheila, beautiful in her own way, with a heart that was absent in Sigrid. He had blown it. He watched her get up slowly, walk to the door, then turn around to look at him one more time.

"I'm glad we've had this meeting, Sam – it's made me realise that I have no feeling for you any more. I've come through, to the other side – and do you know something?" She lifted her head confidently. "It doesn't look too bad – if I keep my eyes on the road ahead."

Paul Roche looked at her admiringly as she left the station, her head held high – no sign of the weeping, vulnerable woman he had encountered on their first meeting. Sam Shaughnessy had told them about the operation overseas, but they would have to wait for the psychiatrist's assessment of his mental state before they could question him any further. He had given them the names, and they had matched their files for the most wanted drug-pushers in the EU. He was willing to tell them more, almost like a confession, eager to get rid of the guilt, to receive some sort of absolution for what he had done. Declan had cooperated, too. Sylvie Reddan had been taken in for questioning, and they had enough evidence to put him away for a long time, get rid of some of the vile dirt from the streets, selling their goodies to innocent, vulnerable teenagers.

Chapter 31

"Sheila – I've been meaning to ask you . . ." Leonard Holmes looked at her flushed face as she took a tray of lasagne from the oven in the kitchen at the back of the restaurant. The place was filling up rapidly. He had got one of the city councillors to do the official opening, and now, as he noted with satisfaction the half-empty premises next door and the mutinous expression on Donal Sheridan's face as he looked at the steady stream of customers going into Leonard's Place, he was excited at the new idea churning over and over in his brain.

"Yes?" said Sheila. "If you just wait until I have these organised . . ."

When she finally took a breather, settling herself on one of the stools in the kitchen, she looked at him expectantly

"The thing is, Sheila – I'm not going to stop here – I have another place I'm interested in, down by the quays, a lucrative proposition, but I'll need somebody reliable to run it for me." He looked at her keenly. He had discussed it with Ellen, of course. He had known she would have her reservations, the Sharon incident still fresh in her memory. But Ellen was a no-nonsense woman, with a good business head of her own. She had said if he thought Sheila was right for the job, then it was fine by her.

"The fact is – I'm offering the challenge to you, Sheila – manageress of the new place, with an option, down the line a bit, of course – of a partnership in the business – if things go as well as I think they will."

He watched the expression on her face. She was looking at him as though he had gone completely mad, her eyes staring at him incredulously.

"Do you mean it? Running the place on my own?"

He nodded. For a moment he thought she was going to refuse, her mouth opening to say something, then closing again.

"You are an asset to any business, Sheila,

trustworthy, hardworking. The customers like you and you have a flair for trying something different, and with your culinary skills and my money we should have a very successful business up and running in no time."

Sheila felt as though her life had just begun to take off, as if she had been living in a limbo for what seemed like years – missing years. Even all those years of being married to Sam, she had been living everybody else's life except her own. Now this was the chance she had thought would never come.

"Thank you – I'd be thrilled to take it on – and it will be every bit, if even more, successful than this place!" She nodded in the direction of the long line of customers waiting to get in the main door of the restaurant.

Leonard Holmes relaxed. He had made a good move – he knew the woman was capable, and trustworthy. He put out his hand to her, and she accepted it in a firm grip, contract sealed and delivered.

* * *

"How are you getting on, love?" Sheila looked anxiously at Sharon as she dried dishes, putting them away carefully in the overhead presses.

"Fine, Mam. I have my rota of duties each day

– I'm on wash-up this week – but I think I'm getting there."

She looked at her mother, and Sheila could have cried when she saw the old, familiar smile on Sharon's lips. Cabhair was doing her the world of good, and Liz Kearney was constantly in touch with her, giving her updates on her progress. "Don't expect too much, Sheila, at the start – it takes a while for them to fit in – and on top of the settling in, there's the constant urge to take a fix."

Liz Kearney was a small, amiable woman in her late fifties. She had remained single, she had told Sheila with a twinkle in her eye, "because my mam always told me the only man who'd have me would have to be a 'jelly man' – ready to bend at my every whim!" She had bought the house when her mother had passed away, a large house in a quiet area of countryside, needing a great deal of refurbishment. Bit by bit, with the help of the residents of Cabhair, the house had started to come together, new floors laid, curtains, a complete makeover in the old-fashioned kitchen. Stephen O'Hara had been a good friend to her, she had confided in Sheila. "Gave me encouragement when I first started to take the young people – and not so young. The basic need they all have is just to be loved." And she had given them that in abundance, so much so that the centre was never empty, occupancy at full capacity twelve months of the year. Sharon had settled in after a few days, much to Sheila's surprise. She had been so rebellious up to the time she had been in the hospital, she wondered if it had been such a good idea to isolate her from the family so soon after her scare with the drugs. But, looking at her now, her face filled out, her long hair immaculately clean with none of the greasy concoction she used to massage into it – "because Declan likes it" as she had protested so many times – Sheila knew that it had been the right decision for her.

"Dee told me about Dad – what happened with Tom." Sharon looked at her, embarrassed. "I'm sorry, Mam – for not being more understanding. I didn't realise the hell you were going through when Dad left – and I'm sorry!"

Sheila put her arms about her, felt Sharon's arms about her waist, a tentative gesture, and knew that from now on their lives would be changed for the better.

"What's going to happen to him, Mam? Will he have to go to prison – for taking all that money from his job?"

"Paul Roche says that he'll have to serve some time – but the fact that he came home, that he owned up to his part in everything – that should be a good mark in his favour." She anticipated the next question, and braced herself for it.

Sharon hesitated. She didn't want to upset her mother, not when they were trying to put the past behind them – but she had to ask . . . "Will he be coming home to us, Mam – home to live with us again?"

"I don't know what's going to happen in the future, Sharon – we just have to take a day at a time." She wouldn't make any predictions. Her life had been turned upside down, had evolved to a situation where she believed, she hoped, she might find some sort of stability, maybe even contentment.

"I'm sorry, Mam – for everything." Sharon looked at her, shamefaced. "I should have been a bit more helpful, helped Dee with Tom, instead of making trouble for everybody." She looked round the large communal kitchen, weighing up her words carefully. "This has been a haven for me, Mam – time out, to get myself together. When I think of Declan now, I feel nothing but revulsion – and I promise you, when I get home from here, things will be different."

"Good girl!" Sheila gave her a hug, feeling her respond as she put her arms about her. She kissed Sharon goodbye.

The hearing was at eleven o'clock. She had to go. She couldn't stay away, not on the day her husband was being tried for embezzlement, and an accessory to a major drugs scam. Today would finish a chapter of her life. She braced herself, hurrying to meet Stephen O'Hara outside the court house.

Chapter 32

The lights on the dockland sparkled in the reflections in the water, the sound of music from the various riverside pubs reverberating through the buzz of the latest 'in' district in town. Inside Sheila's Place the tables were full, some disappointed patrons being turned away at the door, waiters and waitresses skimming expertly from table to table, their hands laden with trays of appetising dishes.

Sheila circulated from customer to customer, a ready smile on her face, asking if everything was to their satisfaction, if they needed anything else? She had come a long way since that dark time in her life when she thought she would never climb out of the misery. Brenda was her second in command, concocting a different menu each week to satisfy the discerning customers, while Sheila took care of the accounts and the promotional aspect of the restaurant. Leonard Holmes had told her to regard the restaurant as her terrain, and she had wallowed in the freedom of running it, hiring qualified, efficient staff, an excellent chef and two commis chefs. The business had gone from strength to strength, and now, after five years, she was a partner in the chain of high-quality restaurants Leonard Holmes had set up in customer-friendly areas in the city.

The telephone rang in the back office and Sheila went to answer it, her voice calm and efficient as she answered. "Sheila's Place – can I help you?"

"The deal's gone through, Sheila – he's agreed a price, and the place is ours – we can look for the planning permission to extend in less than a month's time!" Leonard Holmes sounded excited, and a slow, gratified smile crossed Sheila's face. The wheel had turned. Donal Sheridan had called it a day at Tasty Bits, his business spiralling steadily downwards since competition had got the better of him. He had sold out to Leonard Holmes, and Sheila couldn't help but feel a warm glow of triumph.

"That's wonderful, Leonard – we must

celebrate – why not come over tonight for dinner – you and Ellen?" She looked at her watch, a present from Paul.

Stephen O'Hara had tried to press her a few times, warily asking about her relationship with the policeman, but she had remained tight-lipped: Paul was a good friend, nothing more. And he fitted in to her home life as if he had never been outside of it. Dee and Sharon both respected him, and Tom looked on him as a surrogate father, something that didn't displease Paul, Sheila knew, judging by the heart-to-heart talks she had seen them having in the living room, Tom scratching his head in agitation as he tried to come to grips with some complicated piece of maths homework.

She hurried to the carpark outside the restaurant, her day finished, leaving a capable manageress to deal with business until closing time. She had begun to drive only twelve months ago, and she was revelling in the freedom of getting to places independently, without having to rely on anybody for a lift. Her independence was the most important thing to Sheila. She had found that out during the painstaking process of standing on her own two feet, coping with all the problems of a single-parent family.

She wondered what she could possibly prepare for dinner, something that wouldn't take too much time, something light – maybe some fresh salmon and a lemon sorbet to fellow.

She had taken a bottle of their best Chardonnay from the cooler in the restaurant. She would telephone Paul as soon as she got home, tell him the good news.

As soon as she parked the car outside the front gate, she saw Stephen O'Hara's car pulling in to the kerbside.

"Sheila, I wanted to tell you myself – Paul Roche thought maybe I'd be the best one to break the news – Sam is out. It's been on the cards for a while – good behaviour, an exemplary prisoner – they're releasing him in the morning."

She turned to face him, her hands clenched tightly, steadying herself against the bonnet of the car.

"Come inside, Stephen – we can talk inside," she said shakily and he followed her into the house.

As she led the way through to the kitchen, she heard the sound of Sharon's voice calling from the bathroom.

"Mam, I'm home – I'm starved! Just a quick sandwich – the college Rag is starting tonight, so I won't have much time . . ."

Sharon ran down the stairs and into the kitchen, coming to a halt when she saw the expression on her mother's face. She looked at Stephen O'Hara for an explanation.

"Your father is being released – tomorrow."

Sheila looked at Sharon for a reaction, but there was none, just an indefinable look in her eyes.

"Will he want to see us – to come here?" Sharon asked.

She thought of all the prison visits, the short, awkward silences between father and daughter, when there didn't seem an awful lot to say to one another. She had watched him age in the time he was locked away from them, his dark hair greying almost overnight, the short, tight haircut accentuating the leanness of his face. She had watched Sheila grow stronger, build up a business for herself, take care of them as best she could. Dee was away in college in New York, studying languages and economics. Sharon had decided to take up interior design and was really into her course, loving every minute of it, getting top marks in all her exams so far. It was only because of Sheila that they were making a go of life, because she hadn't given up, struggling through day by day ...

"I'll go and see him – before he's released – see what he's intending to do." Sheila spoke quietly, her voice shaking a little, thoughts of the interview with Sam making her feel depressed. He couldn't come home – she didn't want him home, she had moved too far ahead – and then there was Paul . . .

"Do you want me to go with you, Sheila?" Stephen enquired sympathetically. He could imagine what she was feeling, all the horror of the humiliation she had to endure after Sam had left her visible on her pale face.

"No. I'll go alone – this is something between the two of us and I have to face it, on my own."

* * *

The conversation at the dinner table was low-key, Sheila lost in thought, occasionally managing a smile when some remark was made about the restaurant, or the clientele.

Paul Roche, sitting next to her, could sense what must be going through her head, and for his own part, he had to admit, he was feeling a bit apprehensive. Supposing she felt sorry for Sam, decided to make a go of it again, make a fresh start? He had come tonight with the small package in his pocket, hoping to ask her the all-important question. There couldn't be marriage, at least not for a while yet – but inevitably, that's what he hoped for with all his heart. Sheila was a good woman, a beautiful, successful woman, and any man would be a fool not to want her. He hoped Sam wouldn't think the same thing, want her back with him again, put pressure on her, for the family's sake.

"Here's to us, Sheila – to our latest addition to the gourmet world – long may our success continue!" Leonard Holmes lifted his glass.

Ellen looking across at Sheila, her sharp eyes noticing the worry on Sheila's face. There was something wrong, she could feel it in her bones. And by the look on Paul Roche's face, he didn't appear too happy either. She hoped that things worked out for them. They were a lovely couple, and they deserved some happiness. She smiled as she saw Paul reach for Sheila's hand, and the look that passed between them left Ellen Holmes in no doubt but that everything would work itself out in the end.

Chapter 33

He looked thinner in his casual jacket and jeans. She had only ever seen him in recent years in the navy track suit he wore in the prison, and now, with his hair sleeked back from his face, and the new clothes, he looked older, more vulnerable. Sheila sat awkwardly next to him in the visitor's room behind the exit door of the prison. Just a few more minutes, and he would taste freedom. He had a jail record, but he had done his time, and he could move on – just as she had …

"Sheila – I've been thinking about us for the last couple of days." He hesitated. The truth was that he was afraid to move out of the cosy little cocoon he had inhabited for the last five years. He had learnt how to do woodwork, to paint, to model clay into various pots and containers – and he had been given an address by the Superintendent of a place where he could go, a sort of halfway house, until he got on his feet again. But what he wanted most in the world was to make things right with Sheila, maybe even persuade her to give him a second chance …

"No – Sam – no. I've made a good life for me and the children. You'll always be their father, and you can see them whenever you like – but there can be no going back for us. You see, Sam – I don't love you any more!" She looked at him, the realisation dawning on her, so forcefully that it was almost like a slap in the face. She *didn't* have any feelings for him – he was a stranger to her, not part of her life, just a pathetic figure who had made a mistake, and had paid for it by losing everything that had been precious to them.

"You've found somebody else?" His eyes took in the sudden flush to her cheeks. She was beautiful, he thought regretfully. He wondered, for the hundredth time, what he had ever seen in Sigrid – Sigrid, who was now doing time in her own country, and Dieter – two ghostly shadows from his past.

"I've been seeing somebody – as a friend – and that's all I want for now, Sam. I have a good life, and I don't need commitments, except the children – I've been hurt too much."

He winced at the insinuation. He had ruined her life once, and she wasn't going to take the chance of a repetition of all that hurt. He looked at her neat figure in the fashionable business suit, the steady, assured look in her eyes as she looked at him, and knew that he had lost.

He shrugged his shoulders. He had tried, but he was Sam Shaughnessy, and it would take more than a woman's pride to put him down. He still had a few contacts in the business world, still some telephone numbers to play around with, to start him on the first rung of the ladder once more.

She saw the expression on his face, and felt better. That was the old Sam, the one who dusted himself down and got back up again – and he didn't need much help from his ex-wife.

"Do you need a lift – anywhere?"

She stood up to leave, while he shook his head, taking hold of his kitbag, slinging it over his shoulder.

"No – I've booked a taxi. I'll let you know when I'm settled. Maybe I can see the kids soon for a couple of hours?"

Sheila smiled. They were no longer kids. They had minds of their own, adult minds, and Sam couldn't force them to see him. He would have to tread softly and allow them time, time to get to know him again, to overcome the shadow of the missing years when he hadn't been a part of their lives. But for now she just nodded silently. Sam was still living in the past. Dee was a young woman now, home for maybe a couple of weeks at Christmas time, and that was it. Sharon had her circle of friends in the college, arty types, her engagement calendar booked solid from one end of the week to the next, her drug-taking days behind her. And Tom ... Tom was a young man now, and time out with his father would prove to be uncomfortable to say the least. Yes, Sheila thought wryly, Sam would have to give them all time to get used to him once more – and to come to terms with the fact that things would never be the same again.

"Yes, Sam – whenever you want to see them – it's all right with me."

She felt tired, she wanted to be away from this place back to her work, as much work as she could handle, to keep her mind occupied, stop her from brooding about the past.

"I'll go now – goodbye, Sam – I hope things work out for you." She turned quickly, signalling to the security guard outside that she was about to leave. As soon as she got out on to the courtyard outside the heavy iron door, she took deep breaths of fresh air, filling her lungs, ridding herself of the tainted atmosphere of the prison.

Paul wanted to see her. He was meeting her in the restaurant at lunch-time. He had something important to say, he had told her last night as he was leaving the house …

She steered the car into the docklands, the realisation dawning on her. She was in love with Paul Roche. He was gentle and kind, and in the time she had known him she had discovered that he was somebody she could depend on through the bad times, as well as the good.

The missing years were well and truly behind her, like a dark cloud dissipating and letting the sunshine through. It felt like the start of a brand-new life, and today was the very first, beautiful day.

Instinctively she knew what he was about to say to her.

And, Sheila thought, as she got out of the car, seeing his tall figure pacing up and down nervously in front of the restaurant, she knew exactly what answer she would give him …

The End

Published by Poolbeg.com

THE SEAMSTRESS OF FORTUNE

Terri O'Mahony

Born to poor working parents from the country in the late 1800s, Hannah Sullivan is determined to make something of herself. Armed with dressmaking skills, a determination to succeed and a strong streak of independence, she moves to Limerick city, vowing to return a lady.

In the city, Hannah learns that workers are exploited and work in dangerous and unsanitary conditions, and vows to follow in the honest footsteps of her businessman uncle John.

When she meets Jonathan Mayhew, recently returned from the Boer War, she believes they share something special, but their union is not to be.

So Hannah travels to New York, but finds that the streets are not paved with gold. This is a city beset with injustices, and Hannah's strength and determination is tested beyond her imagination.

As Ireland heads towards the Easter Rising, Hannah returns home. Will she and Jonathan find true happiness in the turmoil of Dublin in 1916 or will fate get in their way?

ISBN 1-84223-201-0

Published by Poolbeg.com

The Windbreaker Season

Terri O'Mahony

Golden sands and a beautiful coastline at Seaman's Point on Ireland's west coast is an idyllic haven for city dwellers desperate to break away.

But while Eva Fitzgerald relies on alcohol to get her through the lonely days with two small children, her husband Tony beds the glamorous Sylvia in the city.

And when Eva discovers she is pregnant again, it's the last thing she needs to mend her marriage. Despairing of her future, Eva encounters a mysterious and handsome stranger on the beach. Is he what he seems and what exactly does he want from Eva?

When you chip away at the surface you never know what you'll find.

ISBN 1-84223-146-4